The Enemy Within

Daughters of the People, Book 3

LUCY VARNA

Bone Diggers Press
www.bonediggerspress.com

For Richard
You know why

Cover design © L.J. Anderson, Mayhem Cover Creations.

Published by Bone Diggers Press, Clayton, Georgia.

ISBN 978-0-9888883-6-4

TITLES BY LUCY VARNA

THE DAUGHTERS OF THE PEOPLE SERIES
Book 1: *The Prophecy*
Book 2: *Light's Bane*
Book 3: *The Enemy Within*
Book 3.5: *Tempered*
Book 4: *In All Things, Balance*
Book 5: *Sanctuary*

THE SONS OF THE PEOPLE SERIES
Book 1: *Say Yes*

THE CULLOWHEE HERITAGE SERIES
Book 1: *A Higher Purpose*
Book 2: *A Wicked Love*

Notes from the Fab Four

Notes on the People compiled by Tom Fairfax, Phil Walters, George Howe, and James Terhune, known at the IECS unofficially as the Fab Four.

Aenkanien. A tattoo inked into the left-hand shoulder blade of a Son who becomes the husband of a Daughter. Once approval has been granted by the mothers of both parties and the tattoo is in place, a formal marriage ceremony is unnecessary; the two are considered married in the eyes of the People, though many couples choose to undergo a civil or, less frequently, traditional ceremony.

Amaetien. The tattoo Sons receive on their sixteenth birthday (the day they become men under the traditions and laws of the People) to indicate their maternal lineage. Usually inked onto the upper left arm, the *amaetien* is a symbol of the mother's eternal protection and devotion, and a warning to any who would harm the Son.

Ankana. Woman. Also refers to the Woman with No Face.

Council of Seven. The People's ruling body, consisting of seven women, one representing the line of each of the Seven Sisters.

Daughter. A direct descendant of one of the Seven Sisters, Daughters may be either immortal (if they have not yet broken their own curse) or mortal (if they have broken their own curse or are the daughter of a mortal Daughter).

Eknon. Student.

Eternal Order. A supposedly mythical group devoted to undermining the ultimate goal of the People, to break the curse of immortality for every Daughter through the fulfillment of the Prophecy of Light.

High Guard. Seven Daughters devoted to eradicating the Eternal Order. A highly secret and deadly group.

Institute of Early Cultural Studies (IECS). Located in Tellowee, Georgia, USA, the IECS is the main historical research branch of the People and serves as a repository for much of its history.

Kaetyrm. Sister, usually used in a formal situation, though not always.

Maetyrm. Mother, usually used as a term of respect for an elder Daughter and not necessarily as a reference to one's own mother. Teachers, for example, are referred to as Maetyrm.

People, The. The name used by the descendants of the Seven Sisters to describe themselves. The People include all immortal and mortal Daughters, Sons, and the mortal descendants of all submitted Daughters to the second degree (i.e. through the grandchildren of Daughters who have submitted their wills and become mortal). Other descendants are not counted among the numbers of the People.

Notes from the Fab Four

Notes on the People compiled by Tom Fairfax, Phil Walters, George Howe, and James Terhune, known at the IECS unofficially as the Fab Four.

Aenkanien. A tattoo inked into the left-hand shoulder blade of a Son who becomes the husband of a Daughter. Once approval has been granted by the mothers of both parties and the tattoo is in place, a formal marriage ceremony is unnecessary; the two are considered married in the eyes of the People, though many couples choose to undergo a civil or, less frequently, traditional ceremony.

Amaetien. The tattoo Sons receive on their sixteenth birthday (the day they become men under the traditions and laws of the People) to indicate their maternal lineage. Usually inked onto the upper left arm, the *amaetien* is a symbol of the mother's eternal protection and devotion, and a warning to any who would harm the Son.

Ankana. Woman. Also refers to the Woman with No Face.

Council of Seven. The People's ruling body, consisting of seven women, one representing the line of each of the Seven Sisters.

Daughter. A direct descendant of one of the Seven Sisters, Daughters may be either immortal (if they have not yet broken their own curse) or mortal (if they have broken their own curse or are the daughter of a mortal Daughter).

Eknon. Student.

Eternal Order. A supposedly mythical group devoted to undermining the ultimate goal of the People, to break the curse of immortality for every Daughter through the fulfillment of the Prophecy of Light.

High Guard. Seven Daughters devoted to eradicating the Eternal Order. A highly secret and deadly group.

Institute of Early Cultural Studies (IECS). Located in Tellowee, Georgia, USA, the IECS is the main historical research branch of the People and serves as a repository for much of its history.

Kaetyrm. Sister, usually used in a formal situation, though not always.

Maetyrm. Mother, usually used as a term of respect for an elder Daughter and not necessarily as a reference to one's own mother. Teachers, for example, are referred to as Maetyrm.

People, The. The name used by the descendants of the Seven Sisters to describe themselves. The People include all immortal and mortal Daughters, Sons, and the mortal descendants of all submitted Daughters to the second degree (i.e. through the grandchildren of Daughters who have submitted their wills and become mortal). Other descendants are not counted among the numbers of the People.

Prophecy of Light. Issued by an unknown person at some distant point in the past, the Prophecy of Light portends a way for the curse of immortality to be lifted from all of the People, and not solely the Daughters who submit their wills and become mortal. (See the Daughters of the People website.)

Seven Sisters. The progenitors of the modern People. The seven women, all sisters, avenged the deaths of their parents by killing the men of the People (the original band) and were cursed by the god An to live immortal lives without the ability to bear sons. The curse was tempered by the goddess Ki, who decreed that the curse could be broken by each one if she would submit her will, in whatever way (except sexually), to the man she loved. (See the Legend of Beginnings on the Daughters of the People website.)

Shadow Enemy. The traditional enemy of the People.

Son. Usually refers to the child of a Daughter who has broken the curse and become mortal, but may also reference the child of a Son or another male descendant of a Daughter.

Tellowee, Georgia, USA. One of the centers of the People, located in rural northeast Georgia.

ONE

INDIGO DUPREE surveyed the packing boxes strewn throughout her new apartment with a light heart. *Home.* For fourteen years, she'd lived out of a suitcase, roaming from job to job, never staying still for long. It was time, past time really, to put roots down again, to settle somewhere. Time to stop running.

It was purely a coincidence that growing roots landed her in Tellowee among the past she'd left behind. Her mother lived here now with her new husband and a baby on the way, hopefully the long-desired son. A new baby to spoil and love and cherish.

The yearning to push life from her body, to become a mother and hold a babe of her own, whispered through Indigo. She had few regrets in her life. Not having a child was one of them.

Another regret, a stronger one, tightened its grip on her, of a boy on the brink of manhood and a kiss she could never forget.

She shoved the memory away and picked up a box.

Being a Daughter wasn't all it was cracked up to be. Near-eternal youth had advantages, true, but it came with a memory that never faded, never blurred. The mistakes of a long past piled up on one another like poorly stacked blocks, resting on the sanity of the moment, waiting for one false move to send the whole stack toppling.

What would it be like to be mortal, worried only about

things like finding a place to walk her dog, if she had one, or saving up for a new pair of outrageously impractical heels?

Indigo paused in the middle of slitting open the tape of the box she'd chosen, turning the notion over in her mind. Mortal women didn't look over their shoulders, trying to stay one step ahead of an ancient enemy. They didn't worry about breaking a curse or finding a lasting love. Ok, sure, they worried about love, but not the way an immortal Daughter did. An immortal Daughter who couldn't find a love strong enough to take her heart and will was doomed to a restless life, always on the run, never to find solace.

The doorbell rang, startling Indigo into dropping the box she held. She frowned at the door. In town less than a day, and already visitors came a-calling. Gossip spread quickly in the sleepy Southern town. A handful of people knew she'd moved back to Tellowee and she'd just left the house where most of them lived, all except Dani Nehring.

Her frown lifted at the thought of her friend, who lived only an hour away. When Indigo had called the week before, Dani had sounded near rock bottom. Indigo had finally teased enough information out of the suddenly tight-lipped Daughter to learn that Dani had had a rough go of it since their time in Sweden, between falling in love, becoming mortal, and finding, then killing, her long lost mother. Indigo had invited her to come out, maybe have pizza and catch a movie, but she hadn't really expected Dani to take her up on the offer, not yet. Still, Indigo hurried to the door, anxious to see her friend.

When she pulled open the door, her heart skittered in her chest, then sank like a stone. Bobby Upton stood at the threshold, a solid six feet of lean muscle, unruly chestnut hair, and hazel eyes. His face was thinner than she remembered, his eyes harder, but he looked strong and fit in a black, form-fitting turtleneck tucked into low-slung jeans.

Her gaze drifted unconsciously down his body and her breath caught in her lungs. He'd filled out handsomely since the last time she'd seen him. He'd always been tough, with the lean, quick build of his father. His shoulders seemed broader now, the muscles more defined under his clothing. The cockiness he'd worn like a badge as a teenager had mellowed to cool confidence, apparent in his loose stance and calm gaze. He held himself like a man ready to handle anything thrown his way, not a boy eager to take what he wanted.

The man before her wouldn't *need* to take anything. He'd simply have to ask and it would be willingly given.

She sucked in a breath, appalled at the direction her mind had taken, and jerked her gaze to his face. His wide mouth was tilted into a smug smirk. A bloom of heat and color worked its way into her cheeks and her mouth snapped into a thin line.

Ogling Bobby Upton. Atta way to keep the upper hand.

"Indigo."

His voice was low and smooth. Awareness shivered up her spine and she closed her eyes against it. Why had he, of all people, shown up at her door?

"May I come in?" he said.

Her eyes popped open as her skin went hot, then cold. She swung the door shut, anything to keep him on the other side, *please, Goddess.*

His hand shot out, catching the door in mid-swing. "We need to talk."

"I don't have anything to say to you," she said, and bit the inside of her cheek at the breathless note in her voice.

His jaw tightened. "This is business."

She threw all her weight behind her hold on the door, and glared at him when his one palm, flat on the door's surface, was enough to counter her strength. His smirk was a little too smug, a little too knowing. Drat him. Fourteen years and he still got the best of her.

She clenched her jaws together and gritted out, "Still not interested."

He shoved the door hard, popping it out of her restraining

hand, and stepped inside, a dangerous glint in his eyes. Her heart raced as she scrambled back. The last time she'd seen that look, bad things had happened, *really* bad things.

Or really good ones, depending on the point of view. His hand skimming under her shirt, teasing her skin with the soft, sure grazes of his fingertips. His mouth claiming hers, demanding her surrender as he pressed her against an unforgiving concrete wall. Her body melting under the onslaught of his heat, then voices spilling out into the hallway and her jerking away, keeping them both from making a terrible mistake.

She turned from him, away from the stain of memory and regret. "What do you want?"

"I'm here about India."

Indigo stifled an irritated sigh. Why did people always come to the good twin when the bad one erred? "What has she done now?"

"Fallen in with some very bad people."

"India *is* very bad people, Bobby."

"Ever hear of Lilith Cæstus?"

She sucked in a breath. Dani's mother, the ancient Daughter who had wreaked havoc on the People and anyone else she could lay hands on over the past couple of millennia, now dead by her only surviving daughter's hand. "Please don't tell me India was with Lilith when Dani stood against her."

"Ok, I won't."

Indigo wilted under the mildly voiced sarcasm. Hearing that would break her mother's heart. India had always been difficult, zagging when Elizabeth told her to zig, lashing out at everything that came her way, good or bad. The reckless anger had only grown worse as she aged.

"She's just the tip, Indigo," he murmured.

His voice washed over her like a caress, a distracting shiver of possibilities. She pushed her reaction away. Duty was a hard mistress, duty to family the hardest, this one in particular. Bobby Upton in her home. The things a woman did for family. "Ok, fine. Come in and close the door. You can help me unpack while you fill me in."

He shut the door and locked it, and walked toward her in a loose limbed gait, like a man ready to claim what was his. *Blessed Goddess.* Her breath caught in her throat and her heart raced and his heat surrounded her as he neared, and she caught his masculine scent and went dizzy with need. She steeled herself against it and brought herself ruthlessly under control.

Bobby dug a knife out of his pocket, picked a box, and carefully slit the tape holding it closed. "It's been a madhouse around here lately."

"I heard." Indigo breathed out a silent sigh of relief when her voice sounded relatively normal. "Have all the Sandby borg artifacts been recovered yet?"

"No." He unpacked china, set it on the counter, and dropped packing material onto the pile she'd started. "The one Lilith stole from the warehouse in New York a couple months back? That one we have, but as far as we know, the Shadow Enemy has the others."

Her hand went to the spot on the back of her head where she'd been hit earlier that year, during the theft of a cache of documents from the Swedish dig. "No word on the original thief, then?"

At his silence, she glanced up and caught him watching her with a peculiar expression on his face, his eyes intense, his mouth set in a thin, hard line. Her hands trembled when he stepped closer, and then his fingers sifted through her hair, probing the back of her head with a light, firm pressure.

She pulled back to escape his touch, to still the tremors in her body and the needy ache pooling low in her gut. He clasped her shoulder with his other hand, holding her in place while he examined the spot where she'd been hit.

"I was worried about you," he murmured. His breath warmed the skin of her face, and she steeled herself against his nearness. He was so close, his heat and strength there if she wanted it. She'd given in to him once for a few brief moments fourteen years before. It had ended with both of them running as far and as fast as they could. How could his mere presence chase that regret and memory away so easily?

"It was nothing." She tried to step back again and he let her go. "Long healed."

His expression closed as he turned away from her and opened another box. "Mom believes someone's actively working against the People, hiding the Shadow Enemy's movements, maybe undermining other common goals, like breaking the curse."

She plucked at the box she'd crumpled beneath nerveless fingers. "There are always a few who go against the grain."

"This feels like a concerted effort. Organized." He caught her gaze, holding it with the intensity of his own. "It's possible India picked up where Lilith left off. If she did, she probably has at least a rudimentary control of Lilith's followers. If not her, then someone else, but our priority is finding India. I wouldn't ask for your help if I didn't need it."

"She and I were never close."

"But you understand her in a way few other people do." His gaze went hard and flat. "I could always ask your mother for help."

She gaped at him. How could he even suggest that? "She's pregnant."

"Hard to miss."

"And you would ask her to go after India? Are you insane?"

"I have a job to do, Indigo."

"And you don't care who you hurt to do it, is that it?"

"I always care who I hurt," he snapped. "That doesn't mean I can neglect my duty."

"Duty," she scoffed. "You're Rebecca the Blade's son, all right."

"You have no room to lecture me about duty."

She flinched away from the harsh grate in his voice.

"Bobby..."

He cut her off with a dismissive slash of his hand. "I'll find India with or without you." He pulled a business card out of his pocket and tossed it onto the top of the box she held. "I'm briefing a team tomorrow morning at ten thirty. Be there if you want to help."

He stalked out of her apartment, shutting the door firmly behind himself. She exhaled a shaky sigh and slumped against a stack of boxes. Her first day in town and she'd totally blown it. Bobby's face popped into her head, the hot rake of his eyes, the gentle pressure of his fingers sifting through her hair. She shivered as the heat he'd stirred reignited. Why had she answered the door?

Right. She'd expected anyone, anyone at all, other than Bobby Upton, the very reason she'd left Tellowee in the first place. If he'd come about anything but India, she'd ignore him. She was good at that, but duty called, that wretched beast, and her duty, if what he said about India was even halfway true, was to chase down and contain her errant twin, whether she wanted to or not.

Her gut roiled and the muscles around her spine tightened. Why did he have to be the one going after India?

Indigo scrubbed her hands over her face and pushed him out of her mind, determined to keep him there as long as she possibly could.

THE NEXT MORNING, the office hummed with activity as duties were assigned and discussed alongside a hefty dose of weekend gossip. Bobby sat in his office with the door open, listening to the hustle and grind with the satisfaction of a man invested in it. When he and two of his closest friends, Hiro Okada and Drew Martin, had started BDH Security & Protection Services two years before, they'd hoped for success and never dreamed of achieving it so quickly. It was one of life's unexpected pleasures, kind of like seeing the woman of his dreams again after nearly a decade and a half.

The night before, he'd left Indigo's more than a little frustrated and spent hours afterward sweating her out of his system. A punishing run on the treadmill and an hour in the pool swimming lap after lap as if the Shadow Enemy were on his heels hadn't been enough to purge her memory. He'd fallen into bed exhausted and dreamed of her soft, lithe body all night long, of kissing her, of sinking into her, of the little mews of pleasure she made when he touched her.

He rubbed a hand along his chest, over the ache he'd lived with for fourteen years. There was no other woman for him. It had been a hard lesson, one learned when he was barely a man. Now if he could just come to grips with it and her rejection, maybe they could both have some peace.

The intercom buzzed, interrupting his mood's downward spiral.

"Mr. Upton?"

Laura Ellenburg's voice drifted through the line, as clipped and efficient as the rest of her. She'd been the first person he, Hiro, and Drew had hired when they'd started BDH. They'd snagged her right out of business college, impressed by her composure and organizational skills, though she'd barely been twenty at the time. In the two years since, they'd never had a reason to regret it. She was always on time, kept the office running like a top, and, with her waif-like figure and doe eyes, was easy on the eyes to boot. Laura was like the little sister none of them had ever had, and they treated her that way whenever she let them.

Bobby scooted his chair closer to his desk and punched a finger at the phone. "Yes, Laura?"

"There's a woman here to see you." Her voice held a prim, disapproving edge under the stiff formality she seldom dropped. "A Ms. Indigo Dupree. Should I have her make an appointment?"

8

A sudden heat filled his veins, enough to have his blood humming under his skin. He stifled it ruthlessly. She was probably there about India, damn them both. "Send her back, please."

He walked around his desk and watched her through the open door of his office as she strode past the reception desk, her heart-shaped face set in the lines of someone undertaking an unpleasant task. Her long black ponytail swished with every step and her eyes glittered like sapphires against the pale ivory of her skin. She wore drab olive cargo pants and a loose white cotton shirt, and carried herself with the innate confidence of a woman who knew how to handle herself.

His traitorous heart skipped a beat, taking his breath with it, and he cursed low and long. When would he learn?

She stepped into his office, shut the door, and caught his gaze with her own. "I'll help you find India, but I have conditions."

He leaned back against the edge of his desk and crossed his arms over his chest. That was a Daughter for you. Always laying down the law and expecting the man in her life to toe the line. If he hadn't gotten tired of it at the age of ten, it'd be funny. "Such as?"

"I work alone."

"No," he said flatly. "No one here works alone."

"Then I work with anyone but you," she shot back.

The pleasure of her presence evaporated abruptly. "Sorry, Indi. Everyone else is taken."

"How can you possibly know that?"

"Because I do."

"Fine," she gritted out. "Then promise to keep your hands to yourself."

"No can do."

She turned on her heel, heading for the door. Hell with that. He was damn tired of her walking out on him, pushing him away, letting his heart rot in the dank heap of loneliness he'd endured nearly half his life.

He caught her arm and jerked her around. "Why don't we just get it over with?"

Her eyes widened with what he would've sworn was panic. "I don't know what you're talking about."

"Another kiss," he explained patiently. "We're both thinking about it. Let's just do it so we can move on."

"In your dreams."

A muscle twitched in his jaw at the snap in her voice. She had no room to talk about dreams, no leave to remind him of everything he'd lost when she'd pushed him away. He yanked until she fell into him, hissed in a breath when she struggled against him, trying to break free. Goddess, it was so good to have her there, to feel her once again the way a man always wants to feel the woman he desires. He hardened his grip, tightened it until their bodies were melded together, and called himself ten kinds of fool for enjoying her weight pressed into him.

She stilled as something very Daughter-like flashed through her expression.

"Don't do anything you'll regret later," he warned.

"I doubt I would regret it."

Her hands gripped his waist hard enough for her fingernails to dig into his skin through his shirt. She raised her head to look at him, and his gaze zeroed in on her lush, red mouth, so close to his own their breaths mingled. The world went still and faded around them, and he lowered his mouth to hers, slowly enough to give her time to pull away, and not nearly fast enough for the desire raging through him.

When his lips were a hair's breadth from hers, she murmured, "The blinds are open."

He tore himself away from the temptation of her sweet lips and the promise of another taste, and glanced up. Margaret Mary stared at them through the windows separating his office from the main hallway, her eyebrows raised. Of all the people in the office who could've caught him fondling the woman of his dreams, it had to be his sister. By the Lady Ki. A Son couldn't do anything without his female relatives knowing about it.

He cursed inwardly and let Indigo go, and clamped down on the need roiling through him as she pushed herself carefully away from him.

She sat down on the love seat and crossed her legs, fixing him with what he thought of as her teacher stare, uncompromising, hard, and always right. "And that is why you need to keep your hands to yourself, Bobby."

Irritation whipped through him, mixing with the need still zinging through his gut. "Forget it."

Her gaze never faltered. "When a woman says no, it means no."

"When you say no, I'll stop touching you."

"I said no." She took a deep breath, let it out slowly. "Repeatedly."

"You've never said no, not once. In fact, I'm pretty sure the last time we did this you were begging for more."

Her brows snapped together into a fierce scowl and she stood abruptly. "This is never going to work."

A knock rapped on the door and Laura poked her head inside. She glanced from him to Indigo and something shifted in her expression, too quickly for Bobby to catch. "Meeting's in five," she said, then closed the door on them.

"That's my cue to leave," Indigo said.

"Wait." Bobby held his hands up when she backed away. "At least come to the meeting. You can always leave after if you decide you really don't want to help."

After a long moment, she nodded and allowed him to lead her to the conference room with a gentlemanly hand on the small of her back. She didn't pull away. A spurt of triumph shot through him at her acceptance of his touch. Small, intimate touches, delivered so frequently and casually she never gave them a thought, seducing her so gently she never saw it coming.

Hell, doing that would be no problem. He slid his hand up

her back until the ends of her ponytail brushed along his skin, teasing him with every step. No, touching her wouldn't be a problem at all. Knowing he could never have her, that was the thorn that kept him from trying for her again.

TWO

HE REST of the leadership team was seated around the round conference table when he and Indigo entered the meeting room. Bobby introduced her first to his partners and former military buddies, Hiro and Drew. Hiro was the great-grandson of Japanese immigrants and the son of fierce traditionalists who'd raised him to respect the customs of their homeland. He was slender and fit, and more disciplined than any of them, except Margaret. Drew was a Yankee from Boston, a Southie with the burly Irish build of his forefathers and a brawling attitude to match. The three of them had been through hell together and seen each other out in one piece, forging a bond of friendship so strong it bordered on brotherhood.

The two men sat with their backs to the left wall. Zenalisa Jones, their tech expert, had taken her customary spot opposite them, her thin frame slumped sulkily in her chair. Not long after they'd opened, Zena had shown up on their door demanding a job. It had taken her five minutes to hack their system, and less than that for them to hire her. When they'd gently probed her background, she'd given them such a dead-eyed look that they'd backed off. Even Hiro, with his soft touch and gentle voice, hadn't been able to pry it out of her.

"You've met Laura, our office manager, and you remember my sister, Margaret."

"Of course," Indigo murmured politely.

Bobby led her to a seat on the far side of the table and sat her to his left next to Zena. "I've asked Indigo to sit in on this meeting since she'll be helping us with a job I've just contracted."

Drew groaned and sat back in his chair. "We're overbooked now, Bobby."

Bobby sat back in his own chair and drummed his fingers lightly on the arm of his chair. "We can rotate this in as people become available."

Hiro pulled his notebook forward and began making notes. "What kind of skill sets are we talking about?"

"Whatever we need to unearth spies and possible traitors," Bobby said bluntly.

Drew pulled his lower lip between two fingers before speaking. "Corporate espionage or treason?"

"That depends on how you look at it. It's for the Institute for Early Cultural Studies." Bobby caught the slight puzzlement in Margaret's otherwise blank expression.

"Wait, your Mom asked you to do this?" Drew's thuggish face twisted into a leer. "Will she be coming by?"

"That's my mother you're talking about," Bobby reminded him.

Margaret leaned forward and pinned Drew with a menacing glare. "Mine, too."

"Her, I'm afraid of," Drew said, then pointed at Bobby. "You, not so much."

Bobby narrowed his eyes. "I can still kick your ass."

"Here we go." Hiro rolled his eyes to the ceiling in a long-suffering look. "You guys remember we're trying to run a business here, right?"

Indigo leaned forward to catch Hiro's eye. "Are they always like this?"

"Usually, they're worse." Hiro gave her an assessing look that had Bobby's temper flaring. "I'm the nice one of the bunch. A good lover, too, when you get tired of Upton."

"We're not lovers," Indigo said with a small smile. At the same time, Bobby said, "Hey!" and Drew said, "Dibs on the new girl."

"Children." Margaret's voice was quiet but firm, and drew everyone's attention. "The matter at hand?"

Bobby cleared his throat and split a dirty look between Drew and Hiro. "I've got preliminary profiles on a list of suspects and info on the possible shark and its victim. Zena and Laura, I need the two of you on research. The rest of us will divide up the list of names."

"I'll need the paperwork," Laura said.

"Everything's on the secure internal server and I'd like to keep it that way." Bobby looked at each of them in turn, allowing the weight of his gaze to hammer in the absolute necessity of his request. "That means no sharing anything over the Internet, no talking about this over an unsecure phone line, and no internal memos."

"Gonna be hard to work that way," Drew said.

"We'll make it work," Bobby said. "Just so you know, Indigo's twin sister is on that list. They're identical, so make sure you're talking to the right one before spilling anything."

Zena snorted. "If they're identical, ain't no way to tell 'em apart."

Bobby clamped down on his impatience. "You'll figure it out. Our objective is to ferret out the traitor and bring him or her in for questioning. The people on this list are dangerous. All of them are trained in hand to hand and multiple weapons, so use caution. Don't be afraid to ask for help."

"What's the time frame?" Hiro said.

"However long it takes. Sooner's better, though." Bobby stood. "Tie up what you can this week. Delegate everything else. I'll speak with each of you in detail over the next few days, but plan on devoting time to this contract in earnest beginning next Monday. Margaret, I need a word."

The meeting broke up as it always did, like a flock of noisy geese heading for warmer weather. When Indigo rose from her chair, Bobby caught her arm. "Stay," he said, and waited until she resumed her seat before turning his attention to his sister.

Margaret appeared to be in her mid-twenties, though she was centuries older, one of their mother's eldest children. At five ten barefoot, she was just two inches shorter than him, though her ice blue gaze regularly cut him down a notch or two. When she worked, which was nearly always, she dressed in comfortable shirts and cargo pants and kept her ash blonde hair pulled back in a ponytail. Today, she was dressed in black from head to toe and appeared ready to take on a small army.

He was pretty sure she could do it, probably already had a time or two in her long life.

At his request, she moved across the room with a lethal grace until she was close enough to carry on a low conversation.

"What do you know about the Eternal Order?" he said.

Her expression remained coldly assessing. "Aren't you a little old for fairy tales, brother?"

He gave her the look that comment deserved and pulled a sheet of paper out of his pocket. "I found this in the file Mom gave me."

Margaret took the paper from him, unfolded it, and read the two lines of text it contained before passing it to Indigo. "And?"

"Don't play games, Margaret. Tell me about the Eternal Order."

"It's a myth." She leaned a hip against the edge of the conference table and folded her arms across her chest. "A tale used to scare children into being good. Nothing more."

"How do you explain that paper, then?"

"I don't," she said calmly. "There's not enough there to explain."

"'The Eternal Order. Margaret knows.'" He barked out a laugh. "Sounds pretty straight-forward to me."

"Sounds like a con to me," Margaret shot back.

"I'll find out sooner or later."

"When you do, let me know." She turned on her heel and left the room.

Bobby waited until the door swung shut behind her before turning to Indigo. She was staring after Margaret with an odd expression on her face.

"What's wrong?"

She shook her head. The light danced off her ponytail as it shimmied. "It's nothing, really."

"Spill it."

She pressed her lips together. "You know what the Eternal Order is, don't you?"

"I've read the fairy tales," he said drily, and she frowned.

"They're not fairy tales." She folded the paper in her hands into a precise, even rectangle. "It's an ancient order made up mostly of immortal Daughters bent on keeping the Prophecy of Light from being fulfilled. They were wiped out centuries ago."

"Are you sure?"

She nodded, though her expression remained uncertain. "Surely the Council wouldn't hide their existence from the rest of the People. They were so powerful then, so dangerous. No one was safe."

Which was an excellent reason to keep their return a secret. "I'll see what I can find out."

"No, Bobby." Her hand shot out to grip his arm and her eyes went round in her face. "Leave it be. If the Order's been hidden this long, exposing them can only bring trouble."

He considered her for a moment, took in the fear on her face and in her warm grip. "If I didn't know better, I'd think you were concerned for my safety."

She dropped her hand from his arm. "I'd show the same amount of concern for anyone."

"Liar."

"Think what you will." She stood and handed him the paper. "I'll try to give you an answer on whether or not I'll help track down India by this weekend."

"That's fine." He rose and inched closer to her, lured by the sweet fragrance of her skin. "I'll be by later tonight with supper."

"That's not necessary."

"I insist," he said mildly. "You need to eat and we have things to talk about."

She narrowed her eyes at him. "You're just trying to weasel your way into a kiss."

He held up his hands in mock surrender and managed to edge closer. "You still need to eat."

"You're not going to twist me around your finger like you do everyone else, Bobby." She put her hands up to ward him off. He slid in under her guard and gripped her waist, reeling her in until their bodies touched from waist to knee. Exasperation flickered through her expression. "You never give up, do you?"

"Would you believe me if I said I can't help myself?" He lowered his head to breathe in her scent, let himself go dizzy with it. "That no matter how much I tell myself to back away, something keeps pulling me to you?"

She rested her hands lightly on his chest and kept her gaze locked there. "That doesn't make it right."

"Doesn't make it wrong, either," he countered. "Now, do you want Italian or Chinese?"

The hesitation on her face lingered for a long moment before her lips tilted into a smile and a ghost of a dimple appeared in her cheek. "Barbecue. Sweden has terrible barbecue."

He laughed even as he reined in the happiness zinging through him. "I know just the place."

"Six o'clock, then. Don't be late."

He let her go and watched her leave, her gait smooth and sensual as she strode away.

He sat back down to give his body time to cool off. He must be out of his ever-loving mind to pursue Indigo, even if she was the only woman to ever hold his heart.

INDIGO VISITED HER MOTHER after leaving Bobby's office, then went shopping for groceries and other essentials. She ran into several people she knew, and said hello, asked about family and work. It was nice to be back among the People again.

She flipped on the radio to keep her company as she put away groceries, sang alone with the songs she knew, and danced to the ones she didn't. Her mood lightened with every song. She slipped off her shoes, padded across the wooden floor on socked feet, threw the windows wide. An early autumn breeze blew in, bringing with it the smell of fallen leaves warmed under the sun shining brightly in the clear azure sky. Indigo leaned out the window and turned her face into its warmth, and smiled from the sheer joy of being home.

With a contented sigh, she pulled herself back inside and surveyed the work waiting for her. The number of boxes needing her attention had dwindled by half in the frenzy of unpacking she'd done after Bobby left the day before.

Her breath shallowed as she remembered his hands in her hair, his body pressed against hers, and warmth of another kind heated her blood. Her heart screamed at her to *Run, as fast as you can*, but Indigo pressed it down with a deep inhale of air. Her mother needed her, needed the comfort of kin during the last few weeks of her pregnancy, and Indigo wanted to be at the birth of her next sibling. Bobby would give up eventually. Perhaps they could forge some sort of friendship when he did, as she had with the rest of his family.

A little nagging voice in her head cried *Delusional!* and her heart twisted at the thought of not holding him again, of never knowing what it would be like to kiss Bobby without guilt clinging to her.

Not that she wanted to, of course.

A chill breeze crossed her skin. Indigo snapped to attention, then groaned at the time on the apple-shaped clock she'd hung in the kitchen. Half an hour spent mooning over a man she didn't want and couldn't have regardless. It was shameful, how easily her thoughts slipped to him. She burst into a frenzy of activity to drive him out of her head.

The afternoon passed quickly as Indigo puttered. By the time the first shadows of dusk crossed the room, she'd unpacked everything she could, polished the few items of furniture she'd kept, and updated her calendar with to-do lists for the week.

She was rummaging through the fridge for supper when the doorbell rang, startling her, and immediately a flush heated her cheeks.

Bobby.

She hurried to open the door. He stood on the other side looking as casual and confident and dangerous as he had that morning. *Run, run, run,* her heart urged as it beat double time in her chest. She ignored it and stepped back to let him in.

"Sorry," she said as she shut the door behind him. "I forgot you were coming by."

"Well, that put me in my place." He set the bags he was holding on the kitchen counter and started pulling containers out. "I thought you might be pining for company by now."

"No," she said, then winced. Butterflies danced in her stomach, so she took a deep breath, hoping against hope for them to calm. "I mean, I've been too busy to pine for anything today."

"So I see." His eyes darted around the room, and she felt a moment of pride that she'd managed to set the apartment mostly to rights before his arrival. "Looks like there's not much left to do."

"Oh, well, there's still lots of work." She busied her hands with the bags he'd brought, pulling out cartons of food and placing them on the counter. "I don't even have a couch or a bed yet. Haven't decided if I really want a TV. What kinds of channels can you get on cable here?"

She glanced up when he didn't answer. He was watching her with an intensity that jangled her nerves. "Or I could try satellite," she finished lamely.

"There are other options." His gaze held hers for another moment before he broke it and turned to the cabinets. "Where are the plates?"

"To the left of the fridge."

She pulled out silverware and serving spoons, helped him dish out food on two plates and pour tall glasses of chilled sweet tea. They sat at the rickety table she'd been carting with her from place to place for nearly a century and a half, one of the few pieces she'd kept over the years, simply because it held so many memories.

Bobby talked her through the pros and cons of cable, satellite, and Internet access while they ate, and teased her gently when she confessed to not being a huge fan of television programming. She relaxed gradually until it seemed like the most natural thing in the world to sit next to a handsome, lethally sexy man, sharing a meal and a long, winding conversation.

Their talk eventually turned to local gossip, then to their families, before hitting a personal topic.

"So, when's your mother due?" Bobby sat back and pushed his plate away, unfolding his mile long legs under the table.

"A few weeks." Indigo scooted her legs out of the way to make room for him. "We're all hoping for a boy."

"I bet." He nudged her legs gently with his own under the table. "Your mom will be happy to have you near."

"I hope so. India's made it a little hard on her."

"Mmm. She was always so bitter."

"That's one word for it." She stood, fighting the restless unease that filled her whenever she thought of her twin, and gathered their plates. "When Mom became mortal and married Glen, India flipped out. Apparently, she screamed at Mom about being weak or some nonsense and Mom kicked her out."

Bobby rose and followed her to the sink. "I bet that was something to see."

"I'm glad I missed it." Indigo took a deep, soothing breath as she boxed up the leftovers and stowed them in the fridge.

"They've always been at odds with one another, fighting over every little thing. That's what it felt like when we were growing up, anyway."

He leaned against the counter and rested his hands against the edge. "And you hid in your books."

She glanced at him, astonished. "How did you know?"

"I know you."

"No," she said with a shake of her head, and eased back at the dangerous glint in his eyes.

"Yes, I do, and if you don't stop running from me, I'm gonna start chasing you."

Her heart jumped into her throat and excitement thrummed along her skin. "I'm not running."

"Indigo." He touched a finger gently to her mouth, traced the line of her lower lip before letting his hand fall back to his side. "You can lie to everybody else. Don't lie to me."

"I'm not..." She sucked her lip into her mouth, trying to quell the tingle his touch had caused, and only made it worse. "This is silly."

"Yes, it is."

His agreement held no rancor, though his body was stiff, ready, and his hazel eyes glittered and bored into her, tracking every single movement she made as if he were waiting to pounce.

This must be what a rabbit felt like when it faced off against a hound.

She ran water in the sink to wash the few dirty dishes instead of using the dishwasher, and struggled to calm her sudden nerves. "Why did you decide to come back to Tellowee?"

His expression relaxed into a knowing half-grin. "Same reason as you. Dad's MS has been a problem over the past few years and Mom needed help."

"I thought it was getting better."

He opened drawers until he found a dish towel and slung it over his shoulder. His hands were quick and competent as he rinsed the dishes she washed, and a little flutter went through her.

What else would those hands do well?

"It comes and goes, but sometimes, they need an extra hand. Charlotte helps out when she can."

"But she's got the babies."

"Gorgeous, sweet babies, but they're a handful, and since our other sisters are gone more often than not..." He shrugged, a casual lift of one muscled shoulder. "I needed to be near family when I got out of the Army, so here I am, helping out where I can."

Her heart melted a little at his admission. "That's very sweet of you."

"Hardly."

She peered at him and saw a slight tint of red on his cheeks. "Are you blushing?"

"No."

His voice was just shy of sullen. She bit her lip against the amusement bubbling up. "What was that you said about not lying?"

"Har." He checked his watch and pressed his lips into a hard line. "I have to go. Early meeting."

"Oh." She'd just gotten used to having him around. "Thanks for supper."

"Any time." He dropped the dish towel over the drainer and cupped her shoulders with his strong, warm hands. "In fact, I vote we do this again tomorrow."

"Can't," she said, and tried to staunch the honest regret she felt, along with the flood of sensation his touch caused. "Girls' night out."

"Wednesday, then," he said, his voice firm.

"Furniture shopping." When his eyes narrowed, she added meekly, "In the afternoon."

"Come by the office when you're ready and I'll go with you. No buts," he said when she protested and brushed his lips across her forehead. "Lock up behind me."

She walked him out, half afraid he'd try more than a soft

kiss, and sagged with disappointment against the closed door when he didn't even hug her. *No,* she told herself firmly as she straightened. *You're happy he didn't try to do anything. Happy, not disappointed.*

She finished straightening up from their meal, made ready for bed, and settled into her sleeping bag with *Jane Eyre.*

And stared blankly at the book, her imagination caught by the kiss yet to come.

THREE

OBBY JANGLED the keys in his hand, flipping them around on one finger as he mulled over the meeting he'd just left. When his mother had given him the names of suspected traitors to the People, he'd decided to take an individual approach to each one, in particular Isolde, a member of the Council of Seven, the People's ruling body.

He'd been raised to understand that dealing with a councilmember should be done carefully, no matter what the reason. Instead of handling her on his own, he'd approached Hawthorne, an elder who was Isolde's aunt, to at least lay some groundwork. Hawthorne had allowed him his say under her carefully impassive gaze, then said *no* in a voice as cold and dead as the dark side of the moon.

Given her reputation, he was lucky she hadn't separated his head from his body on sight.

The elevator dinged, the doors opened, and people spilled out on their way to lunch. Bobby stepped inside, punched at the button for the floor housing BDH, and studied the lighted numbers marking the elevator's progress.

Hawthorne would eventually come around. She'd been halfway there when he'd left, though he wasn't entirely sure if that was because he'd poured on the charm or if she was getting soft in her old age.

His lips twitched into a smirk. Not that he'd dare call her *old*, especially when she appeared to be about his age, if that. Immortal Daughters tended to be a little sensitive about their age, and he liked his head right where it was.

His humor faded abruptly, taking his mood with it. He'd learned the hard way just how touchy Daughters could be about their age, especially when faced with a potential suitor. Indigo had pushed him away quickly enough. Sixteen was young, yeah, but he'd been a man in the eyes of the People when he'd tried to claim her the first time, a claim that would've been legal and binding to his mother and hers. Among the People, those permissions were the most important. Not much else mattered when a Son united his life with a Daughter.

He shrugged his left shoulder, stretched his fingers over his collarbone, brushing the top of the tattoo hidden by his shirt. Permission was one thing. That tattoo was another. It forever marked him as the husband of a Daughter, claimed through love or, in his case, the drunken recklessness of a man who'd had his heart ground under the heels of a woman who hadn't wanted him.

It had taken him the better part of a decade to come to terms with Indigo's rejection, to work out the anger and hurt. They were still there, waiting to pounce, but over time, he'd found a way to chain them back so they didn't eat at him every single moment. He'd spent years atoning for the damage he'd done trying to exorcise that pain. His past would always haunt him, nothing he could do about that, though he and it had made an uneasy truce, sort of.

His mind drifted to the conversation he'd had with his mother the day she'd hired him to track down those who may have betrayed the People. She'd been spot on when she'd said he felt he wasn't good enough for a woman's love. *Indigo.* His heart lurched in his chest. Mom had said he had to find a way to deal with the past or it would eat the heart out of him, but he knew the truth. His heart was still there, even if it was battered and filthy from the things he'd done after Indigo rejected him. It was there, and it still belonged to her.

He'd asked her to stop by today, to let him tag along while she shopped for furniture, and he recognized his request for what it was: A pathetic attempt to be a part of her life, in whatever small way she would have him. He would settle for friends, if that's all they could be, and not wish for more. He didn't deserve more, no matter what his mother thought. Maybe before he'd let his emotions rule his life he could've had Indigo, but not now, not after the things he'd done, not unless they could both forget the past and the hand fate had dealt them.

Goddess knew he wanted her enough to try, even if all they could ever have was friendship.

The elevator doors opened. Bobby stepped out into the reception area and spotted her dressed in a shimmering, red flowy shirt over form-fitting leggings that highlighted the lush curve of her bottom and the strength in her legs. The breath whooshed out of him in a rush and every nerve in his body went on full alert.

Yeah, friends. How's that working out for you?

He shook his head to try to clear it, and noticed the tense set of Indigo's shoulders as she faced off against Laura, whose normally professional face was drawn into a thunderous scowl.

What the hell.

He ignored the sudden ache in his temples and stalked toward the two women, resigned to sorting out whatever problem had cropped up between them.

INDIGO SMOOTHED her shirt down over her flat stomach, then tugged at the hem to make sure the fabric hung correctly. Above her, digitally created numbers lit up in sequence as the elevator rose toward the floor housing Bobby's company. Her stomach jumped when the elevator dinged, signaling a stop. It wasn't because of nerves, couldn't be. Bobby had asked her to drop by today and offered to go shopping with her. She'd made a considered, rational decision to allow him to accompany her, for selfish reasons that had nothing to do with the attraction sparking between them.

No, not attraction. *Tension.* There was still *tension* between them, left over from that unfortunate day. She didn't want to dwell on that. It was in the past and best left alone. Better to look to the future, a bright future where she was welcome in the Upton household among people she'd known for decades prior to Bobby's birth, and could visit there without any *tension* between herself and the beloved Son because she and he had resolved it.

That the Son in question had a strong back and owned a truck big enough for hauling furniture was merely coincidental.

She walked out of the elevator toward the reception desk. Laura was sitting in for the BDH receptionist again. There was nothing sinister or untoward about the young woman, yet her presence jangled Indigo's nerves even more. Laura dressed smartly, held herself well, and apparently managed the office with a ruthless efficiency that would make Rebecca Upton proud. Indigo ignored the niggle of envy and pasted a pleasant smile on her face.

"I'm here to see Bobby," Indigo said.

"Mr. Upton is out of the office at the moment." Laura's wide brown eyes were cold behind her wire-rimmed glasses. "Would you like to make an appointment?"

Indigo tried to ignore the sinking feeling in her gut and failed spectacularly. So, it was like that. What was Bobby doing spending time with her instead of Laura? "Would it be all right if I wait?"

"That would be futile. Mr. Upton indicated he would be out of the office the entire day."

"Since he asked me to meet him here this afternoon, that's unlikely." Indigo gritted her teeth, searching for her normally endless patience. "I'm sure he'll be back soon. I'd very much like to wait for him."

Laura rose and rested her fingers on the phone in front of her. "Mr. Upton did not tell me about a meeting. Therefore, he will not be back. You should make an appointment and go before I call security."

Indigo huffed out an annoyed breath. Before she could reply, the elevator's doors opened. She glanced around. The nerves she'd managed to settle jumped back into play at the sight of Bobby stepping out, his expression caught between irritation and anger.

"What's going on?" he said.

Indigo opened her mouth to reply. Laura beat her to the punch.

"Ms. Dupree arrived without an appointment." Laura shot a heated glare at Indigo over the top of her glasses. "I informed her that you would be out today."

"I will be," Bobby agreed. "Indi and I are going shopping."

Laura pressed her lips together with what was surely disapproval. Indigo just refrained from giving the other woman a *so there* look. When had she stooped to such childish gestures? Right. That would be the day Bobby Upton had sauntered back into her life.

Bobby ran a hand casually down Indigo's back. She shivered at the touch, though it didn't distract her from the venom that flickered across Laura's face a moment before the young woman arranged her features into a professional mask.

His voice dropped as he leaned into Indigo. "I need to make some notes before we go. It won't take long, if you don't mind the wait."

"I'm a little early." Her irritation over the intractable Laura faded. "In fact, I deliberately came early to see if you wanted to have lunch with me. My treat, in return for your expert shopping help."

Laura gave a patently fake cough into her hand.

"Sure," he said. "Want to wait in the office while I catch

up?"

"That would be lovely."

"Go ahead, then." He pulled out a set of keys, selected one, and handed it to Indigo. "I'll be right there."

She took the ring of keys from Bobby's hand. and headed toward his office, ignoring Bobby and Laura's quiet conversation behind her. The blinds were pulled down tightly against the row of glass windows between the main area and his office. Indigo unlocked the door and flipped the light switch on as she went in, closed the door, and dropped the keys on his desk.

She wandered around his office, exploring the books shelved neatly along the length of the wall behind his desk. Pictures and memorabilia sat at regular intervals, interspersed among the books. She examined each in turn as she skimmed book titles. There was a picture of Bobby with his family when he was about ten and another right beside it of him as an infant, held gingerly in his father's arms. Indigo sighed at the love on Robert's face as he gazed down at his son, touched at the depth of expression.

There were the obligatory sports photos and a few snapshots from Bobby's time in the military. In one, he and Drew bracketed Hiro. All three were dressed in camouflage and wore somber expressions. From the thinness of their bodies and their relative youth, she guessed the photo had been taken on graduation day for advanced training of some sort.

She'd deliberately fostered a lack of knowledge about Bobby as subtly as she could. Maybe it was time for that to change.

Two shelves down was a photo of Bobby with Dani draped over his back, both laughing with the carefree zest of youth. The memories of the day it was taken popped into her mind. Labor Day, about a month before Bobby's sixteenth birthday. The whole town had come out for the annual national holiday and made a day of it with races and contests and food and fun. It had been a wonderful day, though she likely wouldn't remember it as brightly if her life hadn't changed so completely not long after, immortal memory or not.

She stroked a finger over the picture, oddly disquieted at the joy in his young face, and the hardness that had grown into it since.

Because of her.

Indigo inhaled deeply and pushed the guilt away as Bobby opened the door to his office.

"Sorry about that," he said. "I don't know what's gotten into Laura. She's usually so good with people."

Indigo moved out of the way as Bobby came around the desk, and took a seat on the sofa beside the door while he leaned over his desk and made notes on the large calendar there.

"Really?" she said.

"Really, what?"

His expression was blank, his body relaxed and loose except for a slight tightening around his eyes. Indigo considered him and couldn't quite tamp down the smug amusement. He really had no clue why Laura had acted the way she had. Whatever feelings Laura had for him, they weren't returned, not in the same measure.

"Nothing," Indigo said.

He speared her with an intense gaze that left her needier than it should've, then shrugged. "I'll give you a key so you can come in and work."

"I haven't agreed to help you yet."

"But you will."

"You have a lot of confidence in your ability to persuade me."

"Mmm. Persuasion, charm, bribery. Whatever it takes."

He jotted down a few more notes, checked his watch, and threw his pen onto the desk. His eyes slid down her body so briefly she would've missed it if she weren't paying attention. A frisson of heated awareness shivered through her at the glint of approval in his gaze.

"So, where are we going?"

"Wherever you want." She stood and noted the way his gaze followed her movements, almost as if he couldn't help looking. His words from a few days before floated through her mind. *Would you believe me if I said I can't help myself?* It appeared he really couldn't. It pleased her, inexplicably, irrationally. "Would you mind driving?"

"I don't mind." He picked up the keys from his desk and crossed the room to stand beside her. "Probably for the best anyway, since I brought the truck."

She pressed her lips together to stifle the humor tugging at her. A strong man with a truck indeed. "I appreciate that."

He opened the door and placed a hand on the small of her back in a touch that warmed her through and through. "Figured you'd want to get that furniture in as soon as possible."

She let him escort her through the building, and noted with uncharacteristic spite that Laura had abandoned her post. "You figured correctly. I don't mind sleeping on the floor once in a while, but it gets uncomfortable night after night."

They entered the elevator and he punched the main floor's button with a roguish grin that made her blush. Why had she brought up *sleeping* around him, of all people?

She blew a silent breath out when he let it go and forced herself to carry on a natural conversation with him that did *not* include anything related to sleeping or beds or the attraction sparking so brightly between them.

BOBBY TOOK HER to a chichi deli a block away from his office and insisted on paying for their lunch. After they placed orders for a turkey sub each, they found a table off to one side, away from the windows and the lunch crowd streaming in.

Indigo sat down across from Bobby. "You know, I was supposed to treat you as a thank you for helping me today."

He shrugged. "Yeah, but I'm the man."

She looked up from the sandwich she was arranging in meticulous portions across the butcher's paper that held it. "What does that have to do with anything?"

"This isn't Tellowee where Daughters run amuck and bully and coddle their men into submission." He grinned at her. "This is America and I'm the man. Here, when we take beautiful women out, we pay."

She paused with one quarter of her sandwich halfway to her mouth. He thought she was beautiful. After all this time and all the things that had passed between them, the heartache and disappointment and anger, he still thought she was beautiful. A gooey warmth nudged at her heart, right where her resolve was supposed to be. How was she supposed to fight him off when he said things like that?

He raised his eyebrows and pierced her with a look that seemed to see right through her. "No rebuttal?"

"I'm not letting you pay every time we go out."

"You say that like this is an official date."

She gave him a quelling look. "Besides, this lunch was my idea."

"Still the man." When she started to speak, he nudged the plastic basket holding her lunch with a finger. "Are we gonna argue or eat?"

"I wasn't arguing," she said primly. "I was clarifying."

"Uh-huh." He took a bite, chewed thoughtfully as his eyes lingered on her. "How did you like working on the Sandby borg site?"

"It was fun, right up until the robbery. Dr. Lindberg, the man in charge of the dig," she said when he raised a questioning eyebrow, "he was a lot of fun to be around. A bit of a rascal, too, but only around his wife. I think they've been married fifty-five or six years now, and are still very much in love."

He glanced down at his sandwich, hesitated, then took a bite of it almost mechanically. She nibbled at her own sandwich as the silence dragged on between them. Why had she mentioned the l-word around him? No matter what had passed between them, he deserved better than to have her prod an old wound. She sipped from her bottle of water, searching for a safer topic. "How did you meet Hiro and Drew?"

His shoulders relaxed as his gaze lifted and a smile tugged at his mouth. "In the Army. We went through, ah, training together."

"Training." She took another bite, waited for him to elaborate. "What kind of training?"

"Can't say." His grin grew a fraction. "Classified."

"Honestly, Bobby."

"You're so fun to tease." He held up his hands at her impatient look. "Ok, ok. We went through OTC together."

She inhaled sharply and said in a harsh whisper, "Delta Force?"

"Mmm. Pretty much everything after that really is classified."

"But the Delta Force, Bobby? That's so dangerous."

His expression hardened. "I enlisted for the danger, Indi."

No, he'd enlisted to escape what had happened between them and the Army had taken him in like the lost soul he'd been. A wave of guilt flooded through her, dimming her pleasure of the day. He could've been killed or, worse, captured and tortured, all because she'd been too cowardly to handle his heart properly. "I can't believe your mother allowed that."

"I was sixteen. Didn't give her a say in the matter."

"You weren't sixteen when you were selected for OTC."

"No, I was a little older." His grin returned, though his eyes held a dangerous glint. "And thanks to your training, Maetyrm, I had an interesting enough skill set to attract the right kind of attention."

"So you slew them with your mad grammar skills, huh."

"That wasn't the only thing you taught, and you weren't the only teacher I had."

Her appetite fled abruptly and she pushed her basket away. Every Daughter and Son went through rigorous training from an early age. Martial arts, gymnastics, outdoor survival, weapons training, and a host of academic skills that placed them well above their mortal human peers in myriad ways. Many wound up in the armed forces or worked as mercenaries precisely because of the intensive training they'd received as children. "How did you make it into the Army at such a young age?"

"How do you think?" he retorted. "Every teenager in Tellowee knows who to go to if they need an ID."

She'd used such services herself over the years, each time she needed to alter her identification to reflect her apparent age, which hadn't changed in nearly a century and a half. "So you paid someone to fake a birth certificate and school records," she guessed.

"Something like that." He nudged her basket again, inching it closer to her. "You need to eat. We've got a long day ahead of us."

"I'm not hungry."

"Eat anyway."

"Bobby." She rubbed her suddenly damp palms over her thighs. Everything he'd been through since the moment she'd fled from him had been her fault. Every day under the Army's thumb, every day in a backwater hell, surrounded by people who would as soon kill him as spit on him. All of that because of her. "I'm sorry."

"Why?"

"You know why." She took a deep breath, tried to exhale the guilt and worry tangled up with her nerves. "You joined the Army because of me, because I pushed you away."

"I joined the Army because I wanted to be there." He speared her with a flinty gaze. "Don't ever try to own that again. Being there was my choice. If I hadn't liked it, I wouldn't have kept re-upping."

She sat back in her chair, nonplussed.

"Seriously. You're not to blame for what I did." He switched chairs, taking the one beside her. "Here, guess I'm gonna have to feed you, since you won't feed yourself."

"You'll do no such thing," she said, though she smiled and ate her lunch, as he'd no doubt intended her to.

Their conversation drifted to other things, to Indigo's relief. How Hiro, Drew, and Bobby had schemed and plotted and finally opened their business together two years before, after they'd gotten out of the Army. About her travels during the last decade, mostly from one archaeological dig to another, with a short stint as a teacher at another of the People's centers in Europe. And about trivialities. Books read recently, the best grocery stores outside of Tellowee, who was dating whom in the insular community.

Gradually, the awkwardness faded between them. Sometimes, she thought Bobby might be holding back, especially when he talked about Hiro and Drew. He was very open about what he did share, though, and she tried to be as well. They were working toward some sort of friendship, after all. If he touched her hair as they talked or held her hand when they wandered through crowds, she put it down to his solicitous nature. He was a toucher. She'd seen him do the exact same things with his sisters, during that *before time* she refused to dwell on. If her hand tingled from the warmth of his touch and sparked off a chain reaction of dizzy heat that rocketed through every cell in her body, well, that was her problem. She could deal with it.

After lunch, he drove her to a huge furniture store in Buford. Once inside, she paused in awe of the sheer size of the selection.

"Bobby, really." She looked around at row after row of furniture grouped into functional settings for every room in the house. "I only need a serviceable sofa and a bed. We'll never sort through all of this in one day."

"Sure we will." He placed a hand on the small of her back. "C'mon."

Indigo allowed him to guide her through a series of artfully arranged living areas. He stopped at a grouping consisting of a large couch, a loveseat, and a recliner, along with a coffee table, matching end tables, and more accessories than she would ever need.

She bit her lip and searched for a polite way to tell him no. "I don't need this much."

"You don't have to take the whole thing." He grinned, took her hand, and led her toward the couch. "Let's try it out."

He sat in the middle of the couch, pulled her down beside him, and draped a friendly arm around her shoulders. A tang of his soap tickled her nose, sharp and masculine, like Bobby. She shivered when his hand grazed her upper arm through the thin sleeve of her blouse.

The couch was soft and cushy, easy to snuggle into. Maybe a little too easy, especially with an attractive man sitting next to you with his arm draped over your shoulders. "This is comfortable."

"Sturdy, too." He patted the cushion with his free hand. "Easy to clean. This model has a fold-out bed."

"A useful addition." She turned to look at him and her breath caught in her throat. His mouth was inches from her own, sensual and tempting. "You've done this before, I take it."

"Mmm." He rubbed a finger over her lower lip, slowly, carefully, as if he were memorizing the shape and texture. "The extra bed comes in handy when you've got a large family."

"I suppose it does," she murmured. His gaze dropped to her mouth and his arm tightened around her shoulders, drawing her closer, and she put a hand on his chest, to stop him or encourage him, she didn't know.

He blinked and drew back a moment before she heard footsteps approaching. Indigo stood, as much to pull herself together as anything, and managed a smile for the salesman walking toward them. The not-quite-kiss she shoved out of her mind. She couldn't do a thing about the heat that lingered from Bobby's touch.

In the end, she chose to take the sofa and a recliner in a deep chocolate brown, not because they were sturdy and easy to care for, but because Bobby looked so comfortable there. Since he looked comfortable, she reasoned others would as well.

Buying the sofa had absolutely nothing to do with her sudden need to encourage him to drop by her home. Nothing at all.

Bobby talked her out of looking for bedroom furniture at that store, saying only that he had something else in mind. She let it go and set her attention to haggling the price down on both pieces, then arranged for them to be delivered to her apartment. When they left the store, Indigo said, "Just out of curiosity, why aren't we taking the sofa back with us?"

"Because we need the room for your bedroom furniture."

He helped her into his truck before walking around and getting in himself. Once they were underway, she shifted in the seat, studying his profile. He drove with his eyes fixed on the road and his left hand at the top of the steering wheel. His right hand rested on the bench seat between them, edging closer to her in tiny increments.

"What was wrong with the furniture at that store?"

"It's not what you're looking for." He merged onto the highway and accelerated to match the flow of traffic. "I saw the way you eyed the coffee table in there."

Her lips curled into an unladylike sneer. "It looked fake."

"It's cheaper wood with a veneer. Still wood, but not the kind you're used to."

"Oh? What kind of wood am I used to, then?"

He glanced at her long enough for his mischievous grin to reignite the desire he'd stirred in her earlier, a heat her body hadn't quite forgotten. "The real kind. Trust me. You'll love what I have in mind."

"How do you know?"

"You liked the sofa, didn't you?"

She settled back into her seat. Following his lead wasn't so hard, but trusting him to pick out furniture for her? What woman in her right mind would allow a man to have a free hand there?

They ended up at a climate controlled storage unit not far from Tellowee. Bobby helped her out of the truck before he unlocked one of the units and rolled the door up. His unit was packed from wall to wall with items draped in protective sheets and cardboard boxes of all shapes and sizes.

She followed him into the cool interior, peering with him under each sheet he lifted. "What is this?"

"Furniture. Mostly wood." He moved a box and pulled the sheet off of a low rectangular object, revealing a Mission-style coffee table. "Some other stuff I'm saving for..." He shrugged casually as his voice trailed off.

"What?"

"Stuff. This table would look great with your new couch."

He appeared so uncomfortable, she let the moment pass and turned her attention to the coffee table. "Is that wormy chestnut?"

"Yup, with a hand-rubbed oil finish. You'll need coasters and can't put anything warm down on it, but it should suit you."

She knelt to run a hand over the smooth finish, down a perfectly aligned joint. It must have taken hours for someone to craft this one piece alone. "I can't take this."

"Sure you can."

He stepped deeper into the unit, lifting sheets as he went.

"It wouldn't be right." She stood reluctantly. "You're obviously saving it for a very special purpose."

"Yes," he agreed mildly. "Here's the bed for you."

He flipped back one of the sheets, revealing an intricately carved headboard. Indigo stepped closer, her body brushing against his in the tight space as she did, and ran a hand over the design.

"It's beautiful." Questions popped into her mind one after another, so many she had a hard time choosing between them. Finally, she settled on, "Where did you get it?"

"I made it. Most of the design elements are from the Book of Kells." He stroked a hand down her hair, then rested it on the small of her back. "The wood's walnut, from a tree that used to stand near the house. Do you remember?"

"The one lightening struck not long after you were born," she murmured, and found herself leaning into his warm comfort.

"Dad did a lot of woodworking back then, before he knew about the MS. He salvaged what he could, had it sawed for furniture." He moved to stand behind her, dropped his hands to her hips, and drew her back until their bodies were pressed firmly together. "I found it when I got out of the Army."

When he spoke, his breath puffed gently against her ear, sending a shiver along her skin. She eased forward fractionally, away from the delicious press of his body against hers, away from the heat and temptation. His fingers dug into her hips, holding her in place.

Distraction. She need to distract him, or maybe herself, before one of them gave in and did something they might both regret or, worse, enjoy. "It must've taken hours to make this."

"Mmm." His hands eased around to her stomach as he nuzzled his face into the juncture of her neck and shoulder. "You smell like wildflowers in the spring."

"Focus, Bobby," she said, and winced when her voice hitched.

"I am." He licked her neck above the collar of her shirt, and she shuddered at the feel of his tongue on her skin. "I'm trying to talk you into taking the headboard."

She breathed out a laugh. "Is that what you're doing?"

"Say you'll take it."

He pressed a kiss to her neck, just above where he'd licked, and blew gently along the moisture left behind. Heat raced through her, pooling between her legs in a rush of warmth and wetness. She melted into him and tilted her head to the side, silently begging him to continue. Goddess above, what he did to her.

He nipped at her earlobe with sharp teeth, eliciting a needy gasp from her. "Say it slowly, though, will you? I kinda like the persuasion part."

She rested her hands on his, to keep them in place, to learn the feel of him, which one, she didn't know or care. "Tell me why you're lending it to me."

His sigh feathered along her skin as he drew away, stealing the warmth of his touch from her. "You don't want to know."

"Yes, I do." She twisted and caught his heated gaze with her own. "What's so bad that you can't tell me?"

"It's not that big a deal." The warmth drained from his expression, leaving his beautiful hazel eyes cautious and cool. He dropped a perfunctory kiss to her cheek and stepped away from her. "This is the stuff I made for my own house. Since I'm living with Mom and Dad and it's just sitting here, I thought you might like to use it."

She held no illusions that he was being completely honest with her. Whatever he was holding back was his secret to keep. She should absolutely respect his privacy, and she would, right after she found a way to weasel it out of him. "I'll take it, but only if you promise to tell me when you need it back."

"I won't, not for a while." He pulled the sheet free and handed it to her before hefting the headboard.

"I can help."

"Not without ruining your outfit, which I like." He stopped and raked a gaze over her body from head to toe, intensifying the memory of him behind her, warm and firm and strong. "A lot."

Her limbs went limp and weak at that expression, edgy, needy, and so very, very appreciative. "Oh. Um."

Her eyes fluttered closed. Could she be any more of a lovesick girl around him? *Friends*, she recited desperately. *We're going to be friends.*

She clung to that mantra as they loaded and unloaded furniture. By the time they made it to a mattress store, she had herself well in hand, right up to the moment when Bobby helped her pick out a mattress by sprawling out on a few of the displays. An image of him naked in the bed he'd made flashed through her mind, and her muscles clenched with a desperate, fierce need to have him there. *Friends* might not be exactly where they were headed. All the ignoring in the world couldn't make that thought go away.

FOUR

BY THE END OF THE WEEK, Bobby managed to squeeze in time to speak with Zena and Laura about their upcoming assignments. Zena's sneer at the extra work had been expected. It was her normal way of dealing with change.

Laura, though, had been downright frigid to him since he'd spoken to her about Indigo, which seemed out of proportion to what he'd told her. *Don't hassle her. She's family.* Somehow, it had been enough to send Laura into a tizzy.

He took a sip of coffee and grimaced at the harsh, bitter taste. She'd stopped making the coffee, too, leaving it to early-riser Drew, who burned water trying to boil it.

A knock sounded on the door. *Speak of the devil*, Bobby thought, and waved Drew and Hiro into his office.

He'd deliberately left briefing his closest friends until last so he could ponder how best to approach them. They'd shared so much over the years, but he'd always managed to hold the story of the People back. He'd never known how to tell them he was descended from a group of immortal Amazons living under a curse, and he still wasn't sure he wanted them to know now. Telling them would help them understand the real threat the People faced. Leaving them in the dark might make them unnecessarily vulnerable.

They'd probably think he was nuts. No, not probably. Definitely. Who wouldn't?

Hiro and Drew sat down in the two chairs placed opposite his desk, and he was struck once again by how different they really were. Each had joined the Army for the same reason he had, to escape. Drew often spoke of his childhood in Boston as a dead-end choice between running drugs or working in the factories. Either one meant a hard life and an early grave. Hiro's choices had been less harsh. His parents had wanted him to go to college, become a corporate schmuck, and marry a "good Japanese girl," who they'd already picked out for him. He'd said no by enlisting the day after his eighteenth birthday.

Bobby had been running from the woman who'd unwittingly captured his heart.

And now here they were, operating a security business catering to corporate schmucks, all still single, and none of them headed for an early grave, an outright miracle given some of the assignments they'd pulled. All in all, it wasn't a bad life, especially now that they were out from under Uncle Sam's thumb.

Hiro crossed an ankle over a knee and rested his elbows on the arms of his chair. "I know we have other business to discuss, but I wanted to get this out of the way. India visited me a couple of nights ago."

Drew straightened in his chair and muttered a curse. "Me, too. Snuck into my house in the dead of night like she owned the place."

Bobby rubbed a hand over tired eyes. He'd have to disclose the whole bit, immortality, curse, and all. "What did she do?"

"Why aren't you surprised?" Drew said. "Goddamn woman broke into my house and you take it like it's nothing."

"Oh, it's not nothing, but it could've been a lot worse." Bobby sipped his coffee and grimaced. "Stop making coffee. I'd rather do without."

Drew's eyebrows snapped into a mulish scowl.

Hiro's expression was calm, his voice even. "What do you mean, worse?"

"First, tell me what she did," Bobby said.

"Other than break into my goddamn house? Tried to bribe me to turn on you, that's what, and then threatened to kick my ass when I said no." Drew crossed thick, muscled arms over his chest. "And if you don't like my coffee, maybe you shoulda been nicer to Laura."

"I haven't done anything to Laura," Bobby said.

"India," Hiro said with some emphasis, "tried to bribe me as well. Do you think she's approached anyone else?"

"If you didn't do anything, then why is she sulking?" Drew said with a pointed glare.

"All I said was, leave Indigo alone. That's it. And I was nice." Bobby heaved a sigh. "India would know better than to approach Margaret, but the others, yeah, she probably has."

"Why not Margaret?" Hiro asked.

"If you were so nice, then why's Laura in a huff?" Drew asked.

Bobby ignored him. "Margaret would've torn her to pieces on sight."

Hiro nodded. "Margaret the Frigidaire..."

Bobby winced. "Don't let her catch you calling her that."

"I'm not stupid," Hiro said.

Drew snorted. "Says who?"

"Margaret might be cold, but she's stronger, faster, and a better fighter than India." Bobby sat back, gauged his timing, and said, "Plus, she's a few centuries older."

"Back to Laura," Drew began, then snapped his jaws together with an audible click. "What was that?"

"I believe he said Margaret's a few centuries older than India." Hiro's voice held a hint of dry amusement. "Exactly how old is Margaret?"

"She'd kill me if I told you." Bobby rubbed a finger across his mouth, hiding the smile threatening to rise. "Just keep pretending she's twenty-nine-ish and your head is safe."

"And how is it that Margaret's managed to live that long?" Drew said. "Takes more than a wish for that to happen."

"She's immortal, or close enough."

"And you are, too, then." Drew's expression lightened as he leaned toward Hiro. "I knew we shoulda had his head checked after that last mission. All the fungi. Went straight to his brains."

"It's a wonder he has any left," Hiro agreed.

"Seriously, guys." Bobby rolled his eyes skyward. "Did you never wonder why we rotate women out of here so frequently?"

"Because we like to keep 'em hot?" Drew said, and yelped when Hiro casually backhanded him on the arm.

"Because people tend to notice when someone doesn't age," Bobby said. "Because these women are busy chasing an ancient blood enemy and protecting their kin."

Drew sat forward in the chair. "You're serious about all this?"

"As serious as death." Bobby took a sip of his coffee without thinking. "Dammit, Drew, stay away from the coffee machine."

"I told you..."

"I think you'd better start at the beginning," Hiro said.

"Right." Bobby pushed his coffee mug away to keep from picking it up out of habit. "About ten millennia ago, Seven Sisters avenged the deaths of their parents and were cursed to immortality by an angry god, and at the same time, were cursed to never bear sons, only daughters."

He took them through a brief history of the People as they knew it, and explained how the Lady Goddess had tempered the curse, providing an out for each immortal Daughter, and how the People had searched relentlessly for a way to break the curse for good, so that no Daughter would be born with the same, crushing burden. He told them of the Shadow Enemy and their thirst for the blood of the People, and the many battles waged over time as the Daughters struggled to find peace. Finally, he filled them in on the recent finds at Sandby borg, of the discovery of the Prophecy of Light and its translation by a team at the IECS, and the hope they all had that the Light would choose the path that would end the curse, if only they could figure out what the Light was.

When he finished, the room fell into a long silence. Hiro stroked his mouth thoughtfully and Drew tapped a nervous beat on his thigh.

When they remained silent, Bobby said, "C'mon guys. Would I lie to you?"

"You bet your ass," Drew said. At the same time, Hiro said, "Absolutely."

Bobby sucked in a breath, straining for patience. "I mean about something important."

"Hunh." Drew stabbed two fingers at Bobby. "There was that time in Reno, with that hooker you tried to pass off as your sister."

"Because she *was* my sister, you moron." Bobby jerked a thumb at the wall behind him. "There's the picture of us together when I was a kid."

"Uh-huh," Drew said, skepticism heavy in his voice. "I guess those drug lords in Afghanistan were your sisters, too."

"No, those were really drug lords," Bobby said. "And that was a little lie for the greater cause, so it doesn't count."

"What about Madrid, when he snuck two hoochie girls into the CO's hotel room and blamed you," Hiro said to Drew. "Islamabad."

Hiro and Drew shared grins and said in unison, "The camel derby."

Bobby dropped his head into his hands. When had he lost control of the conversation?

"Do you remember the name of that jockey?" Hiro said.

"Who cares about him. It was the sister I wanted." Drew sighed out a smile. "Good times."

"I didn't actually lie about the camel or the jockey," Bobby pointed out. "Or the jockey's sister, who, by the way, was a man and not related to the jockey *at all.*"

"Are you sure?" Drew said. "Because I had my hands..."

Bobby interrupted. Some things, a man didn't need to know

about his friends. "Positive, and it's still not a lie."

Hiro spread his hands in a mild shrug. "You didn't tell us about it beforehand, so close enough."

"Ok, all right. I fudged a couple of times." Bobby sat back in his chair and rubbed a hand across his hair, ruffling it. "But I never lied about anything important and you know it."

"True," Hiro said.

Drew shrugged one shoulder. "I always wondered why that hooker looked just like your sister did twenty years ago."

Bobby shot him an exasperated look and ground his teeth together. "Jerusha's not a hooker, and if you call her that one more time, I'm gonna..."

"Boys," Hiro said, and waited until Drew and Bobby exchanged pointed glares before continuing. "Let's say this story is true. Why didn't you tell us before?"

Bobby barked out a laugh. "Do you think you would've believed me before?"

"If you'd needed us to." Hiro's gaze was steady. "Are you immortal?"

"No. Children born to Daughters who've broken the curse are always mortal."

"Are you sure you didn't sniff a fungus or something?" Drew said.

Bobby fixed a withering glare on him.

"Who exactly is your mother sending us after?" Hiro folded his hands across his waist, his dark eyes patient, steady. "Members of the Shadow Enemy?"

Bobby shook his head. "When I said traitors, I really meant traitors. Mom thinks some of the Daughters have, for whatever reason, been manipulating information somehow, either hiding it from the People or giving false data to us. The problem is, these Daughters may be working alone or they may be working together, or some combination, but they aren't necessarily working with the Shadow Enemy."

"What about India? What's her role in all this?" Drew

steepled his fingers together under his chin. "And how do you know Indigo's not in on it with her?"

"For one, Indigo and India have never gotten along," Bobby said through gritted teeth. "And for another, we know for a fact that India runs with a bad crowd. I can't share the details, but Dani wasn't in the hospital a couple of weeks ago with appendicitis."

"India did something to her?" Drew's eyebrows veed over the storm clouds brewing in his eyes, and Bobby winced. Drew had a bit of a crush on Dani. Bobby dreaded having to tell his partner about his adoptive sister's new love interest.

"No, not India, but she was part of it." Bobby sucked in a breath and blew it out slowly. "Look, guys, I'm only telling you this much because India came after you. She's dangerous. So are these other women. Some of them make Margaret look like a school girl out for a walk in the park."

"We can handle ourselves," Hiro said mildly.

"Maybe. Either way, you need to be on alert. The People we're going after are highly-skilled warriors, all of them, and they won't hesitate to kill you and everyone around you if they think you're a threat."

"Eh, why are we doing this job again?" Drew said. "Wouldn't it be better if your people handled it from their side?"

"Mom specifically asked for the Enforcer," Bobby said flatly.

"Well, damn." Drew tugged at his ear. "Hell's come to Georgia and we're all gonna die."

Hiro sliced an impatient glare at Drew. "Bobby wouldn't take any job with a high risk of failure."

"True. I like my hide where it is." Bobby sat back in his chair, amused. "That's why we're going high-tech. As skilled as these women are, most of them cling to the old ways."

"A good sword arm," Hiro guessed.

"And spear and bow, but you get the idea." Bobby shrugged. "Plus, they don't know your faces."

"If the secret weapon is Drew's mug, we're in deep shit."

Drew shoved Hiro, sending the other man's chair bobbling.

Hiro shot Drew a dirty look and righted his chair. "Are you sure Indigo can be trusted?"

"As sure as I can be," Bobby said.

"Is that your dick talking or your brain?" Drew said bluntly. "'Cause she's a smokin' hot piece of meat, bro, but she ain't worth my life."

Hiro rolled his eyes skyward.

Bobby stood and leaned across the desk, pinning Drew with a deadly stare. "Watch what you say about Indigo."

"If that's how you told Laura to leave her alone, it's no wonder she won't make coffee," Drew shot back.

"Laura didn't call her a tramp."

Drew stood up abruptly enough to knock his chair back. "I didn't call her no tramp."

Hiro rose and moved to stand between them. "Indigo's off limits, Drew. She's *the one.*"

Drew's brows drew together with a confused frown. "The who?"

Hiro raised his eyebrows. "*The one.*"

"Oh." Drew's expression cleared. "Ooooh. The lady in the cups."

Bobby glanced back and forth between them. "What?"

"The woman you talk about when you get drunk," Hiro said drily.

Bobby drew back and said flatly, "I never get that drunk."

"Oh, yes you do," Drew said with a laugh. "You used to damn near wax poetic about that woman, with her big blue eyes and her long black hair and her sweet voice. Damn me, why didn't I put it together first?"

"Because you don't pay attention," Hiro said.

Bobby dropped into his chair, appalled. "I can't believe I got drunk enough to talk about her."

Drew slouched down into his chair. "It's no biggie, man."

"You know our secrets, too," Hiro said in a reasonable tone that grated the nerves down Bobby's spine.

"Not like that one." Bobby rubbed his forehead and tried to tamp down on the embarrassment. "Any more questions about this job?"

They let the evasion pass and discussed strategies and tactics for another hour before breaking up. After they left, Bobby spent the rest of the afternoon making phone calls and catching up on paperwork, clearing his schedule. He wanted to have the weekend free for Indigo. They had no set plans, but he hoped to rope her into spending time with him, just because. They were settling into an almost easy friendship, comfortable in spite of the lightning sparking between them at the slightest touch.

He bit back a hard laugh.

Friendship, hell. What he felt for her went way beyond that. Memory teased him until he trembled with it, trembled for her. The way she'd felt in his arms a few days before, small but strong, warm and soft. The way she'd melted against him and tilted her head, exposing the graceful column of her throat to his mouth as she breathed out helpless little gasps. He'd ached and burned with the need to take her, to ease his hands into the waistband of her tights, roll them down, and bend her over the nearest piece of furniture so he could bury himself in her warm heat and forget.

Goddess knew, he had a lot to forget.

He shifted in his chair, adjusted the hard length trying to ram itself through the fly of his slacks. Damn him, he wasn't good enough for her, never would be again. Knowing that didn't kill the fierce urge possessing him, pushing him to claim her anyway.

INDIGO HUMMED as she walked up the stairs to her apartment, juggling grocery bags and keys. It had been a good week, thanks to Bobby. Furniture shopped for and arranged, a budding friendship growing between them. Maybe he would come over so she could repay his help with a hot meal.

And perhaps talk him into helping her pick out a TV.

He was handy that way.

Her breath caught in her throat when a figure stepped into the hallway in front of her. She tensed for a fight until recognition hit.

"Sister." India bowed slightly, traditionally a gesture of respect. On India, the move held enough contempt for three people.

She'd cut her hair in the past few months, chopped it off short and gelled it until the inky locks stood in disordered, finger-combed spikes along her head. The look suited her, especially when combined with the skin-tight leathers India preferred. Indigo touched her own long ponytail, smoothed down the oversized sweater she wore. Why did she always go for comfort over chic and sexy?

"India." Indigo dropped the groceries at the threshold of her door and stuck the key in the lock, leaving the keychain dangling. "What are you doing here?"

"Isn't it obvious?" India's voice took on a playful lilt. "I've come a-calling."

Indigo sighed, suddenly weary. "What do you want?"

"What, no pleasantries for your dear sister?" India tsked almost playfully. "That's no way to treat a guest."

"Just spit it out."

India's face hardened. "If that's the way you want to play it."

"It isn't a game, India. You know as well as I do that the Blade is out for your blood."

"I'm not afraid of Rebecca Upton."

"Then perhaps you should be afraid of her son, the Enforcer," Indigo snapped. "She's set the hounds on you, sister dear."

India tapped a hand against one leather clad thigh and regarded Indigo thoughtfully. "Is that concern for me or him?"

"Both. We may not always see eye to eye, but you're still my sister. If you harm another one of the Blade's children, you're dead."

"I had no hand in Dani's injuries, nor do I intend to harm the Son of the Blade." India pursed her lips. "Unless he gets in my way."

"He'll come after you. You know how persistent he is."

"Not first hand, no." India's mouth curled with mocking humor. "But you know well enough for the both of us, don't you?"

"Please, India. Whatever it is you're doing, please just stop it."

"I can't. Don't you see?" India stepped closer and held out a hand in what Indigo thought might be a genuine plea for understanding. "The Prophecy must be stopped. That's all I'm trying to do."

"That's what this is about?" Indigo breathed out a laugh. "You're trying to stop the Prophecy? By the Goddess, India, how do you ever intend to do that?"

"By snuffing out the Light." India's smile turned cruel in the pale beauty of her face. "Stop the Light, end the Prophecy, and we all live eternally."

"That's insane. No one knows what the Light is or even where to find it."

"Oh, there are people who know."

"People like Lilith Cæstus, who murdered her way across five continents." Indigo swallowed against the bitterness of contempt and fear coating her tongue. "Is that what you've fallen to, India? Murder and madness?"

"Lilith was never afraid to seize what she wanted."

"Nor was she afraid to kill anyone who stood in her way. Don't do that, India. You're better than her."

India's laugh was hollow and harsh. "You're right about one thing. I *am* better than Lilith. At least I'm not stupid enough to fall to the blade of a weakling mortal."

"Dani is no weakling, mortal or not." Indigo drew her

patience around her like a mantel. "It's not too late to change your course. Bobby's asked me to help bring you in."

"Yes, I know." India's voice sounded oddly gentle. "I came to ask you not to."

"Why?" Indigo said, baffled. "I would never allow him to hurt you. You know that."

"You were always so tender-hearted," India murmured. "Even when I hurt you, you would never raise a hand to me."

A ding of metal dropping sounded from the stairwell. Indigo swiveled to check the stairs, then immediately turned back, her gaze firm on India. "You're my sister."

"Such a simple thing, the trust that implies."

India edged closer and held her arms out, waiting patiently, maybe for the trust that had never really developed between them. Indigo couldn't let it go, couldn't bypass a chance to make amends with her twin, the woman who should've been her other half. She twined her arms around India and sniffed back the tears sparking in her eyes. They'd never been close. At their age, wasn't it time for them to be?

Booted footsteps thudded on the stairs. Indigo tensed and tried to draw back, and was restrained by the hard band of her sister's embrace.

"I'll always love you, my sister. Truly, I will," India whispered. "But I can't allow you or the Son to stand in my way."

India shifted her grip and yanked Indigo around until she was secured across the shoulders, her back to India's chest. Indigo struggled briefly against the confinement, and lost her breath when Bobby appeared at the top of the stairs.

Fear stabbed at her, not for herself, but for him, for what India might do to him. "Bobby, no!"

Bobby's gaze zeroed in on India as he fell into a defensive stance, his lean form beautiful and deadly.

"My, my, my, if it isn't the Enforcer." India stepped back, dragging Indigo with her. "We were just talking about you."

"Let her go, India," he said, his voice low, his expression

like granite. "She's the innocent here."

"There are no innocents among the People. Remember that, Bobby Upton."

India released Indigo and shoved her toward Bobby, then took off at a dead run down the hallway toward the staircase at the other end.

Indigo caught Bobby as he made to follow her sister, and threw all her strength into holding him back. "No, Bobby, please. She's my sister."

Bobby halted in mid-stride and pinned her with an incredulous stare. "She betrayed the People and tried to hurt you."

"She was only trying to distract you."

"You're too kind, Indigo." Bobby glanced down the hallway and sighed. "I can't believe you let her go like that, knowing what she's doing."

She eased her hold on him one stiff finger at a time. "She's my sister."

Bobby cupped her shoulders with warm, work-roughened hands and rubbed gently. "That doesn't excuse anything. You know what she's capable of, honey. You have to let me shut her down."

"I know." She sighed and looked up into his lean face, that hard, compelling face that filled her heart and dreams, and her thoughts whirled into chaos. First India and now Bobby. What was it about the two of them that sent her into turmoil every single time they were near? "I can't think about it now."

Bobby squeezed her hard. "You have to. She's dangerous."

"I know, I know." She brushed a hand over her forehead, willing her scattered brain cells into some form of coherence. "Look, come inside and we'll talk. I was going to make you supper anyway."

"Now who's trying to distract me?"

"Is it working?"

"For now, but only for now." He dropped a kiss on her

forehead and let her go. "Sooner or later, you have to face this, Indi. You can't run from it forever."

Indigo sucked in a breath as his words struck home. She'd come back to Tellowee not to face her past, but to at least stop running from it. Maybe it was better that he never knew how hard she would run from something she couldn't face.

Then again, that was a lesson he'd already learned.

FIVE

INDIGO WOKE EARLY Saturday morning with a pounding heart and dread lodged heavily in her gut. She sat up in bed and searched through the groggy fog in her head for some meaning, some rhyme or reason behind the disquiet. When it failed to appear, she threw back the covers with a huff and took a long hot shower to clear her head.

Half an hour later, the fog hadn't lifted, but at least she was clean. She made her bed and took a moment to admire its fine craftsmanship. Bobby had done a good job with it and the matching chest of drawers he'd brought her the evening before. Pride swelled through her as she ran a hand along the smooth, dark finish of the headboard, bringing with it amusement.

Where Bobby was concerned, she hadn't the right to any pride. That she felt it at all showed how completely contrary she was.

A cup of tea, she decided, something to distract herself from the ever present thoughts of Bobby. No better way to start the day.

While it steeped, she threw open the curtains and reveled in the bright day blooming outside her window. A light frost coated the railing of her empty balcony. She assessed the space with a critical eye. It would be lovely filled with a display of pumpkins and corn stalks. A trip to the local produce stand should do the trick.

A firm knock sounded on her door, startling her into a gasp. She placed a hand to her racing heart and laughed at her own jumpiness. "Come in," she called.

Bobby opened the door and stepped inside, a scowl on his face. "Did you leave your door unlocked last night?"

"Of course not."

"Don't leave it unlocked while you're here." He fixed her with a disapproving glare. "And never allow anyone in without checking who it is first."

She huffed out an exasperated breath. "I'm perfectly capable of taking care of myself."

"Uh-huh. You took care of yourself real well with India yesterday."

She turned on her heel, heading toward the kitchen to check her tea. Why had she bothered to let him in? If all he could do was criticize, maybe she wouldn't anymore, no matter how attractive she found him. "I know how to break holds."

He caught up with her and snagged her in a firm grip, locking her arms in place with hard, muscled arms wrapped firmly around her torso. "Prove it."

She rolled her eyes and relaxed into him. A pleasant warmth stole through her when his body lined up with hers, her back to his broad chest and her bottom snug against his manhood. She clamped down on the sudden urge she had to wiggle and squirm, needling him into reaction, just to see what he would feel like all hard and needy behind her. "Is this necessary?"

"Absolutely."

His breath brushed against the side of her face, tickling her.

"I don't want to hurt you," she murmured.

His low laugh vibrated through her where his chest touched her back. "Sweetheart, you're not gonna hurt me."

Anger flashed through her at the smug condescension layered through his voice. So he thought she, a Daughter with decades of training and experience, couldn't take him, a piddling mortal? Weak little Indigo with her soft skin and gracious nature couldn't defeat a Son?

She lifted her legs off the floor, throwing him off balance, then slithered out of his arms when he lost his grip, evading his grabs with deflecting blows. She came around in a crouch and launched herself at him, catching him around the middle, tackling him. Their bodies hit the floor with a solid thud. They rolled, each grappling for dominance, sliding across the slick hardwood floor until they hit the side of the couch, Bobby on top. He grabbed her hands and yanked them above her head, pinning her to the hard surface. She bucked against him, a burning fury fueling her struggle, and scissored her legs, searching for an opening. If she could gain traction, she could flip him, and then she'd show him who was weak.

He dropped his full weight onto her, pushing the breath out of her lungs. Her eyes widened. His breath hit her temples in harsh puffs as his hard length pressed against her core, intimate and sweet and so very, very welcome. For a moment, she lay still beneath him, savoring his touch, savoring him, pressed against her like a lover.

No, *Goddess*, what was she thinking? He couldn't be there, couldn't love her the way he wanted to, the way she secretly yearned to have him. It would spoil everything, their budding friendship, the tender kisses and glancing touches, the warmth and need and desire, all gone because of her lack of control. *Not again, please not another decade without him.*

In a panic, she redoubled her efforts, shoving at him, and gasped out, "Get off."

"When you calm down."

He dropped a heavy thigh over hers, countering her attempt to flip him. Her leg slipped up the inside of his thigh, grazing his groin, and she stilled at his muttered curse. The anger drained out of her abruptly and their eyes met, his narrowed, hers amused.

"Oops."

"You nearly take my manhood and all you can say is oops?" His mouth twisted into a wry smile. "Have a heart, Indi, or at least think of my children."

"You don't have any children."

"Exactly why you should think of them." He levered himself off of her, grabbed the hands she held up to him, and pulled her into a stand. "Another slip like that and I won't have a love life either."

She walked into the kitchen to check her tea. "We wouldn't want that, now, would we."

Bobby followed her and visibly stifled a laugh at the disgruntled glare she aimed at him. "Tea cold?"

"Thanks to you." She dumped it into the sink and rinsed out her cup. "You owe me breakfast now, and an apology."

"Breakfast I'll give you, but why the apology?"

"Because you didn't believe me when I said I could take care of myself."

"No, I believed you, but I'm no fool." He grinned and rubbed the side of his jaw where a red spot roughly the size of her fist lingered. "It was as good an excuse as any to hold you."

She shook her head, torn between disgust and laughter, and held herself erect when he stepped forward and cupped her shoulders, rubbing them gently through her sweater.

"Have you been working out?" he said.

The concern in his voice touched her. "There's a gym here."

"Yeah, but are you using it?"

He cupped the back of her neck with one hand and trailed the other down her arm, entwining his fingers through hers. She stifled a shudder at the warm shock of desire coursing through her from such a simple touch, wiping her mind clean of their conversation. What had he asked her? Right, the gym. "Um. Not yet. No time."

"Monday morning, then, we'll start working out together. No buts," he said when she made a half-hearted protest. "We have a great training center at the office, one floor up. You'll love it."

"Oh, well." His fingers tangled in her hair, pulling gently, and her breath caught in her throat. "I suppose."

His satisfied look should've made her angry, but when he dropped a kiss to her nose, she closed her eyes and bit her lip to keep from begging him to *just kiss me already,* and forgot all about the way he'd manipulated her into agreeing with him.

They drove his truck to eat breakfast at a diner in Rabbit Town. By the time they arrived, Indigo was so hungry, she ate twice as much as she normally would, and groaned when Bobby tried to get her to eat more.

"We've got a long day ahead of us," he said as he pushed his toast toward her.

She placed her hand on top of his to stop him. "I'm stuffed, really," she said, and he let it go with a skeptical look.

He helped her pick out a TV and lamps, and when she tried to buy bookcases to hold the collection of books she hadn't yet pulled out of storage, he told her *no* in a voice that brooked no argument.

"Should've brought some from the storage unit," he said gruffly.

"You have book cases in storage. That you made?"

"Sure. Back in the back, behind your bedroom suite."

"You can't keep giving me your furniture, Bobby."

He shrugged. "It's mine to give."

"Yes, but you're going to want it back when you get married and..." The truth shuddered through her, a wildfire of knowledge and knowing. "Bobby."

"What?" He caught the sweet sadness in her look and hunched his shoulders. "It's not like that."

"Are you sure?" she said gently. "Because that's what it looks like to me."

He glanced away, but not before she saw the loss and sorrow fill his expression. "You turned me down."

"You were sixteen, Bobby. Still a child in so many ways, and my student on top of that." She wrapped her hands around his firm triceps, holding the man he'd become. The echo of that day pounded through her, the horror and embarrassment that had chased her through fourteen years of running. They bounced through her until they diminished, leaving only regret behind. "What else was I supposed to do?"

"Nothing." His face hardened into an impassive mask, sending uneasy chills down her spine. "We should head back now."

Her heart sank. She followed him through the checkout line, then out to his truck, and waited patiently while he started it, searching for the man she'd come to know behind the shell he'd erected around himself. When they hit the highway, he flipped the radio on, filling the silence that stretched between them, taut and cold and frighteningly empty.

THE COOL NIGHT AIR chilled India Furia's skin as she climbed up the side of Hiro Okada's apartment building, boosting herself from balcony to balcony in a zigzagging line upward using ropes, grappling hooks, and the strength of her own body.

It would've been easier to climb down from the roof, if he lived in a building without roving security guards and keycard locks on all the entrances, including the one in the lobby. Those effectively sealed off access to the roof. Using the balconies, which had no such protection, seemed more prudent than trying to trick his building's security. The only risks she took were being caught by night owls peering out their windows and bypassing the locks on the balcony's French door once she reached Hiro's floor.

With any luck, he'd left it open to catch a good breeze while he slept, but she doubted it. During their one brief meeting, he hadn't struck her as being either careless or a fool.

She pulled herself silently over the railing onto his balcony and stripped off her gear, piling it in one corner of the empty landing while she caught her breath.

She'd approached Hiro as she'd approached the others working with Bobby Upton, only after much research and thought. She'd initially hoped to stall the investigation or stop it all together, but they were a loyal bunch, for the most part. Of all the people she'd approached, Bobby's two Army buddies seemed the least likely to betray him. Yet here she was, on Hiro Okada's balcony, about to try again to gain his help in some way.

His face drifted into her mind as she wound the ropes she'd used into neat coils, and with it came a sensation she had difficulty pinning down. Sharp as anger, but without its rancor, and holding something close to tenderness, which was just ridiculous. Her heart held no tender emotions. They'd all been burned out of her a long time ago.

The door behind her slid open. She turned to find Hiro standing in the open doorway, braced against the frame, bare chested and wearing loose pajama bottoms. Security lights from the parking lot below played along his body, throwing his muscled torso into relief above the low-slung bottoms. She risked a glance downward, traced the sparse hair below his navel as it disappeared beneath the waistband, and caught sight of his bare feet as her gaze went lower. They were long and narrow and graceful, much like the rest of him, and her breath caught in her throat as she imagined his long, slim body nude.

She bit back a groan. What a fool she was, to risk blowing her mission because she was attracted to a man. She turned her back on him and stooped to gather her gear so she could leave, then popped upright when he spoke.

"Bit chilly tonight," he said, with no inflection in his voice, as if they'd met on the street instead of on his balcony in the middle of the night.

"A bit." She winced at the insipid reply, grateful he couldn't see her face.

"A little late for a visit, though."

She flushed at the mild reprimand, then scowled at her reaction. "You didn't have to open the door," she snapped.

His chuckle skimmed over her skin like a touch from his elegant hands, leaving her deliciously warm in places that should've been untouched. "If I hadn't, you would've broken in, and I like my locks the way they are."

She whirled around as anger rose, drowning out the softer feelings he drew from her. "I'm not so clumsy that I would've broken them."

"That temper's going to get you in trouble one day." He stepped away from the door into the shadows filling his bedroom. "Since you're here, you might as well come in."

She waffled for a moment, then stepped inside, closed the balcony door, and listened to the sound of his footsteps as he padded across the carpeted floor in the dark. The squeak of the mattress came to her. Her eyes adjusted to the darkness, picking up the dim light as it filtered through the door's glass. She zeroed in on the bed, where Hiro sat with his back against the headboard cushioned by pillows, his legs spread out in front of him.

"If you're here to try to proposition me again, you're wasting your time." He patted the mattress beside him. "I was about to watch a Godzilla rerun. As I recall, that's what you were watching the last time you broke into my apartment."

She gave a half laugh at the reminder. "So you think you've got my number now, is that it?"

"I'm just trying to be a good host." His chest rose and fall on a deep breath. "Let's not play games tonight, India. It's late, there's a good movie on. We might as well enjoy it before you try to bring me over to the dark side."

It was tempting, more than she'd ever admit. To lie beside a man, to absorb the warmth of another body through her skin with even the most innocent of touches. It had been so long since she'd had that. The loneliness of her life, usually so easy to ignore, pinged through her with a suddenness that took her breath, leaving her uncomfortably vulnerable. Was it him she wanted or would any attractive man have pulled at her emotions?

He turned the TV on with a remote, flooding the room with the flickering light of Godzilla rampaging through Tokyo. The sounds of hordes of fleeing Japanese faded when he turned the volume down. He placed the remote on the nightstand beside the bed and crossed his arms over his chest, stifling a yawn.

He looked tired. She bit her lip as another unfamiliar emotion hit her. It took her a moment to recognize guilt, and when she did, she turned to leave, then felt all the more foolish because she hadn't hardened herself against it and pressed her advantage.

"Shoes off."

She paused with her hand on the door.

"Weapons, too."

Indecision tore at her, and she huffed out an irritated breath. She never waffled. Waffling was for children and mortals, not immortal Daughters with a high-stakes mission. So he looked tired. So what? She needed information. More, she needed an in with Upton's people. Hanging around with him might bring one or the other into her grasp.

That she would be sitting on a bed in a darkened room with a man whose feet turned her on didn't enter into the equation.

"I'm bringing my gear in so it'll stay dry."

"Condensation's hell on gear," he said.

She ignored the laughter in his voice and retrieved her equipment, stowing it in a tidy pile inside the door, out of the way but close enough to grab if she needed to leave quickly. She balanced herself against the wall next to the door to take off her boots and placed them by her equipment before shucking her weapons.

Awareness crept down her spine. She glanced up and found Hiro watching her, his face an unreadable mask. "What?"

"I can't believe you took off all your weapons."

She hid genuine amusement behind a snarky smile. "I don't need weapons to defend myself against you."

She padded across the room and crawled into his massive bed, settling against the headboard a good foot away from him.

"I've got a spare set of pajamas, if you want them."

"I'm fine," she said, and ignored the small shifts he made to close the distance between them.

He ran a finger down the outside of her thigh and her muscles jumped in response. "Those leathers can't be comfortable."

His voice held just enough reasonable patience to spark her temper. Of course, the leathers weren't comfortable. She'd worn them to protect her skin against a fall, not because she'd expected to crawl into bed with him. She opened her mouth to scald him.

"Temper," he said, interrupting her.

She snapped her jaws together and started to scoot off the bed. "This isn't going to work."

His hand shot out, closing on her forearm. "It will if you'll unbend a little. You know how to relax, don't you?"

She furrowed her brows, not wanting to admit that, no, she didn't know how to relax. It was damned near impossible for a woman in her position to do so.

"Put the pajamas on, stay a while." He loosened his grip and rubbed his hand up and down her arm, sending tingles of heat across her skin. "I won't tell a soul."

She peered at him over her shoulder, taking in the sleepy plea, the soothing tone of his voice, the hand stretched toward her on the bed. He was watching her again, his impassive gaze piercing through her as if he saw everything, the aching loneliness, the years of servitude to a cause that separated her from her kin, always apart, always alert. He saw and accepted her anyway, and because of that, she yearned for him, *him*, the man who drew her like a moth to a flame, mission be damned.

So she helped herself to his pajamas and stripped down with her back to him.

A tiny thrill of satisfaction ran through her when his breath hitched.

Mmm. She stepped into the pajama bottoms as satisfaction purred through her. *He noticed the lack of underwear.*

Indigo would've gone to the bathroom, for modesty's sake. Then again, Indigo would never have placed herself in this situation to begin with.

Being the bad sister had distinct advantages.

India tugged on the pajama top before crawling back into the bed next to Hiro. He draped an arm over her shoulders, as casually as if they'd done this a thousand times before, and she accepted his touch, snuggling into him as the rest of the world faded away.

SIX

MONDAY MORNING dawned bright and early, a perfect October day with the promise of clear blue skies, once the sun rose fully.

Bobby could not have cared less. After dropping Indigo off at her apartment Saturday evening and helping her unload her purchases, he'd gone home and spent the rest of the weekend brooding. The scene in the store played over and over again in his mind, and then, just for fun, his memory had thrown in the day he'd made a play for Indigo, the day he'd become a man in the eyes of the People and decided to take the woman he wanted.

He closed his eyes, lost in the taste of her lips, the press of her hips against his, the smooth silkiness of her skin when he'd eased a hand under her shirt. Then her startled gasp and the look of pure horror on her face when she'd shoved him away, raking his young heart over the hot coals of rejection.

What was it about women that made men feel like perfect fools?

He rubbed his hands over his face, trying to wipe away the fatigue and the memories, all of them. The sooner he faced reality where Indigo was concerned, the better off he'd be. While she accepted his touch, welcomed it, even, she didn't seem to want more than friendship.

As much as he logically knew that he should stick with *just friends*, he couldn't deny that in his heart he would always want more, no matter how wrong he was for her. Friendship was just the beginning, and he hadn't even figured that out until she'd poked him in the gut with the past.

Now, how did he convince her to go beyond friendship, or should he even try? As much as he wanted her, that very past hung between them, a stain that blossomed and oozed when he least expected it. Nothing he did could ever erase it.

A tap on the door snagged his attention. Indigo poked her head in, a hesitant smile on her face.

"Hey." He forced himself to stay seated, when his body begged him to run to her. "I didn't think you'd show."

The dimple in her cheek flashed as she slid all the way inside his office. She wore skin tight black yoga tights paired with a loose sweatshirt that hung off of one shoulder, revealing the strap of a matching top. His heart nosedived somewhere south of his knees. He'd never get through a workout with her in those clothes, not without his body giving him away.

"You said you'd work out with me." She held up a workout bag and waggled it. "I hope you don't mind, but I brought clothes to change into afterward. Is there a shower?"

A vivid image shot into his mind. Indigo in the shower, water running down her back and over her firm ass. He bit back a groan and tried to rein in his imagination even as his body hardened.

"Or I could go work out in the gym at my apartment complex." She sighed deeply and sat on the edge of one of the chairs in front of his desk. "Look, Bobby, I know we parted a little awkwardly over the weekend."

"I hadn't noticed," he said drily.

She pressed her lips into a straight line and gave him a prim look. "But we're still friends, aren't we? I mean, we're working toward friendship, don't you think?"

The plea in her voice was so earnest, he hated to shoot her down. "Yeah, but it's not the only thing."

Her gaze slid from his to a point somewhere over his left shoulder. She was about to lie, sure as he was a Son. *Dammit.* When would she shoot straight with him? He stood abruptly, irritation pushing him to action, and rounded the desk. She sat back in the chair, panic written all over her face, and a spurt of satisfaction pinged through him.

She should be wary of him.

He rested on the edge of the desk and pulled her up from the chair into the cradle of his widespread legs. She smelled like spearmint and soap and warm woman, and it was all he could do to keep his hands on her hips and his mouth to himself when she landed against him. His erection pressed into the juncture at her thighs, and he shuddered when she shifted and her body rubbed against his.

"Feel what you do to me, Indigo," he murmured.

She looked away, and his irritation shot straight into anger. He tangled a hand in her hair and tugged gently until she met his gaze. "Don't lie to me, ever," he warned.

"I wasn't going to lie." Her fingers curled into the thin material of his t-shirt where her hands rested against his chest. "I was just..."

"Going to lie." He slid his free hand around, cupping her lush bottom, and inched her forward, molding her to him, their cores separated by material so thin it revealed every inch of his erection, and hid nothing of her heat from him. "Feel what you do to me."

A flush spread across her cheeks. "That's a biological reaction. Any man holding a woman this way would do the same thing."

He ignored the scold in her voice. "I've held plenty of beautiful women, Indigo."

Her eyes narrowed. "Really."

"Lots of beautiful, attractive women. Dozens, even." What he thought might be jealousy flickered through her expression. "And I've never felt this way about any of them."

70

"You've had sex before."

The mild accusation in her voice was hard to ignore. He tamped down the guilt. So he'd sought refuge in the arms of other women after she'd rejected his young heart. What had she expected? That he'd pine away for her, forever a virgin? God knows he'd given her his dues, starting with that drunken night nine years before when he'd bound himself to her forever and forsaken his chance at happiness along with it.

Dammit, he wouldn't feel guilty about the past either, not one second of it.

"I'm a man." He managed a casual shrug. "And I know how it feels to want a woman. There's no one like you."

"Oh." Her brows furrowed and her gaze came to rest on his mouth.

"That's it, just *oh*?"

"Well." She pursed her lips into a little moue he ached to nibble and tease. "I suppose now would be a good time to talk about where this all might lead."

"You're kidding," he said flatly.

"Or you could just kiss me." She slid a hand to the nape of his neck and scraped her nails along his skin. "If you promise to stick with a kiss."

His hand tightened in her hair and she gasped. "I don't know if I can."

"Just try," she murmured.

He let go of her hair, slid his hand down, cradling her shoulders. Her eyes fluttered closed and her breath hitched. Sweet Goddess, she was ready for him, her lips parted and slick, her face flushed with the same need gripping him. His heart raced and fluttered as he lowered his mouth to hers, and fourteen years worth of longing and memory pounded through him.

He groaned at the first touch of her soft lips on his, tried to temper the need rising in him to grind against her, to take what she so freely offered, to claim her in a primal rush. He slanted his mouth across hers and their breath mingled, hers sweet and

71

hot on his tongue. She arched into him with a moan and slid her fingers into his hair, and his muscles tightened with a burning desire. When it threatened to spiral out of control, he pulled back to nibble at her lips, to lick at the sweet lushness and savor it, to savor *her*.

He'd waited so long for this, too long between her first sweet kiss, taken by a boy on the verge of manhood, and this one, given freely by a woman eager to have him.

She opened for him, deepening the kiss until it raged through them both. Her tongue darted out in a teasing taste along his lips, then licked against his, and his control teetered and smashed. His fingers dug into her shoulder and the firm flesh of her bottom, and he shuddered when she curled her nails into his back through his t-shirt.

A heavy fist rapped on the door.

He jerked away from her, gasping for breath through the roar in his ears and the ache in his groin. Indigo opened her eyes and he fell into the passion shining from the sparkling depths. Her lips were red and full from the kiss, her cheeks flushed, and her breaths came in short pants. Savage need rippled through him. She wanted him. Sweet Mother, she wanted him. "Indigo," he breathed, and lowered his mouth to hers.

The door opened and Drew stepped inside. "Whoops," he said, and stepped out again, closing the door behind himself.

Bobby cursed under his breath, dropped his forehead to Indigo's, and struggled to bring the desire rampaging through his body under control, to stifle the impulse to back her up against the door, push her pants down, and surge into her over and over again until she cried out with release. Need shuddered through him. *Soon, please, let her need him with the same fierce urgency.*

When the need to claim her dimmed enough for him to think around it, he said, "Why didn't you lock the door when you came in?"

"Mmm. Because we were going to work out, remember?"

He rubbed his nose against hers and loosened his grip so

she could pull back enough to catch her breath. "All I remember is you telling me to kiss you."

"Selective memory," she accused gently, and nipped at his lower lip, sending a pulse of heat down his body. "Do you need to go after Drew?"

"I'll talk to him later. Kiss me again." He smacked her bottom lightly when she tried to pull away, and grinned when she yelped. "I want to make sure we're doing it right."

She pushed at his shoulders and he let her go, and braced his hands against the edge of the desk, willing himself not to reach for her again.

"This is neither the time nor the place for that, Bobby Upton."

He cocked his head and considered her. It wasn't a no, exactly. "You say that like you're afraid it might go beyond a kiss."

"It might," she said mildly. "I'd rather not take that chance."

"Does that mean there's a chance we might do this again?"

The look she gave him was both prim and haughty, and made him snicker in spite of the aching need.

"A man can hope."

"A man should get ready for the gym." Her eyes drifted down his body and widened when she spotted his erection, clearly visible through the nylon of his running shorts. She patted her chest absent-mindedly, as if trying to contain her heart, and nibbled at her bottom lip before her cheeks flushed and she jerked her gaze back to his. "Do you, ah, need a moment?"

"Probably a few."

"Right." Her gaze dropped again and her lips curved into a secretive, womanly smile. "I'll just..." She pointed at the door.

"I'll catch up."

She snagged her bag, turned part way toward the door, then stopped abruptly. "I almost forgot. Do you have time later to talk about India?"

The desire slid from him in a rush. "I can make time.

Why?"

"Something she said to me on Friday." She shook her head and jerked at the bag in her hand, obviously troubled. "About stopping the Prophecy by snuffing out the Light. Her exact words."

A cold stillness filled him, chilling the heat left by her passion. "The Eternal Order?"

"Maybe." Her eyes rounded in a face gone suddenly pale. "I should've mentioned it earlier."

"We got a little caught up."

"That's an understatement," she muttered.

He laughed and pushed himself away from the desk to walk across the room and drop a kiss to her lips, and fought the urge to deepen the brief taste, to finish what they'd started earlier. "Let me get my things and I'll go with you."

"All right. I'm sorry I didn't agree to help you right away." She shifted her stance from one foot to the other. "You know. To track down India. I shouldn't have hesitated like that."

"Don't worry about it." He drew his workout bag from under his desk and hefted it. "She's your sister. I know you love her, in spite of everything."

"I do."

Her voice was gentle. A light shone from her eyes that he'd never seen before. When he reached her side, she stood on tiptoe and pressed a kiss to his mouth, a light, friendly gesture that startled him.

"What was that for?"

"For understanding." She smoothed down the material of his shirt, her hands lingering on his chest. "I appreciate it."

He cupped her shoulder and squeezed. "Hey, what are friends for?"

Her dimple flashed as she smiled, and he followed her to the elevator with his body still tingling from her touch.

INDIGO HUMMED HAPPILY as she made tea in the fully equipped break room at Bobby's office. The kiss they'd shared before their workout, and his reaction to it, lingered in her mind. The glorious touch of his lips to hers. The hard press of his erection at the juncture of her thighs.

He'd needed her, really needed her judging by the husky moans rumbling from his throat when she'd pulled him down and opened to him. Her breasts had grown heavy and wet heat had pooled in her nethers, and she'd reveled in the feel of his fingers biting into her skin. Every brush of his body against hers had sent a wonderful rush of feeling through her. Heat, desire. Need.

And not a whit of guilt or shame.

She licked her lower lip and closed her eyes to savor the taste of him clinging to her mouth, and relished the thought of touching him again without the horror of that long ago day tainting their passion.

When her tea finished steeping, she pulled the tea leaf strainer out and stirred in a touch of honey before sipping delicately at the steaming liquid.

Would he want to kiss her again?

She huffed out a laugh. *Silly Indi.* Of course, he would. He could barely keep his hands off her when they walked through a public area fully clothed. And when they were alone...

A rush of heat shivered through her. When they were alone with that heavy need between them, what would he do?

So far, he'd been a gentleman, or as much of a gentleman as a man like Bobby was capable of being. So maybe his hands strayed where they shouldn't a time or two. Maybe his mouth touched her where it oughtn't more often than not, but that kiss. *Mmm, that kiss.*

What if she enticed him?

No. They were friends, and friends didn't try to seduce one another.

Did they?

She knit her brow, mulling over the ethics of seducing a friend.

Of course not. That would be...wrong. And deceitful.

The memory of his hand on her bottom, pressing her against him, popped into her mind. She wanted to feel that again, feel his need, let it consume her.

Dare she seduce him?

No, she thought again, and allowed her lips to curl into a secretive smile. But she could think about it, couldn't she?

The break room's door opened. Indigo glanced over her shoulder and barely stifled a groan at the considering stare on Margaret's face.

Margaret Mary, Bobby's oldest and most deadly sister, who had nearly caught them kissing the week before.

"Margaret," Indigo said.

"Indigo." Margaret stalked forward and grabbed a mug from the cabinet above the sink, helped herself to the coffee. "How's your mother?"

"Very well, thank you."

"I'd like to drop by when the baby's born, pay my respects."

Indigo sipped her tea and watched Margaret carefully, waiting for the other shoe to drop. One could never tell what was going on behind Margaret's cold eyes. "I'm sure she'll love to see you."

Margaret leaned her bottom against the counter and regarded Indigo with equal caution. "Do they know the sex yet?"

"They wanted it to be a surprise."

"Mmm. Are you fucking my brother?"

"No." Indigo sighed and gripped her mug tightly. "Not that it's any of your business."

"Maybe I think he can do better."

"Maybe you should let him decide," Indigo shot back.

"If you hurt him again..."

"Is that what this is about? Protecting your brother?" Indigo compressed her lips into a thin line. "Or are you using him as an excuse to keep me from helping him?"

"Maybe a little of both," Margaret admitted. Her gaze was fixed on Indigo as she sipped from her mug.

Indigo weighed her options, considered the other woman, and took a calculated risk. "Are you a member of the Eternal Order?"

Margaret sputtered out a laugh. "What makes you think that?"

"Oh, get real, Margaret. Like I could draw any other conclusion after you brushed Bobby off last week."

"I'm not a member of the Order," Margaret said evenly.

"What about the High Guard?"

Margaret's expression remained blank and cold. "I couldn't tell you even if I wanted to."

Indigo tapped a finger against her cup. "Will you hinder Bobby's efforts to track down the People's enemies?"

"Why would I do that?"

"Because he might get in your way."

"No." Margaret's lips twitched into what might have been a smile. "In this instance, his agenda is my own."

"I see."

"Do you?"

The two of them locked gazes and shared a moment of understanding Indigo would've been hard pressed to explain to anyone else.

When the silence stretched thin, she said, "I care about Bobby."

"See that you do."

Laura walked in and flushed when she spotted Indigo.

Margaret freshened her coffee and lifted the mug in a salute to Indigo on her way out. "Have fun."

"Thanks," Indigo said drily, and girded herself for the next battle.

SEVEN

BOBBY SQUEEZED TIME from his schedule to drive to Tellowee and see his mother without making an appointment. It would likely piss her off, but that was ok. He wanted answers. Now that Indigo had confessed her fears about India's ties to the Eternal Order, he would damn well get them.

He caught Rebecca as she entered her office.

"Bobby." She raised on tiptoes to kiss his cheek before continuing into her *sanctum sanctorum*. "What a pleasant surprise."

He followed her in and closed the door behind them. "Do you have a minute?"

She turned a puzzled look on him, an elegant one, and his heart softened. He'd heard the stories of her youth, about the young girl who had wielded a sword with such dazzling cunning that it had been given to her. She'd used it to cut a swathe through generations of armies in Europe, Africa, and Asia, first as a soldier and eventually as a leader. That sword rested in a case in the corner of her office, protected by glass, unlike the woman who stood before him. Her heart had fallen to his father, the charming history professor with a bent for genealogy, and now it was Bobby's as well.

He waited for her to take a seat behind her desk before

dropping into one of the chairs in front of it. "How's Dad?"

"Better. The new medicine is working very well." She leaned forward in her chair and pierced him with a questioning stare. "We missed you this weekend."

"I stayed at the office. We officially started work on the IECS job today and I wanted to be ready."

She dropped her eyes to the desk and shifted a paper.

Uh-oh.

"I thought you might have spent the weekend with Indigo."

"Why would you think that?"

"You're working with her, aren't you?"

"That doesn't mean I'm seeing her." Which he wasn't. Exactly.

"True. Are you at least on speaking terms?"

His mind drifted to the kiss they'd shared that morning, the weight of her body against his, the way she'd curled her fingers into his hair and pulled him down for more. "Sort of."

"Are you trying to get along with her or are you being stubborn like your father?"

Bobby breathed out a laugh. "Mom, really. We're getting along fine."

"Well." She narrowed her gaze on him and he struggled not to shrink beneath it like a child caught with his hand in the cookie jar. That steely gaze had likely brought down a hundred armies all on its own. "As long as you're trying."

"I am." And he was. If he were trying any harder, they'd be married with babies on the way.

A little girl with Indigo's sapphire eyes, holding her hands up and calling him Daddy.

Indigo round with child, glowing softly the way expectant mothers did when they were happy and healthy.

Indigo under him, her ebony hair spread out across his sheets, her body caught in rapture as he stroked into her until she came, over and over again.

"Bobby?"

He looked up to find his mother watching him with raised eyebrows.

"Sorry. Work." He cleared his throat and shifted in his seat. "Lots going on."

"Of course."

A knowing smile played across Rebecca's mouth, and heat rose in his cheeks. Dammit, why couldn't he get his mind under control and off of Indigo?

"What brings you by today?" she said.

"India Furia." He leaned forward and pinned her with a sharp stare. "She's been visiting my team members, threatening them if they don't back off."

"Not an unexpected development."

"Not much of one, anyway. She stopped by Indigo's on Friday, mentioned her plans for stopping the Prophecy."

Rebecca's gaze remained steady. "Any specifics?"

"Just a threat to snuff out the Light." He kept his gaze as careful as hers. "Indigo thinks India's part of the Eternal Order."

The corner of Rebecca's eye twitched in an otherwise neutral expression, and his heart sank. "When were you going to tell me?"

"About what?"

"Don't play games with me, Mom."

They faced off against one another, cool stares clashing across the desk.

"Some things are better left unknown."

The careful note in her voice set him on edge. "I'm not risking my people on an unknown."

"Life is an unknown, Bobby." She swiveled in her chair to look out the windows running along one side of her office. "You're old enough to understand that."

His jaws clenched at the reprimand. "I've been old enough to understand that for a long time."

"True."

She sounded sad, regretful even. For the first time, he

noticed the faint lines around her eyes and the gray in her ash blonde hair. His gut twisted into a hard knot. Sweet Goddess. When had she gotten old on him?

"Tell me about the Order," he said softly.

She sighed and swiveled back to face him. "I can only tell you so much."

"Then tell me what you can."

He reached across the desk and waited for her to take his hand, as she'd done when he was a little boy. She'd always been there for him, protecting him, loving him. Now, maybe it was his turn to return the favor.

"Sweet boy." Rebecca clasped his hand in hers. "You were always my favorite."

He grinned. "You say that to all of us."

"And it's always true." She squeezed his hand gently before letting go. "I suppose you're going to share everything I tell you with your team."

"Not all of them. Hiro and Drew, yeah."

"And Indigo?" she said with a coy tilt of her head.

"Let's not go there again."

"I want you to be happy."

He let his gaze go flat over the humor. "You're stalling."

"Only a little. So you'll tell Hiro, Drew, and Indigo, whom you aren't seeing."

"Mom."

"Don't approach Margaret," she warned.

"Too late. Now spill."

Rebecca pressed her lips into a thin line. "The Eternal Order is real."

He rolled his eyes skyward. "I got that part."

"Don't be smart, young man." Rebecca tapped the top of her desk with one finger. "I can still put you in your place, if needs must."

He rubbed a finger across the smile that rose. She could indeed, and would probably always be able to. "Yes, ma'am."

"And don't think I can't see that smirk. Honestly. Kids these days."

They shared a grin, and then Bobby listened while his mother told him everything she could about the Eternal Order and its struggle to stop the Prophecy from being fulfilled.

REBECCA LEANED BACK in her chair and watched her youngest child as he left her office. Trying to find a balance between giving him the information he needed and protecting the larger interests of the People had exhausted her.

Bobby had probed her knowledge relentlessly, seeking the information he needed to close in on India Furia and other possible traitors to the People. An intelligent mind focused ruthlessly on the overall objective, exactly what the People needed to defend themselves. Her mother's heart filled with pride that her son would be the one to solve this problem and bring their enemies to justice.

The intercom buzzed, announcing her next appointment. She picked up the phone's handset and instructed her receptionist to give her a moment before sending anyone in.

She took a sip of cool water, relished the feel of it trickling down her throat, and ignored the fatigue that seemed to dog every movement she took these days. A quick make-up check in the hand-held mirror she kept in her desk reassured her that she didn't look nearly as old as she felt.

Of course, if she felt her true age, she would feel old indeed.

She still had a couple of decades before she hit the millennium mark, and hoped she'd be around for it. Robert had promised her a party to end all parties as a celebration. She intended to hold him to it, but first, she had to lead the People through their current crisis.

The door opened to admit Sigrid Glyvynsdatter, their in-house genetics specialist, and George Howe, a young man whom Rebecca had invited to the IECS to assist Sigrid in gathering and analyzing DNA samples from living members of the People, as well as from the remains of the dead.

The two were opposites in nearly every way. Raised in the time of the Vikings to be a ruthless and fierce warrior, Sigrid had, like most immortal Daughters, maintained her warrior's form, lean and quick, and had the grace and confidence to match. George was slightly dumpy, and fidgeted himself into a nervous frenzy whenever his co-worker's frosty gaze rested on him. Though they were both brilliant scientists, their mindsets were often at complete odds.

Strangely enough, it brought out the best in both of them. Rebecca had personally hoped the two would find love together, but the unpretentious Mr. Howe had apparently already given his heart to another Daughter. Sigrid showed no signs of challenging the other woman's claim.

George sat down in one of the chairs situated in front of Rebecca's desk. Sigrid handed Rebecca a folder before seating herself.

"Our report," Sigrid said in a voice still thick with her native tongue.

Rebecca flipped it open and skimmed through their latest findings. "Anything of special note?"

"Nothing untoward or unexpected," Sigrid answered.

George slumped slightly in his chair.

Rebecca closed the folder and pinned him with a curious stare. "Would you like to add something, Mr. Howe?"

"No." He cleared his throat and slid a little lower. "Only, if we could just..."

Sigrid turned a glacial stare on him, and he halted in mid-word.

"Yes?" Rebecca prompted.

"Mr. Howe would like to send some of our samples to off site labs," Sigrid said.

He tugged at his collar and shifted in his seat. "It would speed up our work tremendously."

"And leave it open to infiltration by others." Sigrid dismissed his argument with a decisive blink. "I'm concerned about receiving results that have been deliberately tampered with, or possibly having samples stolen outright."

"Concerns noted," Rebecca said. "Mr. Howe, our labs will simply have to be sufficient."

"Yes, ma'am." His shoulders hunched miserably. "Can we at least bring in some more people, maybe equip another room to use as a lab?"

Rebecca raised a questioning eyebrow at Sigrid, who looked briefly skyward.

"It would ease some of the workload and hasten our work," Sigrid admitted.

"All right. I'll expect a formal request on my desk by the end of the week, along with a list of names of appropriate personnel," Rebecca said. "Have you made any headway on identifying the Sandby borg Daughter?"

George perked up. "Some. We found a small amount of DNA in her bones and are testing it now."

"Good. I want to be informed as soon as you know anything." Rebecca clasped her hands together and rested them on the desk. "How's testing of the general population going?"

"Slowly. Many of the older Daughters are resistant to being tested." Sigrid unbent enough to twist her lips into something resembling a wry grin. "But it's coming along. It would be helpful if we could dedicate one person simply to record keeping."

"Whatever you need."

George and Sigrid exchanged a look.

"What?" Rebecca asked.

George leaned forward, confidence entering his posture for the first time since he'd entered the room. "We've started testing the skeleton found at that nightclub Bones a couple of weeks ago."

"Very interesting," Sigrid murmured.

"How so?" Rebecca asked, intrigued.

"The bones are old." George's cheeks flushed with excitement. "Possibly old enough to be a Sister, if I understand the timetable correctly."

"Perhaps not that old," Sigrid cautioned. "But old, indeed. This could help us cement some of the lineages that are in question now."

Rebecca pressed her lips together, trying to quell her own excitement.

"I'd like to expand testing to later generations," George said. "Later, of course, once we've finished testing the remains held at the IECS and known members of the People."

"Of course," Rebecca said. "I bow to your good judgment."

George burst into a frenzy of technical talk that went straight over Rebecca's head, about mitochondrial DNA, which she had at least heard of, and a host of new tests and research that left her dizzy. When Sigrid jumped in with her own opinions, Rebecca sat back and listened to them argue, and allowed the promise of their research to lift her hopes. Perhaps one day, the mysteries of the People's history would be fully unraveled.

EIGHT

THE LONGER INDIGO SPENT around Bobby and his crew, the more impressed she was by their efficiency and effectiveness. By the end of the first week, Hiro and Drew had rounded up and questioned two of the Daughters on their list.

Of course, it had taken a whole team to persuade each of the Daughters to answer questions and BDH had run through its in-house supply of bandages as a result, but the job had been done. They'd questioned the Daughters, thoroughly checked their stories with the help of Zena and Laura, and let the Daughters think the scrutiny was done. It wasn't. Bobby assigned rotating teams to keep tabs on the women's movements and contacts, funneling the whole through his own hands to stay on top of their progress. Hiro and Drew were equally as bad, focusing intensely on each step of their assignments, seemingly to the exclusion of everything else.

She and Bobby worked closely together, though she focused on India and he on coordinating the entire operation. When they were at BDH, they usually holed up together in his office with her set up on the couch and him at his desk. More often, they were on the road, tracking leads and gathering information.

The days were long and hard, lasting well beyond what Indigo had expected, and effectively kept her from acting on any tentative thoughts she might have had to seduce Bobby. Not that they didn't spend time together, because they did, but it was usually at BDH or on the road.

He hadn't stopped touching her. His hands lingered on her waist, brushed through her hair, slid under her shirt when they were alone, caressing the skin of her torso. His lips found hers in odd moments, at times tender and fleeting, at others fiercely demanding, until Indigo gasped with pleasure and bit her tongue to hold in pleas for more.

More was something he never requested, never pushed for.

It bothered her more than it should have. She replayed their kisses over and over again in her mind until her body hummed with frustrated passion, and began to wish she'd never said no to him in the first place.

That day still stood between them, not because she couldn't move past it, but because Bobby couldn't. His eyes lingered on her far more than he likely realized. In them she caught a haunted longing that left her wondering exactly what was going on in his stubborn, male head.

On Halloween, she took a short break to pass out candy with her mother and step-father at their house in Tellowee. A bittersweet envy filled her as she watched Glen fuss over her mother's rounded form. They were so in love, so intent on one another. As soon as was polite, Indigo made her excuses and slipped out, ashamed of the jealousy gnawing at her over their obvious happiness.

Another week passed, the list of suspects grew, and more people were brought in for questioning. Word got out that Bobby was on the prowl and some of their sources dried up.

Hiro and Drew were only too happy to take teams out and renew those sources.

Margaret, on the other hand, seemed content to observe and take a back seat to the main action.

Indigo hadn't told Bobby about her conversation with his sister in the break room or shared her suspicions that Margaret was more heavily involved than she let on. Indigo hadn't forgotten, though, and in her spare time began to dig quietly into the other Daughter's movements over the past few centuries, searching for answers to a conundrum only she could define.

By the middle of the third week, Indigo's nerves were stretched thin. They were no closer to discovering India's whereabouts or her possible connections to the Eternal Order, and had been unable to fully eliminate any of the other names on their list. Bobby seemed as focused as ever on their end goal.

She was ready to scream with frustration.

The only things that kept her from doing so were their morning workouts and their evening work sessions. Each morning, they met at the gym on the floor above BDH and spent an hour lifting weights, swimming, or sparring. Each night, they would grab supper and eat it at Bobby's desk or in the break room, or go to her apartment to continue working.

As gently as she prodded, their conversation never lingered on the past. It ate at her, the things she'd done, the things he'd done because of her.

Nearly two weeks after Halloween, they met at her place for supper, a roast she'd put in the crock pot that morning before she'd left for work.

Bobby sidled up behind her while she stood at the counter, waiting for the microwave to heat the mashed potatoes. His arms came around her waist and she leaned back, drawing comfort from his warmth.

"Mmm." He nuzzled the side of her neck and pressed a chaste kiss there. "How can you still smell so good after the day we've had?"

"It's called soap," she said with a laugh.

His tongue raked over her skin, sending a wave of heat through her. "I think it's called Indigo."

The microwave dinged and she pulled free to check the potatoes. Bobby took plates out of the cabinet. His clothes tightened over his lean, fit body as he stretched up. She bit back a sigh. What would he say if she yanked his shirt up and licked her way down his torso? Surely he wouldn't mind if she took just a nibble or two.

That's depraved, Indigo, one part of her chided, and another answered with, *Yes, but do it anyway.*

"What are you smiling about?" Bobby asked, bringing her abruptly back to reality.

A flush crept up her cheeks and she cursed her fair skin. "Nothing," she said, which was true enough. Her inner ramblings were nothing he needed to hear.

The phone rang, saving her from the inquisition gathering behind his narrowed eyes. Without moving his gaze from her, Bobby reached out a long arm and picked up the receiver. "Hello."

She crossed her arms over her chest, struggling between laughter and outrage. If he felt free to answer her phone, maybe he was a little too comfortable in her home.

He leaned back against the counter while he listened and gave her an arch look. After a moment, he said, "We'll be there," and hung up.

He turned to rummage through her silverware drawer and she huffed out an exasperated breath.

"Who was that?" she said.

"Who was...? Oh, on the phone." He pushed the drawer shut and dropped forks and knives on the counter. "Your step-dad. He's at the hospital with your mom."

Nervous excitement flitted through her, making her bounce. "The baby?"

Bobby grinned as he picked her up and whirled her around once, right there in the kitchen. "On its way."

She clutched at his shoulders, as much to hold him as to counteract the dizziness. "We have to go."

"Supper first."

He let her slide down his body, and she hitched in a breath at the feel of his hard muscles rubbing across hers.

"No, no time," she said and caught his hand. "We need to go."

"You need food, sweetheart." He dropped a kiss onto her forehead and turned to dish up two plates. "Besides, babies are slow. You can spare five minutes to fuel your body."

"Oh, fine," she huffed, but took a plate when he offered it. He was right. It could take hours for the baby to come, and they hadn't eaten in so long her stomach dug into her backbone in protest.

They ate standing at the counter, then stored the leftovers in the fridge and washed up before leaving. Bobby drove, leaving her to fret during the short distance to the hospital. To distract herself, she pressed a hand against his thigh and held on as if he were her anchor, and not the man she found herself wanting more and more with a need that bordered on desperation.

BOBBY EDGED THE TRUCK up over the speed limit in the twenty minute drive from Indigo's apartment to the hospital outside Tellowee, not enough to get caught, but enough to shave time off the drive.

Indigo's face was pale and tense. Nerves or excitement, he figured, or maybe both. Two minutes after hitting the highway, she'd latched onto his thigh as if she were afraid he'd abandon her. Her fingers tightened hard enough to leave bruises, sending a pulse of pleasure through his muscles at the sweet pain of her touch.

Maybe if she'd placed her hand a little lower on his leg, it would've been different, but she'd unthinkingly rested it so that her pinky brushed against the fly of his jeans every time he moved his leg.

So maybe he jiggled it a little more than he should have, but by the Goddess, even that small touch sent him to heaven.

He took a curve a shade too fast and inhaled sharply when her hand slipped and her knuckles grazed his erection through his jeans. When the road straightened out, he grasped her hand and reluctantly moved it closer to his knee where it wouldn't be so distracting.

Hospital first. Touching later.

The paleness of her hand contrasted starkly with the dark blue of his jeans in the night's shadows. Would she touch him like that if they were alone in her apartment? Maybe if he coaxed her into it she would. He glanced furtively at her, ran his gaze along the drape of soft fabric over firm breasts, the toned muscles of her thighs, and shifted as the heat and need ratcheted higher. Yeah, maybe he would.

He parked in the first empty parking spot he came to and hustled Indigo out of the car and into the hospital's after-hours entrance. She held his hand as they took the elevator to the floor housing the maternity ward, her breath humming shallowly in and out of her lungs as she watched the elevator's numbers light up. When the doors opened, they stepped off it into a crowd of friends and family.

Bobby trailed behind Indigo, letting her lead the way, speaking to the people he knew, which was nearly everyone. Tellowee was a small community and his mother a well-known member. Politicking, as she called it, had been bred into him at an early age.

After Indigo found a nurse and received an update on her mother, they squeezed onto one of the waiting room's couches. He draped an arm over her shoulders and pulled her close, as much because of the tight space as anything.

She completely missed the curious stares directed their way.

Bobby met each one with a steady gaze, raising smiles on some faces and scowls on others.

As much as they all liked to believe otherwise, there weren't so many People that gossip didn't spread like the wind, and was remembered far longer. Nearly everyone who knew him and Indigo had probably at least heard that they'd had some difficulties when he was a teenager, although few would know exactly what those difficulties were. For him to show up at an important family event with her and show such casual affection was bound to raise a few eyebrows.

What would those same people say when Indigo took him as her lover?

It was bound to happen, maybe would've already if they hadn't been so busy at work. He hadn't missed the way her eyes followed him, the flush that crept up her pale cheeks when he caught her staring, shy and sweet and sexy all rolled into one. She had the cutest habit of drawing the corner of her bottom lip into her mouth when she was thinking about sex. Every time she did that, his penis saluted. Every. Single. Time. It was getting so he couldn't be around her without the damn thing standing at attention.

He'd taken to jerking off in the shower, his senses surrounded by steamy heat and the memory of her fingers tangling in his hair, the taste of her skin on his tongue, the curve of her ass under his hand and her back arched, pressing her breasts into his chest; and his fist, working his erection hard and swift, willing himself to come just so he could maintain a little control around her.

Sometimes it even worked.

He shifted on the couch, cleared his throat, leaned forward over the near painful erection pushing against the fly of his jeans. The need he had for her never eased. The urge to sink into her and feel her slick heat wrapped around him was never far away. Just the thought of being with her like that, of joining his body with hers and having her accept him, sent desire pulsing through him, low in his gut. He pushed it back, fixed his attention on the game of Rummy someone had started while he'd been lost in thought, and breathed a silent prayer.

Sweet Lady Ki, please let her be ready soon.

An hour passed so slowly Bobby shook his watch to make sure it was running, and was still surprised at the digital numbers on its face. People came and went, stopping by to offer their good wishes or staying to help pass the time.

His mom dropped by, took one look at Indigo squeezed up against him, and furrowed her brow. He wasn't sure if she was issuing him a silent order to behave or if she was concerned about the implications of his and Indigo's position. Since several people were squeezed into tighter spots in the waiting room, he thought it was probably the latter.

Indigo barely noticed. She pretended to play cards, but her eyes roamed continuously to the area where her step-father would come out when the baby was born.

Another hour passed before that happened, and when it did, a cry went up around the room at the happy smile on Glen's face. Indigo stood and pulled Bobby with her.

"It's a boy," he said, then held up his hands when a cheer rang out. "And a girl. We have two blessings tonight."

Indigo whirled and threw her arms around Bobby. He held on as she laughed and cried and pressed sloppy kisses to his cheeks.

"Oh, I have to go talk to him for a minute. Be right back." She pressed a final kiss to his mouth and darted off, pushing her way through the crowd.

He shoved his hands into the pockets of his jeans and watched her go until she disappeared with her step-father into the delivery room. Rebecca stepped up to him and threaded her arm through his.

"The day you were born," she said in a soft voice meant for the two of them alone, "your father passed out before we could even get here."

A swift, nostalgic ache rose in Bobby's chest at the familiar tale.

"Charlotte had to drive us to the hospital, and you know what her driving's like. By the time we arrived, your father was a nervous wreck, poor Charlotte was in tears, and you had nearly pushed your way out. You were always in such a hurry."

"I know," he murmured. It had gotten him into trouble

more than once, and not solely on the day he'd become a man and tried to claim Indigo.

"You've slowed down a little in your old age," she teased.

He grinned at her. "Not so much as you'd think."

She placed her hand on his cheek, pressed gently until he turned his face toward hers. "There's no hurry, Bobby. There never was."

"It feels like there is, like if I don't hold her to me, she'll slip right through my fingers again."

Rebecca patted his cheek, then dropped her hand. "I think you'll find Indigo more receptive to your suit this time around."

An unwarranted hope lurched in his chest. "How so?"

"You'll see," she said simply, and he nodded, though he didn't see at all.

Indigo came out not long after, beaming, and pushed through the crowd until she reached him.

"Congratulations," Rebecca said.

Indigo's smile dimmed a notch. "Thank you, Director Upton."

"Rebecca," his mother said. "How's everyone doing?"

"Wonderful, thank you. They've brought the babies to the nursery and said we could go look."

"Then look you should." Rebecca squeezed Bobby's arm, though she directed her remarks to Indigo. "Please give your mother my best wishes. Tell her I'll stop by in a day or two to check on her."

"Thank you," Indigo said.

Bobby watched his mother make her way through the crowd with the ease of a knife through butter before letting Indigo tug him toward the nursery. His whole conversation with his mother had been off somehow, pointed in that mysterious way women had of conveying information without tipping their hand in the slightest. What could she possibly know about Indigo that would give him hope?

"Oh, Bobby, you should see them." Indigo's voice was

hushed as they walked hand in hand along the corridors. The crowd fell away behind them, a distant murmur of family and friends. "They're so tiny and perfect. The nurse said I could hold them if I wanted, though I think I'd rather wait until they're out of the nursery. Don't you think?"

He let her chatter, content to wander the halls with her, enjoying the smooth silkiness of her hand gripped in his own and the light patter of her happiness. When they came to the nursery, he was surprised that her siblings were the only two residents. A nurse spotted them at the window and hurried to let them in.

"If we had other babies, you'd have to stay outside," she explained, "but since it's just these two angels and they're perfectly healthy, you'll be fine."

Indigo led him to a spot between the two hospital cradles and bounced from one to the other, cooing softly over the sleeping infants. When she wound down and found a spot halfway between, he pulled her into his arms with her back against his chest and held her. A strange feeling gripped him as they stood there, flanked by newly born babies, and he remembered the vision he'd had of a little girl with Indigo's beautiful sapphire eyes.

A sudden longing to make that child a reality hit him, hard enough to stagger him. He tightened his hold on Indigo as his heart stuttered in his chest, turned over, and thumped hard.

She sighed and leaned her head back over the yearning in his heart. "Aren't they beautiful, Bobby?"

"Mmm." He brushed his cheek against her midnight hair, breathed in the clean scent of her. "They look like little wrinkled frogs to me."

She gasped out a laugh and smacked his arm. "I can't believe you said that."

"I can't believe you took me seriously."

"Oh, you," she said, and settled back against him with a happy sigh. "Seeing them makes me want my own."

"I'm happy to oblige," he said, and felt the quiet rumble of her laughter more than heard it.

"I'm sure you would." She turned in his arms and rested her hands against his chest. "Don't you want to have children?"

Oh, if she only knew. How could he tell her that he'd dreamed of her having his children since the day she'd walked into his English class as his teacher, less than two months before his fifteenth birthday? Would it scare her off to learn how often he pictured her in his mind, round with his child, her eyes full of love and promise? "Some day. Why did you never have any?"

"Oh, well, you know. It was never the right time. Never the right man." Her gaze dropped to her hands and the happiness slipped from her face. "Growing up with India and Mámá fighting all the time was difficult."

"That was a long time ago," he said gently.

Her face lifted and her eyes filled with regret. "The past has a way of clinging to the present, no matter how hard we try to shake it."

He knew that, knew it all too painfully well. She didn't have to suffer for it, though. He kissed her then, a soft press of lips meant to comfort, to soothe, to bleed some of her sadness away so that the pleasure could fill her up again. Her fingers curled against his chest and she sighed into his mouth, and he took it, all of it and her, everything she was willing to give him.

When he could tear himself away, he said, "Let me take you home."

"Ok," she said, and her eyes lit with the promise he'd dreamed of seeing there. His heart jumped into his throat, the racing beat roaring through his ears as heat sprang between them. *Blessed Goddess.* Unless he was mistaken, she wanted more than a drive home.

NINE

I T TOOK THEM an hour to make their way out of the hospital. Her mother was being moved to a regular room when Indigo and Bobby came out of the nursery. Indigo said goodbye to her step-father and promised to visit the next day, and then there were all the well wishers and family members to deal with, and by the time they left, second thoughts pinged around Indigo's head.

Had she really agreed to have sex with Bobby or had that been her imagination?

She peered at him out of the corner of her eye as he drove, his left hand draped over the top of the steering wheel. His right one held her hand against his thigh in a casual gesture. He'd let her hang on to him on the ride over, held her hand while they were inside, stroked her back, easing her nerves.

Coming from him, such affection could mean anything. After all, this was the man who'd admitted to holding *dozens* of attractive women over the course of his young life.

Her breath faltered in her lungs and a flush crept up her face. She'd totally misread the situation. So what if he'd kissed her senseless on a dozen different occasions over the past few weeks? He'd walked away every single time in spite of the erection he nearly always sported afterward.

A shaft of pain twisted its way into her heart, bone deep and hard.

What was she doing? If he still wanted her, he would've acted by now. This was Bobby, the same person who'd tried to claim her as soon as he'd become a man in the eyes of the People. Bobby, who didn't lollygag or wait around on someone else, but stepped forward, manned up, and got the job done.

This was a man who held his sisters' hands and showered everyone he knew with affection of one sort or another. Her heart twisted again. She was no different, nothing special. Why had she allowed herself to believe she meant something to him still, just because she once had?

Indigo tugged gently at her hand, trying to slide it from beneath his. His grip firmed around it, and he lifted her hand to his mouth and kissed her fingers in a tender gesture that stung her fragile heart.

Damn him for making her believe, for making her *want*.

The minute he pulled into the parking lot of her apartment complex and parked, she jerked herself away from him and out of his truck. Her tennis shoes squeaked as she all but ran up the sidewalk and the two flights of steps to her apartment without checking to see if he followed. She fumbled with the lock, let herself in, and made it three steps inside before he caught her.

His hands gripped her waist, swinging her around until her back hit the closed door. He braced his forearms above her and leaned in until their noses touched. Her breath hitched in her lungs, caught by the heat in his hazel eyes, so deep and needy, almost desperate. She pressed her hands flat against the door, holding them there to stifle the aching need to touch him, to curl her fingers into his shirt and pull him down until their lips met. Heat pooled between her thighs and her skin tightened in anticipation and she bit her lip hard, willing herself not to give in.

"I love it when you do that," he said.

"Do what?"

He shifted and moved, traced her mouth with one finger. "When you're thinking about sex, you nibble the corner of your mouth. It makes me hard."

"Oh." Her breath came in shallow gasps. "I didn't know..." That she was doing it, that it provoked him sexually.

His laugh was low, gritty, and sent his breath feathering across her lips. "I like it."

"Oh."

His finger traced her lips again. Her lips tingled at the teasing touch and she opened her mouth and flicked her tongue out, tasting the tip of his finger. He sucked in a breath and stilled, and an embarrassed flush heated her cheeks. She turned her face away from him, away from temptation. "Sorry."

"Why? It felt great."

"Is that what this is, then? A way for you to feel great?" She pushed him away with a hurt fury that surprised them both. "Anyone will do, huh, especially poor, weak little Indigo. Is this payback for rejecting you Bobby?"

His eyes widened as he huffed out a breath, dimming the heat in his gaze not one whit. "What are you talking about, Indi?"

"I'm talking about you toying with me."

"I'm not toying with you." He gave a half laugh. "I'm trying to seduce you."

She crossed her arms over her chest and regarded him with narrowed eyes. "Really."

"Well, yeah, but that's nothing new. I've been trying to do that since I was sixteen." He ran a hand through his hair and mumbled, "Thought I was doing pretty well there, too."

She sucked in a breath. "You've been playing with me since the moment you walked through that door, with your casual hugs and kisses and those sexy little licks on my neck."

"Sexy, huh?"

"I thought we were friends." She glanced away, covering the hurt, her pride begging her to hide it from his astute gaze. "I thought you wanted me."

"I do. We are." He rubbed a finger over his forehead, shook his head. "What is this about?"

"I don't know!" She met his confused gaze with her

miserable one. "I guess I just got carried away in the nursery, surrounded by babies, and you were there and made me want you, like you always do, and I'm tired of being alone when you're right there, underfoot all the damn time, tall and sexy and charming, and really, do you have to be such a good kisser?"

A gentle smile tugged at his mouth. "You said damn."

"I know." The humor of it hit her and a laugh bubbled up. "Sorry."

"No, it's ok. You should vent more often."

He held out his arms and she walked into them. The tension bled out of her in a swift rush. It felt so good, so right to hold him like this, like she was supposed to be there, surrounded by everything he was. She rested her head against his chest and breathed in the lingering hint of spicy cologne, the masculine scent that was all Bobby. "I feel silly."

"Don't." He rested his chin against the top of her head, tightened his arms around her. "Next time, though, maybe you should talk to me instead of bottling it up."

"Maybe." She drew back until she could meet his gaze. "So, was it my imagination or did you really want to have sex with me?"

"That was definitely not your imagination." He dropped a kiss on the tip of her nose. "I'll understand if you don't want to, though."

"But you're, er." She stuttered to a stop. How did one describe a man's erection in polite company?

His laugh was low and shaky. "I've been *er* since the first time I saw you."

She bit the corner of her lip, and he groaned.

"You have no idea what that does to me." He rested his forehead against hers. "It's late. I should probably go."

"What?" She clutched at his shirt. "No, wait."

"Indi, sweetheart, one more kiss that's not a goodnight and I might not be able to stop."

"Maybe I don't want you to."

He heaved a breath and looked skyward. "Maybe's not gonna cut it, not this time. If I stay, you have to be sure it's what you want."

Her heart tipped into overdrive. "I'm sure. No, I am," she added when his mouth twisted into skepticism. "I want to be with you, have for a while. I just needed time to work up to it."

"Yeah?"

She answered him with a slow, womanly smile as she took his hand in hers and backed toward her bedroom, watching the burning need in his gaze build until it encompassed them both. She left the overhead light off, flipped on the bedside lamp instead, and wavered as uncertainty flicked through her. It had been so long since she'd been intimate. None of those men had been anything like the one who stood before her, strong and confident, intent only on her. It was scary and good all at the same time.

And she *wanted* it to be.

He yanked his BDH polo over his head and dropped it to the floor, his eyes hot, demanding, and just a little dangerous. "Touch me."

She reached out and ran a finger down the center of his torso from the top of his sternum to his belly button, marveling at the taut, smooth expanse. He shivered and she pulled back, only to have him grab her hand and place it more firmly against his skin.

"It tickled," he said in a gruff voice that sent tingling chills up her spine.

She circled her fingers along his chest. His skin was smooth under her touch, the hair scattered there crisp and warm. Satisfaction purred through her when he shuddered and she did it again because she could, because he'd given her permission to touch him, freeing her to do as she pleased.

Emboldened, she moved closer and ran her hands up his ribs. On the way back down, she slowed her touch and memorized every dip, every ripple of muscle over bone. His skin

101

was warm and firm, tougher than her own, but still smooth as satin. She ran a fingernail along the edge of his pants, teasing him. The hair under his navel was silkier, warmer, and oh so tempting. She slipped a finger into his pants there, rubbing in and out of his waistband as he sucked his stomach muscles in with a low moan that shivered through her.

"I want to put my mouth on you, here." She traced her fingers lower, skimming over the hard length hidden behind his zipper, learning the width and breadth of him through the worn fabric. "May I?"

His breath whooshed out in a rush. "Anything you want."

Oh, yes, she wanted, burned so hard with the need for him, it consumed her.

She pressed nibbling kisses along his collarbone while her hands wrestled with the fastening of his jeans, fumbling in her eagerness to touch him. He rested his hands on her waist and watched her with an intensity she could feel, his eyes taking in every touch, every breath.

When his jeans were undone, she pushed her hand into his underwear and stroked the backs of her fingers along the velvet skin of his erection. His hands dug into the skin at her waist. "That's it, baby," he murmured, and threw back his head on a gasp when she circled him with finger and thumb and stroked downward.

Desire washed over her, and power. She wanted to feel him shudder and moan while she sucked his erection into her mouth, to bring him pleasure and taste his release and know that she was the one who had given that to him.

She pulled her hand out and stood on tiptoe to take his mouth in a fierce kiss while she worked his pants down over his hips, over the firm curve of his bottom and the thick length of his manhood. He moaned when his erection broke free and rasped out her name in a voice harsh and needy, urging her on with his fierce cry. His skin glimmered in the low light. She followed the play of shadows along his muscles with her lips, darted her tongue out, tasting the saltiness of his skin, and sucked and nibbled her way down his torso until the hardwood floor dug into the bones and skin of her knees.

His erect penis jutted proudly from his body, the tip wet and ready, eager for her. She cupped his firm bottom with a steadying hand, circled his erection with the other, and licked along the slit at the end of his manhood. His hips jerked forward at the first touch of her tongue, pushing his length into her mouth.

"Sorry," he said. "Feels good."

She *hmmd*, reveled in his answering moan, and eased the head of his erection deeper, sucking gently and licking the underside until he tangled a hand into her hair, urging her to take more. She did, slipping him as far into her mouth as he would go, then let him slide slowly out as she drew away. In and out she pulled him, suckling him in the age-old kiss of a woman for the man she desired. His body arched, pressing his hips forward, and his muscles trembled under her fingers, flexing and bunching with each wet stroke.

"Indigo, please," he moaned. "I need you, so much. Let me have you."

A hint of saltiness hit her tongue and she drew back, even as his hands tightened in her hair. She glanced up and found him gazing down at her, his hazel eyes hot, his expression taut with need, and a thrill ran through her. "You want me to stop?"

He laughed, low and unsteady, and shook his head. "I don't want to come yet, either."

He pulled her to her feet and their hands tangled together, yanking at each other's clothes, dropping them onto the floor in a careless pile of his and hers, and then she pushed him onto the bed and looked her fill of him. His skin glowed golden in the low light and his eyes glittered beneath hooded lids as his own gaze drifted across her body, lingering on the lush weight of her breasts, the soft slope of her stomach, the curls at the juncture of her legs. His feet were flat on the floor, his thighs a wide frame for his erection, and the muscles of his torso bunched with the curve of his body.

He was the most beautiful man she'd ever seen, and he was *hers*.

She pressed her lips together, needing him so much. Where did a woman start with a man like Bobby, with his dangerous eyes and godlike body and a touch that sent her soaring higher than she'd ever been?

"When you do that, I want to lick your mouth until you open for me."

She huffed out a breath. "Do you catalogue every gesture my mouth makes?"

"Every. Single. One." His gaze heated her where it flicked down her body. "Come to me."

The low command shivered through her, leaving her weak and helpless.

"Don't make me wait, Indi." He held out a hand, beckoning her closer. "I need you."

She clasped her hand in his, let him tug her forward as she crawled onto the bed and straddled his waist, lifted herself above him and guided his erection with her fingers until the tip nudged at the entrance to her wet heat.

"Don't stop," he said.

"I won't. Not this time."

She shifted her hips, taking him in little by little until he was completely sheathed and her sex stretched, deliciously full. He rested one hand on her thigh, ran the other down her stomach, down, down, and delved his fingers into the folds of her sex, rubbing against the little nub hidden there.

Wild pleasure streaked through her. "Bobby," she breathed, and braced her hands against his chest. She moved over him, undulating her hips slowly, sliding over his hard length. Heat flooded through her, overwhelming her with a suddenness that took her breath. He made her *want*, made her *feel*, and it was so good, *so good*. She threw back her head and closed her eyes and met the rhythm he set with the upward thrusts of his hips and the downward push of his hand on her hip and the rub of his fingertips along her sex.

Faster and harder they flew, their breaths gasping in time to the union of their bodies. She lost herself in the need and the pleasure he gave her, in his low moans and the feel of his hands on her, until she hung on the edge of a precipice, waiting for him to join her.

He thrust up one last time and came with a groan, his release throbbing into her, and then he pinched the little nub he'd been rubbing, thrust into her again, and sent her tumbling under wave after wave of her own release.

Bobby tucked a hand under his head and stroked Indigo's back, waiting for their breaths to slow and their bodies to cool. Her weight was supported partially by her own thighs. He wished she would slide her legs down and lay fully on top of him. He wanted that, wanted to feel her skin pressed against his when she was sated and full.

She slid to his side with a sigh and rested her head on his chest, leaving him bereft at the loss of her weight.

"You're still hard." Her hand glanced along his hip and landed softly on his lower stomach, just above the base of his penis. "I thought you came."

"I did." And Goddess, it had been wonderful. The wet heat of her sex, the soft mews in her throat. Desire stirred and he reined it in. "I'll probably be like this for a while."

"Why?" Her fingers slipped closer to his sex through the thick hair protecting its base. "Was it not good?"

He laughed softly. "It was beyond good, Indigo. Better than it ever was in my pitiful dreams."

Hesitation filled her expression. He pushed her onto her back and settled on top of her. His erection slid along the wetness at the core of her body, a remnant of their shared pleasure, and he groaned with the beauty of it.

"Trust me, sweetheart." He dropped a kiss to her lips, savored her sweetness for an all too brief moment before levering himself off the bed. "We're gonna do this again soon."

Her eyes slid closed. He took advantage of her inattention to snag his shirt off the floor. In his rush to have her, he'd nearly exposed himself and the mark he carried on his back. She couldn't see it, could never know it was there.

"Is this one of those *wham bam thank you ma'ams*?"

"What? No." A choked laugh escaped his throat. "Geez, Indigo, where do you get this stuff?"

"That's what it feels like." She propped her head on an elbow and studied, her eyes cool pools of sapphire. "I'm not complaining. It was really good."

"Glad it met your approval."

She ignored his sarcasm with a quiet blink. "Great, even, but the last time I did this, I'm pretty sure there was more than two minutes of cuddling afterward."

"So you feel cheated, is that it?"

He crawled back to the bed, taking his shirt with him, and aligned their bodies. Goddess, he hated to leave her when her body was sated from their shared pleasure. He wanted her again with a greedy desperation that surprised him. Not tonight, though. Tonight, their first time, once was enough. Any more and it would hurt her. Any more and she might see the *aenkanien*.

She shifted and rested a hand against his chest. "Yes, absolutely. Also, I'm trying to figure out why you're rushing out of here when we've barely started."

"Mom's expecting me home."

Her neck was too tempting a target to pass up. He dipped his head and licked, taking his time exploring her skin.

"Can't you, um... Do that again," she said when he nipped. "Can't you text her or something?"

"I could, but I'm not going to."

She tangled her fingers in his hair and tugged until he lifted his head. "You're really not staying the night."

"Nope," he said firmly, and hoped she didn't hear the regret or remember the erection he still sported.

She arched her hips and rubbed against him, and he sighed. She hadn't forgotten the erection.

"I can't believe this." She pushed him off and sat up, and he backed hastily away. "This is so not what I expected from you."

"Sorry," he said, and winced when she hit him, a full-blown punch in the shoulder.

"Don't you lie to me, Bobby Upton." Her voice hit him like a battering ram, beating at the guilt gnawing its way through him, degrees harder than her fist had been. "What's going on here?"

"Nothing. I just have to go."

He eased back again and she pounced, tackling him onto the bed. He fought her in a panic, deflecting her hands as gently as he could while she grappled with his limbs and tried to turn him over. Her hand slipped through his guard and grasped his penis in a firm grip. He stilled, careful not to shift suddenly. Her hand tightened, making his breath hitch.

"Indigo, be careful."

"Oh, I'm going to be careful, you weasel." She squeezed again and his breath whooshed out of his body with the pressure of her hand, somewhere between pleasure and pain. "I want to see your back."

Fear shot through him, as wild and desperate as his need for her. "No, baby. Please don't ask me to do that."

Her other hand latched onto his balls and her fingernails dug into his scrotum. "Turn over."

Her face had gone cold, expressionless, though her voice was choked with anger and hurt. He sat up slowly and, when she let go, gave her his back, exposing the tattoo he'd tried so hard to hide from her, and with it, yet another reason for her to run from him. He squeezed his eyes closed against the regret and the fear, and breathed a silent prayer to the Lady Goddess.

Please let Indigo forgive me.

The hope that She would hear his plea eluded him.

"Whose mark is it? No." Indigo's breath came in heavy,

uneven pants and her hands fell away from him. "I don't want to know. Just tell me, Bobby. Tell me how you could have sex with me when you wear another woman's mark on your shoulder."

"Indi, honey, it's not like that."

"Don't call me that. Don't you dare call me that, not after we..."

Her voice quavered and broke, and with it, his heart.

"I got this the day I turned twenty-one." He shifted to face her and blanched at the tears on her cheeks. "Me and Hiro and Drew, we were home on leave and they got me drunk as a skunk. I'm not sure exactly what happened after that."

"You got married."

She said it the way other people would say, *Well, duh, you idjit*, but with a flat rancor he'd never heard from her.

"No, not exactly." He scooted closer, rubbed his forehead with shaky fingers when she cringed away. "I had this picture in my wallet, a drawing I made a long time ago when I was still young enough to believe I could have the woman of my dreams."

She curled her legs up and wrapped her arms around them, her wide sapphire gaze scrutinizing him as if he were a snake coiled to strike.

"Anyway, I guess I showed it to Hiro and Drew, probably told them where it was supposed to go. Next thing I know, I'm, er, getting sick outside a tattoo parlor with my shirt off and my back on fire."

Her tears had dried, though she held herself stiffly. "Whose mark is it?'

He breathed out a laugh. "How could you even ask?"

Her lips pressed into a thin slash across her pale face. "That tattoo is my mark, my *aenkanien*?"

He turned, putting his back to the light cast by the bedside lamp. "A dove in flight carrying an olive branch in its beak and two intertwined circles in its claws."

"It's beautiful." Her fingers touched him gently, softly tracing the intricate black line tattoo on his left shoulder blade.

"Why didn't you tell me?"

"I didn't want you to feel obligated." At her sigh, he said, "It wasn't your fault that mark ended up on me. I couldn't make you take responsibility for it."

Her hand dropped away. "Who else knows about it?"

"My family." He stood and kept his back to her, ashamed to face her for the first time in his life. Of all the things he'd done to her, this was the worst. "No one knows whose mark it is, though."

Her bark of laughter held enough bitterness to have the shame curling into despair. "Your mother does."

He jerked around so quickly his head spun. "No. I never told her."

"Bobby, she knows."

"She'll never make you claim me."

"She doesn't have to." Indigo slid off the bed and stood next to him, her chill gaze steady and even and determined. "I claim you willingly."

"No." Cold anger washed over him, chased by fear. She would never love him if she were forced to take him as her mate, never, and eventually it would kill any kindness she held for him. He'd rather let her go than live with that. "Not like this."

"What else is there to be done?" She took the shirt gently from his hand. "We'll sort it out tomorrow, ok? I'll talk to your mother, pay the fines, and we'll work it out."

"So that's it, then. Bobby's made a mistake and you're gonna make it all better."

A puzzled frown crossed her face.

"What about the years I spent hacking my way through drug lords and terrorists and anyone else the Army threw in front of me, all the time I spent burning through the anger of your rejection by killing as many people as I could get my hands on?" He yanked her to him. "You gonna fix that, too?"

"Bobby, please." Indigo's eyes were round in a face that had gone pale. "I thought you'd want this."

"Oh, yeah, I want you," he ground out. "I want you so bad it hurts. It's hurt for a long, long time, Indigo."

Her hands came up, placating, seeking to gentle him as if he were a wild beast. "Bobby, please. Come to bed and we'll sort it out, I promise."

"Yes, let's do that." The fury dropped away in a rush, taking any softer emotion with it, leaving him as steely cold as the barrel of his gun. "Let's go to bed."

He rushed her, capturing her in a quick grab, and threw her onto the bed, following her as she scrambled back.

"What are you doing, Bobby?"

"Living up to my nickname."

He grabbed her foot and brought the inside of her ankle to his lips, licking the salty sweetness of her silky skin into his mouth.

"I don't understand," she said. "Can't we just talk about it?"

She tugged at her foot and he nipped at her skin, not enough to hurt, only enough to keep her still.

"Oh, but we are. Don't you want to know what you're in for?" He licked up her leg and when she squirmed, he grabbed her other ankle and held it against the mattress with a hard grip. "Don't you want to know what kind of man you're taking on?"

"I know what kind of man you are, Bobby."

He licked into the crevice of her knee. Primal satisfaction ripped through him when her breath hitched and her fingers curled into the bedspread. "Do you, Indigo?" He ran his hands up her shins and pinned her legs down just below her knees. "I was very effective at what I did."

"I know that's why you were called the Enforcer." Her muscles trembled when he sucked the tender skin of her inner thigh, scraped his teeth there. "That was a long time ago."

"What was it you said about the past clinging to the present?"

He braced his hands along the outside of her thighs, pressed butterfly kisses to her stomach, licked gently into her navel. She sucked in a breath and brought her hands up, cradling his head against her abdomen.

"You have to let go of the past sometime, Bobby."

"Not today. Today, I'm teaching you a lesson."

"What..." She moaned when he raked his tongue across her nipple. "What lesson?"

"The Enforcer is not to be trifled with." He captured her nipple in his mouth and suckled until her eyes fluttered closed and her head fell back. Her skin tasted like the sweetest nectar as it hit his tongue. He laved the velvet of her nipple over and over again, willing her to *feel*, willing her to *need*. "Tell me no, Indigo."

"Um." She cleared her throat, rolled her head against the pillow. "What am I saying no to again?"

He stifled the laugh that rose over his anger, washing him clean with its goodness. Goddess, she was cute when she was lost in passion.

"Sex. Tell me you don't want me." He rose over her and prodded the core of her body with the tip of his erection. It was all he could do to hold back, to keep from slipping into that tight, wet heat. "Tell me to stop and I will."

Her eyes popped open and she gaped. "You want me to turn you down now? Are you crazy? If you stop now, I'll kill you."

He hooked an elbow under one of her knees and pressed it against her chest as he surged up into her, burying himself in her heat in one smooth stroke. His own muscles trembled with the need to stay there, to love her until the pleasure lifted them high and her heart cried out for him. "Be certain," he gritted out.

Her hands cupped his face and her eyes softened. "Don't make me beg."

"Hook your leg around my back," he said, and when she did, he pushed into her with sharp, hard thrusts of his hips. Her eyes drifted closed and her hands gripped his shoulders so fiercely, his blood welled up under her fingertips. He welcomed the pleasure-pain and used it to focus, to hold his body in check even as she gasped and arched against him and her sweet little pussy rippled around his erection in a frenzied release.

He pulled out of her, stopping the build of his own release as her hands slid limply off his shoulders.

"Holy Mother." A secretive smile tilted her lips upward. "Remind me to make you mad again tomorrow night."

He huffed out a half-laugh. "I'm not finished yet."

She lifted her head and raked a gaze down his body. "Bobby," she said, and fell back onto the bed with a lusty sigh.

He captured her hands and pinned them above her head with one hand. Her body was slick and pink from their play, and he'd left too much of it unexplored. She shifted under him, rubbing her hardened nipples across his chest. They were round and firm and begging, and he couldn't deny them a minute longer.

He licked across her skin, tasted sweat and woman and sex. The heat in his body skyrocketed to an unbearable level at the little whimpers she made deep in her throat. He let go of her hands and flipped her over, pressed open mouthed kisses down the hollow of her spine, exploring her slowly, filling in the long years of yearning. All that time, dreaming of how she would feel under him, imagining the way she would move and sound, the way she would beg for him. Those piddling hopes had never come close to the reality of holding her, of joining with her so intimately, they became one.

He built her passion one trembling sigh at a time, savoring every inch of her until she clutched the covers in her hands and squirmed beneath his mouth. His control broke when she arched her bottom up, offering herself for him. He knelt between her legs and urged her onto her knees with her head cradled in her arms and her back sloped downward, thrusting her lush bottom into the air, and drove into the slick clasp of her core. *Sweet Mother, yes.* This is what he'd waited for, this moment when she was his, only and ever his. He'd never let her go again, not until the last breath left his body.

She moaned and pushed back against him with each thrust and he fell into her, lost as his heart thudded and his muscles tightened and she drew him in, welcoming his touch as desire built to a fevered pitch. He pounded into her until she came and called out his name, and her body clamped down on his, pulsing and fluttering, pushing him past desire into release. He gentled his thrusts as it went on and on, spilling his seed into her until he had nothing left to give.

TEN

INDIGO STRUGGLED to catch her breath, to bring her body down after the seeing to Bobby had given her. When he'd pulled out of her after that marvelous display, they'd fallen to the bed with him spooned behind her, their sweat slicked bodies sliding until they fit together, just so.

He'd lashed out, trying to scare her into backing off maybe, and given her a telling glimpse into the man hidden beneath the carefree, fun-loving veneer.

She'd reveled in the sting of his teeth on her skin, the force of his thrusts, the throb of his release. Never before had a man taken her like that, like he couldn't live another minute without being inside her.

And he'd been right. Bobby Upton was not a man with which one trifled. Lesson learned.

Giddiness swept over her and she laughed to herself until her body shook.

"Shh." Bobby spooned against her and stroked her hair. "It's ok."

She shook her head. No, it was not ok. It was wonderful, fabulous. Absolutely exhilarating.

She couldn't wait to do it again.

His arms tightened around her, pulling her flush into his sweat soaked nudity. "I'm so sorry. Do you want me to leave?"

She blinked and rolled over. His face was pale under his tan, his expression pinched and full of regret, like he'd committed the most horrible of sins.

"Why would I want that?" she said, honestly baffled.

"I hurt you." He dropped a kiss to her forehead and pulled away. "Let me get something to clean you up."

She grabbed his arm. "Wait. It's not like that. I mean, yes, you hurt me, but not..." She blew a breath out. "It's a good kind of hurt."

How could she explain the fullness in her body, the delicious tenderness between her legs, and the power of knowing that he wanted her, fierce and rough and hard and urgently, as no man had ever wanted her before? That having him bear her mark made it all the more beautiful and real?

"Hurt is hurt," he said with a skeptical look.

"Not this time." She sat up and held out her hand, waiting patiently until he took it. "I want to tell you something."

He curled around her, rubbing her nose with his in a gesture so tender it took her breath. "What?"

"I don't care what happened in the past."

He stilled in mid-rub and his eyelids slid shut. "I don't want to talk about that."

"No, listen." She grabbed his arm, holding him in place. "What you did after, well, after that day, the things you did in the Army, I don't care about that. It doesn't change what's between us."

"Indi, baby. You don't know what I did back then, all the people I hurt, all the..." He swallowed hard and nuzzled his face into the crook of her shoulder. "Don't tell me it doesn't matter."

"It doesn't," she insisted. "If you can't let it go..."

"Who says I haven't?"

She gave him the look that comment deserved. "Do you love me?"

His gentle laughter feathered across her skin, chilling her, arousing her. "You have no idea how much."

"And after all this time," she murmured. She'd always heard that once a Son gave his heart, it was no longer his. Could it possibly be true? Hope fluttered in her stomach, as jittery as nerves and twice as elusive. "Let it go, for me. Let the past not come between us anymore."

He held himself still against her for long moments, his muscles clenched, his breath a gentle brush across her throat. At last, he said, "I'll try. I swear to you, Indi, I'll try."

She exhaled the breath she hadn't known she held. It would have to be enough. "Share a shower with me?"

He drew back, studying her as desire pushed the worry out of his expression. "Are you sure I didn't hurt you?"

"Not the way you mean."

He shook his head as she led him into her bathroom, reveling in the soft smile playing around his mouth, the sheer beauty of his perfectly muscled form. As the water warmed and the tiny room filled with steam, she ran his fingers through hers, marveling at the rough callouses, so different from the tender warmth of his gaze.

"You're doing it again," he said.

"What?"

"Biting your lip." He dipped his head and licked at the corner of her mouth, catching her teeth. "Keep doing that, sweetheart, and I'll keep pleasuring you, as long as you want me to."

She laughed softly and pulled him into the shower's warm spray. Bobby posed her with her hands against the shower wall and her legs spread wide, and washed her in gentle strokes, murmuring softly to her as he ran his hands down the column of her neck and the curve of her spine; over the roundness of her bottom and into the sensitive creases beneath it; down the backs of her legs and up again, sliding over her stomach to cup her breasts and knead them; into and around every inch of her body in a slow, torturous route. Her heart thumped in her chest and her breath caught in her throat and her muscles trembled under the heat of his calloused touch.

He eased her beneath the spray, rinsed her skin off, and tilted her head back to wash her hair, rubbing her scalp with the pads of his fingertips until she tingled. By the time he finished, she was trapped somewhere between gentle need and bone deep relaxation.

"You give awesome showers," she said.

He laughed and rubbed soap across his chest. "I've always wanted to do that."

"Mmm." She leaned against the wall of the shower and trailed a finger through the soap bubbles on his chest, tracing the letters of her name, branding him in this small way as hers. "Can I do that to you?"

"Not unless you want to have sex again."

"I'd love to, but I think we probably need to talk." Still, she couldn't resist running her finger in slow spirals around his nipple. "Plus, I'm a little sore."

His eyebrows snapped together as he put the soap away. "I knew I hurt you."

"Only a little and it was good."

"You're sure?"

She gave a half laugh. "Any better and I would've melted into a puddle on the bed."

After toweling each other off, Bobby helped her dry her hair, using her blow dryer set to low and her brush to comb through the long strands, soothing her.

"Are you sure you've never done this before?" she said.

"Only in my mind." He put the dryer and brush away, and rested his hands on her bare hips, stroking the skin tenderly. "My sisters never trusted me with their hair."

"Their loss," she said, and he grinned. "Do you still need to leave?"

"Mom's expecting me." He rubbed a hand across his hair, brushing out some of the water lingering from their shower. "I can text her, let her know I'm not gonna make it home tonight."

She peered at him over her shoulder. So, his earlier excuse for leaving had really been about hiding the *aenkanien* from her. "Remember when you told me not to lie to you?"

He wrapped his arms around her, propped his chin on the top of her head. "Yeah."

"Ditto."

"That wasn't a lie, exactly."

"Close enough."

She took his hand and led him to the bedroom, and hesitated yet again, uncertain over dressing for bed or not, over where they would each sleep or how. Would she ever learn to be comfortable with this intimacy?

"Do you want to talk about it tomorrow?" He picked up the watch he'd laid on her nightstand before their shower and checked it with a slight frown. "It's getting pretty late."

She couldn't talk to him while she was stark naked. It sent her mind down too many dangerous paths. Bobby working his way up her body with nips and licks and knowing touches. Bobby filling her with his hard length and sending her over the moon again and again. She shivered as need stirred in her nethers. A nightshirt it was. She walked to the chest of drawers and rummaged for one. "I want to see your mother first thing in the morning."

"You don't have to do that." He sat on the edge of the bed and watched her pull the shirt on, his eyes following the quick stretches and jiggles she made as she shrugged it on. "I told you. There's no obligation here."

"Yes, there is." She flipped her hair out of the neckline of the shirt and sat down beside him, taking his hand into her own, his rough touch comforting in a way she could never explain. "It's not just about duty, Bobby. I'm a hundred and sixty two years old, well past the age for a Daughter to have her first child."

His breath shallowed. "You want to have my baby?"

"Yes." He looked so vulnerable, so insecure. She leaned forward and placed a gentle kiss on his mouth. "You'll be a good father."

"You don't have to claim me to have that."

"No, but since you already bear my mark, it seems like the sensible thing to do."

And she wanted it, so very much, to wake next to him each morning, to feel him move within her each day, to bring him pleasure. To feel special, needed, and to make a difference in someone else's life.

His expression shifted, as if he were waging an internal war. "Why me?"

"Because you're kind and sweet and funny." She kissed him again, let her lips cling to his for a moment. "Because you make me feel like I'm the most beautiful woman in the world."

"You are." He wrapped a hand around the nape of her neck and touched his forehead to hers. "Like a flesh and blood cross between Snow White and Wonder Woman."

A giggle bubbled over and she fell back against the bed, taking him with her. "Really? Wow." She traced a hand over his shoulder, marveling at the way his body was put together. "I can't decide if I'm flattered or not."

"Be flattered," he said firmly. He slipped his hand under her shirt and stroked the backs of his fingers along her stomach. "Are you sure about this?"

"I've never been more certain of anything."

That much was true. The number of things she was sure of at any one time wouldn't take two hands of fingers to count. The decision to take Bobby as her mate was easily the most certain thing in her life, though she refused to dwell too heavily on the whys.

"I want to live with you." His fingers moved up into longer strokes down her abdomen. "If you want me to."

"I do. We can find a house later, if you want."

"I've already got the furniture built," he said with an easy grin. "We'll need a big yard with room for a garden and a swing set."

She arched an eyebrow. "Planning ahead?"

"Since I was fifteen. I know this place near Tellowee.

So much had changed the second time Bobby walked into her life. A few weeks ago, knowing that he'd wanted her since he was little more than a child would've sent her running scared. Now, she wanted to make a life with him.

Of course, now he was a grown man.

She ran a hand over his *aenkanien* and a secret thrill shivered down her spine. He was hers now, only hers. She would find a way to make it work. "Your mother has to agree to the claiming first, and she might not. She may be offended at my treatment of her precious son."

"She knows you had nothing to do with the *aenkanien*."

"Mmm. Well, we'll see."

Bobby took a minute to text his mother, and Indigo didn't rag him. Even in these relatively safe times, the People lived in the shadow of danger. Sons and Daughters alike were still hunted and harmed on a regular basis. No need to worry Rebecca unnecessarily with those fears.

Indigo flipped off the lamp and scooted under the covers next to Bobby, and drifted into sleep as he cradled her through the long, autumn night.

INDIA SLIPPED THROUGH the balcony doors into Hiro's apartment and placed her gear in a neat pile to the side. In the light shining dimly through the glass, she could barely make out his sleeping form. It was late and she shouldn't have come. Still, it wasn't the first time she'd slid into his bed in the middle of the night, and it probably wouldn't be the last.

The hospital had been quiet when she'd snuck into the nursery to see her new siblings, the favored son and another girl. She'd stood over them as they slept, watching them as a good sister should, and her chest had tightened with unaccustomed emotion. Tenderness at the miracle of their birth. Love that they hadn't earned and wouldn't appreciate for years, if ever. And a sweet longing to have a child of her own.

Her mother must be happy.

India unlaced her boots in jerks and tugs, set them beside her gear, and yanked her leathers off as a storm of conflicting emotions raked at her. Frustration, bitterness, anger. They rolled over her, pushing out the softness, leaving her heart hard and cold.

She padded across the room on silent feet and eased into the bed next to Hiro.

He stirred, shifted, and his hand snaked under his pillow.

"It's me," she said softly, so he wouldn't pull out the knife he slept with. She wanted a fight, not a massacre.

"Mmph." He reached for her and she went willingly, letting his warmth seep into her. His hand made small circles on her back, drifting down until he cupped her bottom. "You're naked."

"I am." She rested a hand on his chest and draped a leg over his hip. "Is that a problem?"

"No. Mmm." He yawned and pulled her closer. "Let me wake up."

She kissed him instead, trying to be gentle for some reason that was beyond her when all she wanted to do was bite and punch and kick. He inhaled sharply and groaned when she nipped at his lips, maybe a little harder than she should've.

"You're in a mood." His hand squeezed her bottom. "What's wrong?"

"Mámá had her babies."

"So you snuck into my apartment and crawled naked into my bed?" he murmured sleepily.

She bit back her first smart remark and said, in the most reasonable tone she could manage, "You left the door unlocked."

He yawned again and rubbed his face against hers. "Knew you'd be back."

His comment stung, though she couldn't have said why. "I

shouldn't have come."

"Wait, no. God, you're sensitive."

She reared back, not just stung but hurt. Tears popped into her eyes as her heart ached and withered. Damned if she'd let him see them.

She rolled out of his grasp and slid from the bed. The covers rustled behind her and she sensed more than heard him draw closer, following her across the room. His hand fell onto her shoulder and she shoved it away.

"What's gotten into you?" His voice was a hard, impatient rake across her raw nerves. "Jesus, India. Any other woman would be happy I left the damn door open for her."

"I'm not any other woman." She snatched her shirt from the pile on the floor. "Guess you didn't notice."

"Oh, yeah, I noticed all right." His hand snuck out, quicker than she could follow, and snatched the shirt from her hand. "If I noticed any harder, everybody else would, too."

She reached for her shirt and let out a frustrated growl when he held it out of her reach. "Give me my shirt."

"Not until you calm down." He backed up a step. "You go out there angry and you're liable to fall."

"I'm as likely to fall as you are to lose your dick." She grabbed at her shirt and stifled a scream when he held it away from her. "What is this, kindergarten? Give me my shirt and I'll get out of your hair."

"Is that what this is about?"

He dropped the shirt and lunged for her. She evaded narrowly and swung her arm out, hitting his forearms in a sweeping blow, knocking his hands to the side.

A smile flashed across his face, part satisfaction, part danger, and then he came at her, hard and fast, his hands quick and sure. She fought back, blocking and weaving, allowing him to learn her defenses while she studied his offense.

They circled around the room exchanging swift blows that flew out like lightning. The third time his strike snuck past her guard and nipped at her, barely grazing her hip, her temper flared. He was toying with her. She wanted a fight.

Her next blow caught him in the ribs, hard enough to bruise, not hard enough to break a bone. He stepped away from her, dropped his hands, and studied her, his expression flat and unemotional.

She stiffened under the discomfiting weight of his stare. "What?"

"You don't know how to play, do you?"

She'd disappointed him. Her breath shallowed in her lungs and her head went light. She shrugged, trying to throw the odd feel of it off. "Life is a struggle, not a playground. Either you win or you lose. There's nothing in between."

"India." He shook his head, snagged her shirt, and held it out for her. "Sometimes I feel sorry for you."

She sucked in a breath at the ache that sprang up in her gut. She could take a lot from him, but not his pity.

And she wanted so much more.

But there he was, watching her with an unnerving steadiness, holding her shirt out. Why didn't he just say it, just tell her to leave? Why did he have to be so gentle about it?

She dug her fingernails into the palms of her hands until the urge to apologize passed. She wouldn't beg. Men were a dime a dozen. Another one could be in her bed before the sun rose, if she wanted.

She didn't, but that wasn't the point. She could have anyone. Somehow, though, the only man she wanted was the one who stood in front of her, telling her to go without saying a word.

She reached out to snatch her shirt away and he grabbed her wrist and twisted, bringing it up and back, using it as leverage to push her face first onto the bed. He pinned her wrist to her lower back and followed her down, straddling her thighs with his own. She bucked and wiggled trying to unseat him, and he smacked her bare bottom hard, stopping her cold.

"Now that I'm awake," he said, "let's talk."

Her arm ached where he'd jerked her around and her bottom stung. She wiggled again, trying to break free, and he smacked the other cheek, a sharp blow that sent pleasant tingles radiating through her. Her muscles tightened and heat pooled between her legs. She buried her face in the bed, stifling a moan.

"Don't do that," he said in a voice as sharp as the blow he'd landed.

"What?" She kept her face buried so that her voice was muffled by the comforter. "I stopped fighting."

"Hunh. Right." His hand dropped onto her bottom over the area he'd smacked and rubbed gently. "Don't hold back your response. If you're turned on, let it out."

"I'm not."

Of course, she was. Worse, she wanted him to do it again.

"And now you're lying." His hand squeezed her bottom. "If I let your arm go, will you promise to be good?"

"Define good," she hedged.

"No more fighting."

She could stand the pain, and would have, if the fight hadn't drained out of her. "Ok."

He held her arm for long moments before releasing her. She pushed halfway up, swung her arm around gently, and prodded her shoulder, checking for damage.

"Here, let me."

He braced a hand beside her head on the bed, using the other to push her hand out of the way and rub the sore muscle. She crossed her forearms and dropped her head onto them, and sighed as his fingers dug into her skin, kneading the tension away.

"Feel good?"

"Mmm." She sighed again, a deep cleansing breath, and closed her eyes. His hand shifted to her neck with firm strokes, teasing a moan from her. "You don't have to do that."

"I want to." He shifted behind her, brushing his body against her back, and pressed his mouth where his hand had been. "If I didn't, I wouldn't keep leaving the door unlocked, which any other woman would know."

His tongue darted out, rasping across the skin of her spine, and she lost track of the conversation.

"I love your skin." His breath blew across the damp spot his tongue had left behind, and she shivered. "Soft and sweet. A little salty."

He licked again, lower down, then lower and lower, touching his tongue to the skin above each of her vertebrae in turn, and working his way back up with butterfly kisses. She grasped the comforter, wrinkling it in her fists, and bit her tongue to hold back the fire, to contain it and keep it from spilling out of her.

His teeth sank into the skin at the juncture of her neck and shoulder, hard enough to pull an involuntary moan from her. He pressed an open mouthed kiss to the spot and sucked lightly, and her muscles quivered with need. What was it about this man that left her weak and aching, desperate for more of anything he would give, yearning to give him something in return?

He pulled back and she shivered from the loss of his body heat. "Under the covers," he said.

She pushed up from the bed with trembling muscles and, for the first time in her life, didn't curse the weakness. He'd made her this way, made her feel something other than fury and anger and frustration, and it was good. She crawled under the covers, turned on her side, and watched him strip his underwear off, drinking in his perfectly formed beauty.

He crawled into bed beside her and draped a hand on her hip, his expression in shadows. "I want you to stop coming up from outside."

Desire drained abruptly from her. She closed her eyes and turned over, away from him, suddenly so tired it hurt.

"Could I sleep here tonight? Just for a little while." Her voice broke. She swallowed to clear it and didn't even notice the tears. "I won't come back, if I can just..." *Have a little longer*, she thought, but couldn't bring herself to say it.

"Shh. Hey." He scooted up behind her and spooned her. "I meant I want you to come up the stairs like normal people do. You can use the spare key card."

She breathed out a relieved laugh. "I knew that."

"Sure you did. That's why you're crying." He brushed his face against her hair. "I never thought I'd see that from you. Maybe a roundhouse kick or a punch to the mouth, but not tears."

"Gimme a break." She peered at him over her shoulder, catching his dark gaze in the shadows. His eyes glittered in his narrow face. Even she could see the concern etched there. "It's been a rough day."

"You want to talk about it?"

She shook her head. "That's not why I came here."

"Why did you come here?"

"You know why," she said softly.

"You could've had that any of the, what, dozen or so times you've dropped by, before, during, or after our Godzilla marathons. Preferably all three." His hand stroked her hip, soothing her. "Why now?"

Because she'd reacted instead of thinking, like she always did when her temper was high. Because she ached for him and needed him, and knew it, deep down where she never looked, in the part of her heart that craved a soft touch and a gentle voice and an end to the constant bitterness.

Not that she'd ever admit it, not to his face, especially not the part about needing him.

"When I saw the babies, it just, I don't know, made me want more. Maybe I'm tired of being alone."

"I can cure the alone part," he said. "But we should probably hold off on the babies until after the second date."

She gaped at him, saw the mischief in his eyes, and laughed, letting it roll over her until her stomach muscles hurt with the goodness of it. "Thank you," she said when her laughter died off, leaving only a pleasant warmth behind.

"For what?"

"For letting me stay."

His features tightened and her breath caught at the passion gathering there.

"I wouldn't have it any other way," he said, and kissed her like he meant it.

ELEVEN

B OBBY WOKE INDIGO before he left for work, while the sun was still skimming under the mountains on its way into the sky. She mumbled and shifted in the bed, and winced when she moved her legs.

He wanted to ease the soreness with his mouth on her skin, and would when the sun finished its journey for the day. He settled for teasing kisses along her neck when she turned her face away from his, and laughed when she pulled a pillow over her head and snuggled into it.

His lover wasn't a morning person. Who knew?

He let himself out of her apartment, pulling the locked door shut behind him, and jogged down the stairs as quietly as he could. The pre-dawn air chilled his skin through his thin jacket. Time to pull out the winter one.

His truck started on the first try and he let his mind wander while it warmed up.

He could grab enough clothes to last him through the week when he went home to change before going to work.

Maybe Mom would've already left for the IECS by then.

He checked his watch and huffed out a breath that fogged in the cool air. Nope. She'd still be in the middle of her workout when he got home.

Not home anymore, though. Satisfaction filled him,

followed quickly by a sharp worry. Indigo was ready to claim him, but how long would that last when she hadn't submitted to him and become mortal?

Probably not long. He'd heard the stories of immortal Daughters who settled down with lovers. It hardly ever ended well, no matter what emotions were involved. Inevitably, the man aged while the Daughter didn't, and things got ugly when one of them wanted to move on.

He couldn't imagine ever wanting to leave Indigo behind, though it wasn't much of a stretch to imagine the opposite.

She'd run from him once, devastating his young heart. A second time would kill him.

He worried over it during the short drive between Indigo's apartment and his parents' home. If he could find a way to make her love him...

No. He of all people knew love couldn't be forced. Hadn't he learned that the hard way?

But they were friends and she cared for him, and his past didn't seem to bother her nearly as much as it bothered him. Those were good places to start.

His optimism lasted until he eased his way into the back door and saw his mother sitting at the kitchen table, drinking a cup of coffee.

Well, damn.

Resigned to the inevitable, he poured himself a cup and sat down across from her, facing her without any shame, though he felt like a kid sneaking in past curfew after a night of hell raising that ended up in the morning paper.

"Good morning, Bobby."

Her voice was light and even, her gaze sharp, and he was suddenly glad he was wearing a collared shirt. He was pretty sure there was nothing to see. Indigo wasn't a kid to leave those kinds of marks and neither was he.

"Morning, Mom. Dad not up yet?"

"He's sleeping in today." She set her cup into its saucer with the barest clink. "He has a doctor's appointment later."

"I can take him," he offered.

"He informed me last night that he would drive himself." Her smile was gentle. "This new medicine has given him back a good deal of his independence."

"That's good." Bobby sipped his coffee, stifled a curse when it scalded his tongue. "Tell him to call if he needs me."

"I shall." She folded her hands on the table. "Thank you for texting me last night. I know you're a grown man and you're free to come and go as you please, but I worry."

"I know." He put his mug down, reached across the table, and grasped her folded hands, chafing gently. "I'm sorry."

"Don't be." She unfolded her hands to hold his. "I knew this day would come. I'm trying to be happy for you."

"You know how I feel about Indigo."

"I do." Her hands tightened on his and her lower lip trembled once before she pressed her lips tightly together. "I've known since you were just a boy that she would capture your heart and I would lose you to her."

"No, Mom, don't think that." He scooted forward and clasped both her hands in his. "Geez. You women with your crazy notions."

She laughed, a short sound that carried as much heartache as it did joy. "Even when you tried for her, I knew you were mine. While you were gone in the Army and out building your company. All that time, you were my little boy, right up until the moment you walked through that door and sat down across from me like the man you've become. I'm going to miss you so much."

"Mom." He huffed out a laugh. "I'm moving ten minutes away. You'll hardly know I'm gone."

"It's not the same." She sniffed and patted his hands. "I assume you want my blessing, and your father's."

"Of course, I do."

"But you'll do what you want, regardless of what I think," she said in the cool voice she reserved for adversaries, or people who'd pissed her off.

He met her steely look with his own. "As you said. I'm a man, not a child."

A flash of pride crossed her face and was quickly replaced by the hard mask of a warrior. "If she breaks your heart again, I'll have to deal with her."

"As the law allows, but only that." He picked up his mug, sipped the strong brew. "Even if she hurts me, I'm duty bound to protect her."

"And you know your duty well," she murmured.

"I'm my mother's son."

She acknowledged that with a cool nod. "Yes, you are."

"She's going to come talk to you today." He tapped his thumb against the rim of his mug. "Don't penalize her too harshly."

"You've borne her mark for years, Bobby, years when she forsook you."

"That's not fair and you know it. She only learned about the *aenkanien* last night. The decision to put it there wasn't hers."

"Still, the law is the law and I have my own duties to consider. I won't have you cast aside penniless when she's finished with you."

He hunched his shoulders, uncomfortably reminded of his earlier thoughts. "I can take care of myself."

"That's not the point. She has a financial obligation to you in the eyes of the People." She compressed her lips into a thin line. "The care of a Son who's been claimed is one of our most sacred laws."

"Just keep in mind that I'd like to have children before I'm too old to enjoy them."

Her lips curled into a smile and held such cunning, apprehension stole up his spine. "Don't worry, dear. I'll make certain you have those children."

"Mom," he warned. "Don't meddle."

Her eyes widened innocently. "I would never meddle."

"Yes, you would. Try to be good, ok? When she becomes my wife, she becomes your daughter."

"I know. She'll be a good daughter." Her smile softened and a gleam entered her eyes. "But I should be allowed a little fun, shouldn't I?"

He groaned. His mother having fun wasn't necessarily a good thing.

He checked his watch and grimaced. "I've got to get to work."

"Do you want some breakfast before you go?"

"Thanks, no. I'll catch some on the way in." He stood and dropped a kiss to her forehead, carried his coffee mug to the sink and rinsed it out. "I'm moving into Indigo's apartment tonight."

"So soon?" She rose and brought her cup to the sink. "Don't you want to wait until after a formal ceremony?"

He coughed to hide a laugh. "Ah, we've already consummated our relationship."

She blinked. "I don't like to think about you doing those things."

"You know I've had sex before," he said, and grinned when she gave a mock shudder.

"My son is as pure as the driven snow."

"If it makes you happy to think that, who am I to argue?"

He touched his forehead to hers, then raced up the stairs to shower, change, and pack enough clothes to last the rest of the week. His mother was waiting for him when he came down. She opened her arms and held him tight, and sent him off with a kiss and a look that said she had a special kind of fun in mind for Indigo.

He started his truck and rolled the worry around in his mind. Sooner or later, Indigo would have to learn to deal with his mother. She was woman enough to do it or he would never have fallen for her in the first place. Still, the worry lingered as he drove to work and spent the day trying to focus on running a business instead of on the upcoming meeting between the two women he loved best.

HOURS LATER, Indigo sat on an overstuffed love seat in the waiting area of Rebecca Upton's office at the IECS. She smoothed a hand over the bun she'd twisted her hair into, touched icy fingers to the pearls draped around her neck, and nearly jittered out of her skin in her nervousness.

Claiming Bobby wasn't the problem. That morning, she'd awakened to find him gone with only a vague, lingering memory of his goodbye kiss. In the cold light of day, she'd taken the time to consider the matter without lust clouding her mind and discovered a keen yearning to make Bobby hers in the eyes of the People.

To do so, she would have to seek his mother's approval. There was no way around it. The People's traditions blended and melded as societies changed and grew, but some things remained sacrosanct. A Son was not forsaken. There was no wiggle room there, not in their laws and not in her mind. Her duty was clear. Bobby must be claimed, regardless of the circumstances surrounding the *aenkanien* he bore.

It wasn't solely duty that drove her. She acknowledged that and then ignored it. Better to leave it alone until she could ponder the ramifications of her inner motivations.

"The director will see you now, Ms. Dupree," the receptionist said.

Indigo rose and took a deep breath before straightening the black business suit she wore. It was her least favorite outfit, but a necessity. Bobby's mother was a powerful woman. One did not face her without being well-groomed and ruthlessly prepared.

She gripped the handle of her briefcase and marched across the reception area, turned the handle of the door leading to the director's office, and entered.

It was a large room, well-appointed with a graceful Queen Anne style desk at the back and a small sitting area to the front, off to one side. Hand-woven rugs decorated the hardwood floor. Books and memorabilia rested in shelving on either side of the door. From the corner of her eye, Indigo caught a glimpse of the director's primary weapon, a sword that was thankfully still encased behind protective glass.

Negotiations such as these had gotten violent in the past. Hopefully, this one wouldn't.

Rebecca rose gracefully from behind her desk and walked around it. Her carnelian red suit hugged her figure, highlighting the power of her form and position. "Indigo. Thank you for coming by," she said, as if the meeting had been her idea instead of Indigo's.

Indigo bowed slightly. "Director."

"Rebecca. I insist."

"Of course."

Rebecca's eyes held a craftiness that sent a niggle of worry through Indigo, in spite of the accompanying smile.

"Won't you have a seat?" Rebecca held her hand out toward the sitting area. "I think we'll be more comfortable here, don't you?"

Indigo's heart stuttered in her chest. What was Bobby's mother up to? She perched carefully on the edge of a plush chair and set her briefcase on the floor beside it.

Rebecca sat down on the settee, resting comfortably against the cushions. "How's your mother?"

"She's doing well, thank you. The delivery was normal and she's recovering quickly."

"And your siblings?"

"The babies are fine." Indigo softened automatically at the thought of the babies, then pulled the emotion back, certain the director was about to strike. "They and Mámá should be able to go home tomorrow."

Rebecca folded her hands in her lap, her face a polite mask. "How is India?"

And there the hit, a subtle reminder of Indigo's

connection with a rogue element of the People. *Damn. Should've seen that one coming.* "I haven't seen her in some weeks, but I assume she's doing well."

"When you do see her, please tell her I'd like to have a word with her."

If she wanted to see India, the director would have to get in line, right behind Indigo. "As you wish."

"I understand your work at the Sandby borg site is complete. Have you decided to settle here in Tellowee permanently or will you be moving to another job soon?"

Indigo struggled to keep her expression neutral, her muscles relaxed. *Should've seen that one coming, too.* "I expect my stay in Tellowee will be long-term, considering my relationship with your son."

A flicker of amusement flashed across Rebecca's face. "Oh?"

Why had she bothered to be polite? "In fact, he's the reason I'm here."

"I'm aware." The politely amused expression never wavered. "I wonder, though, how a woman of your means and stature could possibly have the temerity to ask for my son."

Shit.

Indigo clenched her hands reflexively and nearly groaned at the mistake. *Never show weakness in front of the Blade.* It was the number one rule when dealing with a Daughter as old and powerful as Rebecca Upton.

"I assure you, Director, my means are more than adequate to care for a Son of Bobby's standing." She reached for her briefcase, pulling it onto her lap. "I have extensive documentation of my financial status, including investments and real estate holdings."

"Leave it," Rebecca said in a hard voice.

Indigo slid the briefcase onto the floor, her hope for a peaceful settlement sinking with it.

"I'm much more concerned with the matter of your

abandoning him, first at sixteen when he tried for you, and then at twenty-one when he took your *aenkanien.*"

"In my defense, Director, Bobby was my student when he was sixteen. It would have been unethical for me to accept his suit." Sweat pooled under Indigo's breasts and her heart fluttered against her ribs. "As for the *aenkanien,* I only learned of it last night."

"The law is the law." Rebecca pinned Indigo with an unforgiving stare. "As his mother, I have the right to seek Retribution before the Council."

Indigo's eyelids slid closed and the blood rushed from her head, leaving her dizzy. This was her greatest fear, that Rebecca would invoke the old ways of physical punishment and eschew the newer fine system. The penalties were great either way, but the fines were a relatively small matter for most Daughters, especially older ones who'd had time to accumulate wealth of one sort or another.

Physical Retribution, on the other hand, usually involved flogging the skin from the offending Daughter's back. Indigo had seen it done once, as a child, to a Daughter who had forsaken an abusive Son. It had taken weeks for the skin to grow back and years, she'd heard, for the scars to fade completely.

She'd felt the sting of the lash before. Her body jerked involuntarily at the memory. Such a punishment wouldn't kill her, but it would hurt for a long, long time and brand her as a pariah.

Bobby would be lost to her forever.

She opened her eyes. Rebecca's lips had curled into a smile that held the faintest hint of triumph.

"What Retribution will you seek?"

"Since my son is fond of your skin, I shall forego the right of Retribution through the Council and ask for a monetary penalty instead."

Indigo held in her sigh of relief. "Thank you, Director."

"Rebecca. Twenty five thousand dollars per year of your

neglect, with interest retroactive from the date of the *aenkanien*, as well as five thousand dollars per year from the date of his suit to the time of the mark's application, without interest. You will put this money into a trust for the benefit of any children from your union, to revert to Bobby should your union fail or if there are no legal issue."

Indigo sat back in the chair, nonplussed. That was far less than she'd anticipated, all things given, and actually quite reasonable, given Bobby's status. "Of course."

"When will you next ovulate?"

"I fail to see..."

"Do not test my patience, child," Rebecca said. "When will you ovulate?"

Indigo clamped her teeth together. "By spring."

"Good. If you conceive a child by my son within the next two years and bear it within three, I shall waive the penalty for refusing his initial suit." Rebecca folded her hands in her lap. Indigo tensed, preparing for another strike. "If you have two children within that time, I shall match the amount of your penalty from my own coffers, to be paid into the trust."

Indigo compressed her lips together, hiding her astonishment. "That's very generous."

And the requirement of children aligned neatly with Indigo's own goals, which couldn't be a coincidence. Somehow, Rebecca was two steps ahead, while Indigo was still trying to figure out which game they were playing.

"I want my son to be happy."

"He will want for nothing."

"That's not the same thing as being happy." Rebecca leaned forward and laid a hand on Indigo's arm. "Is there any chance you could love him?"

"I care for him," Indigo said carefully. "He's a good man and treats me well. If I were to love anyone, it would be him."

Rebecca considered her, searching for something in Indigo's expression. After a moment, she squeezed Indigo's arm and sat back. "His father and I wish to pay the Son's gift."

Indigo relaxed for the first time since entering the building. "That won't be necessary."

"Oh?"

"Bobby has paid it himself, in furniture for our home."

"Ah." Rebecca smile held genuine amusement. "Still, we would like to contribute."

"Bobby is contribution enough." Indigo shifted in the chair. "If you wish to contribute beyond that, I'll leave it to him to negotiate the gift."

"I'll speak with him then. When will the ceremony take place?"

"We haven't set a date. I'd like to wait until after our current business is finished."

Rebecca nodded. "I understand you've already consummated the union."

A heated blush crept up Indigo's face. Drat her fair skin. "We have each submitted physically to the other."

"I see." Rebecca's gaze remained steady. "I shall have the contract drawn up by the end of the week. Will ninety days give you enough time to establish the trust?"

"Yes, thank you." Indigo couldn't bring herself to say Rebecca's name, no matter how often the director insisted. "I'd like to present Bobby to my mother this weekend. After that, we would love to have you and Mr. Upton for dinner."

"We'd be delighted." Rebecca rose. "I'll look forward to your call."

So much for having Bobby deal with his mother. Indigo grasped the handle of her briefcase and stood.

"Take good care of my son, Indigo." Rebecca stepped forward and clasped Indigo's shoulders in a surprisingly gentle grip. "He deserves some happiness."

Didn't they all. "I shall do my best."

Rebecca nodded and stepped back, her expression caught in a mixture of triumph and resignation.

Indigo bowed and left. When she closed the office door behind her, she took a deep breath and let it out slowly, and sent a thankful prayer to the Lady Goddess that she'd made it out of Rebecca Upton's lair in one piece.

TWELVE

INDIGO DROVE CAREFULLY from the IECS to her apartment and changed clothes before heading to the hospital to visit her mother.

No. *Our* apartment. A home that, Goddess willing, would be filled with the sounds of children by the end of the following year. A little girl with Bobby's daredevil nature and sweet smile.

Or the blessed Son.

She held that wish to herself, savored it for a long, precious moment, then let it go. It was too soon to think of becoming mortal. Her heart was still her own, even if her body wasn't, and Bobby had made it clear the night before that her body was no longer solely her own, as his was now hers as well.

Maybe he would *teach her a lesson* again that evening. A pleasant throb pulsed between her legs and she pressed a hand to her racing heart. *Mmm.* Something to look forward to.

She parked and made the short walk from the hospital's parking lot to her mother's room.

Elizabeth Andrews was a beautiful woman, tall with the black hair and blue eyes she'd given her daughters. Her heart was kind, though not always sweet, and she had no tolerance for disobedience in her children, disobedience often meaning holding an opinion other than one that aligned with Elizabeth's own.

India was just as hard-headed, though she lacked her

mother's kinder attributes. She lived in a black and white world without room for compromise or softness, and had always been determined to forge her own path, regardless of the consequences. It often seemed as if Indigo's twin deliberately chose paths that would provoke their mother's temper.

It had made for a difficult childhood on all sides.

Indigo pushed the door to her mother's room open and stepped quietly inside. Elizabeth lay on the hospital bed situated in the middle of the room, Indigo's brother held to her breast. His twin occupied a rolling glass cradle between the bed and the opposite wall. Pictures flashed across a television mounted to the far corner, the sound muted. Flowers, stuffed animals, and gifts covered nearly every inch of the institutional furniture decorating the room.

"Mámá." Indigo kept her voice soft as she closed the door behind herself.

"Darling." Elizabeth smiled and held her hand out. "I'm sorry to have missed you last night."

Indigo bent and pressed a kiss to her mother's smooth cheek. "You were a little busy having babies."

"True." Elizabeth ran a gentle hand over her son's head. "I would wish this for you, Daughter."

Indigo placed the gift she'd brought on the chest of drawers, then sat in the room's only chair. "Perhaps next year."

Elizabeth's gaze sharpened. "You've taken a lover?"

"A mate," Indigo said. "Bobby Upton, though we haven't sorted out all the details yet."

"Well, well, well. That's quite a step up."

Indigo rolled her eyes skyward. Why did everyone keep saying that? "I'm not that low on the social ladder."

"That's not what I meant. Here, take Joey, will you?"

Indigo stood and took her brother, cradling him gently. His delicate eyelids were closed in sleep, his mouth puckered as if it still suckled his mother's breast. A wave of tenderness swept through her. "So this is Joey."

"Joseph, after Glen's father." Elizabeth cleaned her breast and righted her gown. "And your sister, Beth, bless her heart. I couldn't bear to saddle her with my mother's name."

Indigo's lips twitched. "Uriana is a bit unusual."

Elizabeth laughed softly. "Poor Mother. She always hated her name, but refused to change it, even after she married. Stubborn woman."

Like mother, like daughter. Indigo wisely kept that thought to herself.

"Would you like Joey back?"

"No, you hold him for a while." Elizabeth pushed herself up in the bed until she sat straighter. "I want to talk about Bobby Upton."

Indigo sat down, using Joey as an excuse to avoid her mother's curious gaze. "You'll be up to a formal presentation this weekend, won't you?"

"If that's what you want."

"It's traditional."

"And you were always so bound by duty and tradition." Elizabeth sighed. "Have you submitted to him?"

"No." Joey's face scrunched up. Indigo shifted him to her shoulder and rubbed his tiny back. "He bears my *aenkanien.*"

Elizabeth's eyebrows rose. "I heard he carried a dove on his shoulder, though I thought that could only be rumor. Rebecca would never allow her son to be forsaken."

"Believe me, she extracted a hefty fine."

"So you knew about it."

"Not until last night. Apparently, he got it on his twenty-first birthday after getting really drunk."

"And she still penalized you?" Elizabeth blew out a disgusted breath. "The old biddy."

Indigo laughed. "Mámá, really."

"Well, it's true."

"She made a very reasonable offer, all things considered."

Elizabeth snorted. "Not before putting the screws to you."

"Well, there is that. But it's all settled, except for the formalities. Bobby's moving in with me tonight and we'll likely be married next year." Indigo rose and placed Joey in his own cradle, then took a moment to admire Beth. "If I have children within three years, she's promised to waive part of the fine."

"That bitch." Elizabeth drew in a sharp breath. "You should've taken someone with you to help you negotiate."

"I handled it fine." Indigo moved to her mother's side and sat gingerly on the edge of the bed. "Besides, Bobby and I were planning on having children anyway, so that provision is less harsh than it sounds."

"You were always too accepting, darling. Why didn't you fight for a better deal?"

"What makes you think I didn't?"

Elizabeth's expression turned skeptical. "Because I know you."

"Honestly, this is what I want. If I didn't, I would never have approached her with a formal claim."

"Be careful, darling." Elizabeth grasped Indigo's hand. "Rebecca Upton is devious and cunning. I can't believe she let you off that lightly."

"Not too lightly, I promise. The fine alone is significant enough to affect my investments."

"Do you need money? Your grandmother's funds..."

"No, really, Mámá. I'm fine." And even if she weren't, she wouldn't accept the money. A Daughter who couldn't care for her own mate was sorry indeed. Indigo had enough pride to want to care for Bobby on her own. Thank the Goddess she was frugal. "Can we come by on Sunday?"

Elizabeth hesitated, worry lingering on her face. "Of course. You're welcome anytime."

"Good." Indigo leaned forward to brush a kiss along her mother's cheek. "I have to get back to work now. Bobby's expecting me."

"Come by again, if you can. We're going home tomorrow."

"I will."

Exhaustion followed Indigo from her mother's hospital room to her car, all the way to BDH. Dealing with two strong-willed women in one day was not something she wanted to do again anytime soon.

On the way up the elevator, she remembered the traditional ceremonies, and slumped against the elevator's wall with a weary sigh. Her mother and Rebecca Upton in the same room, staring each other down, on top of the downright embarrassing rituals the traditional claiming demanded? No way.

Maybe they could just elope. Las Vegas was nice this time of year.

The elevator dinged, its doors opened, and Indigo stepped out. She made her way through the reception area to Bobby's office. Laura walked out and closed the door behind herself, and gave Indigo a thin smile that seemed a tad too self-satisfied. Indigo veered off, following the young girl. Whatever Laura was up to, she intended to nip it in the bud once and for all.

In fact, she'd be more than happy to set Laura straight on a number of items, starting with Bobby's availability.

Indigo stalked after the other woman, her fatigue forgotten, replaced by a stony determination that would've made her mother proud.

THE HOURS dragged by. Bobby tried to focus on work, knew he needed to, but his mind drifted and his eyes wandered to his watch. How long could it possibly take for two women to hash out a marital contract?

He checked the time again and pushed sharply back from his desk with a muttered curse. Only five minutes had passed since the last time he'd looked.

Indigo had texted him with the time of her meeting with his mother. Even with traffic, she should've been here by now.

He glared at the paperwork on his desk, picked up a pen,

and tapped it in rapid beats against the top of his desk. *Patience.* She had to deal with this on her own, and he needed to let her.

He focused on the paperwork and forced himself to go through it point by point. Half an hour passed and then another one. Margaret poked her head in requesting a meeting. Drew stopped by with an update on one of their field teams. Laura came in needing his signature, and after that, Bobby gave up trying to work. He grabbed his empty coffee mug and headed for the break room. If Indigo hadn't made it back by the time he finished another cup, he was going after her, tradition be damned.

He left his office door open and stalked down the hallway, trying not to snap at the people he passed. They didn't deserve the lash of his temper, though it wouldn't be there if Indigo was around to soothe it away.

What could possibly be taking her so long?

He slapped the door to the break room open. Margaret stood at the coffee pot, filling her own mug.

"That better not be the last of the coffee," he said.

"There's a little more." She placed the pot back into the machine and moved aside. "Sounds like you don't need any more caffeine, though."

"Hunh. You're one to talk."

"I'm not the one walking around with a thundercloud hanging over my head."

"I'm not..." He let out a sigh. Yes, he was. "Forget it. What did you need a meeting for?"

"I have some interesting info for you on the manhunt you're doing for Mom." She eyed him levelly. "It can probably wait until you're in a better mood."

He grimaced and rubbed a hand across his nape. "Yeah. Sorry about that."

"Want to talk about it?"

And give her ammunition for sisterly blackmail? He wasn't that stupid, no matter what his sisters thought. A man couldn't get away with anything around that bunch. "Maybe later."

"Is it about Indigo?"

He returned her cool stare evenly. "Why would it be?"

"Because you've been groping her for the past few weeks, and mooning over her for a lot longer." Her mouth curled into a smug smirk. "I hear congratulations are in order."

Bobby opened his mouth to retort and was interrupted by Indigo, marching through the door to the break room, dressed in khakis and a BDH shirt with her coal black hair pulled into a ponytail. Her eyes glittered and red spots of color graced her cheeks. She looked ready to crush someone under her heel, if she hadn't already.

"Uh oh," Margaret muttered.

Bobby set his mug down on the counter.

Indigo's gaze zeroed in on him. "I need to speak with you."

"Sure. What's up?"

"Alone." Indigo stepped back, holding the door for him. "In your office, if you don't mind."

His heart took a nosedive and landed somewhere south of Peru. She'd changed her mind. *Dammit.* He knew he should've gone with her to see his mom, knew he should've gone after her sooner. Nausea rolled through him and a cold sweat popped out on his skin.

He was going to lose her.

"All right," he said, and barely stifled a wince at the crack in his voice.

He ignored Margaret's look of sympathy and followed Indigo out of the room. She stalked ahead of him to his office, ponytail swishing with her steps, her body taut and angry. Her ass twitched under her khakis and his body hardened with need, even as he steeled himself for rejection.

At least you had one night. His heart tightened painfully in his chest. One night and thousands more to endure without her, alone with the memory of her scent clogging his head, her soft skin under his hands, the ecstasy on her face when he filled her.

As soon as she entered the room, she moved to pull the blinds shut. He closed the door quietly and watched her. Her hands were shaking. Did she think he was going to hurt her when she let him down? Is that why she was closing the blinds, because she didn't want anyone to see his reaction after she let him go?

He rubbed a finger across his brow. Was he really that much of a bastard? *No.* He'd been good to her, given her his best, except for the night before, and she'd seemed to like that. Surely she didn't think he would hurt her. Maybe she just wanted privacy.

"We can do this somewhere else," he said.

Her laugh was as shaky as her hands. "I can't wait that long."

He flinched.

"Lock the door," she said, and her words were a sucker punch to his gut.

It was going to be bad.

He pinched the bridge of his nose, trying to breath through the agony building in his chest. One night. Sweet Goddess, he'd wanted more than one night.

She finished shutting the blinds and turned, facing him. Her mouth was set in a thin line and her chest rose and fell so rapidly, he thought she might be on the verge of hyperventilating.

"Did you lock the door?" she said.

"Yeah. Why don't we..."

Before he could finish, she crossed the room, fisted her hands in his shirt, and yanked him into a scorching kiss. He stumbled while his mind reeled and his body shouted, *Hell, yeah.* Her tongue pushed against his lips, so he opened for her, and groaned when she made sweet little forays into his mouth, teasing the corners of his lips and his tongue and shooting fire straight down to his groin.

She pushed him back and pulled her top off, then her bra. "Shirt off," she said, and her voice wasn't shaky anymore, it was hot and heavy and needy.

He pulled his shirt off and dropped it onto the chair, and

helped her strip down until she stood nude under the harsh, fluorescent lighting. He reached for the waistband of his khakis, and she pushed his hands away and took his mouth in a greedy kiss. Her hands worked the fastening of his pants, dipping under his clothes in heated strokes while she edged him backward, and he went, eager to see what she'd do next, ready to meet her halfway. When the back of his legs hit the couch, she shoved his pants and briefs down to his ankles and pushed at his chest until he plopped onto the couch.

She straddled him and took him into her body in one long, heated stroke, engulfing him until he wasn't sure where he stopped and she began.

"So good," she gasped, and threw her head back with a low groan when he thrust up into her. Her hips began a slow, undulating rhythm, pulling him deeper into her wet heat, and her sex clenched around him with her movements, and his control slipped and shattered, and he didn't care because she was there and she was his and he wanted her so much, wanted whatever she would give him.

He wrapped an arm around her back and pulled her closer, and sucked her nipple into his mouth, laving it with his tongue, and put his other hand on her hip to urge her into a harder, quicker rhythm. He rocked up into her as her hands roamed over him, clutching his head to her breast, stroking his back and shoulders, digging into his skin, and he was so thankful she wanted him, *Goddess, yes*, but all he could think was *love her, love her* and his chest filled with it, filled with emotion and the beauty of their passion until he fell down, down, down into Indigo.

Her hips were a frenzy of movement, sharp thrusts that stoked the heat higher and higher until he was ready to burst, and her breaths came in pants. She pulled his mouth away from her breast and claimed it, moaning her pleasure against his lips, and braced her hands against the back of the couch. Her hips worked against his body, faster, faster, until she cried out and her body shuddered and her sex clamped down on his erection in hard throbs that sent him over the edge, and he thrust into her so that he was fully sheathed and his seed spurted into her in hot waves that pulsed through him again and again until he was spent.

She collapsed against him, gasping for breath, and nuzzled her face into his neck. He cradled her head and smoothed a hand down the sweat soaked skin of her back, and felt her shaky laugh caress him inside and out.

"Sorry." Her breath puffed across his neck and her hands curled into fists against his chest. "I shouldn't have done that here."

"Here was fine. Great, even. In fact, I vote we do this at least once a day until we're both gray headed." He brushed her hair back, dragged in a shuddering breath around his rocketing heartbeat. "I thought you were leaving me."

"What?" She jerked upright, her eyes wide with shock. "Why would you think that?"

"You were late." He shrugged as casually as he could. "Mom acted like she was gonna be difficult, and I thought you might've changed your mind."

"You talked to her?"

"This morning when I picked up some clothes." He pulled her down, tucked her against his chest, enjoyed the weight of her body draped over his. "Was she really bad?"

She cupped the nape of his neck and relaxed. "She was...merciful."

Merciful? *Shit.* That did not sound good at all. "What did she say?"

"Forget it, Bobby, I'm not telling you. She got what she wanted and now we can be together. That's the important thing, right?"

Not so much. What had his mother done to drive Indigo into sex in a semi-public place? Awesome hot monkey sex that had his dick hardening just thinking about it, but still. Not very Indigo-like behavior. He'd bet his bottom dollar his mother's *fun* had stepped over a line or two or, more likely, ignored those lines completely.

Indigo nipped at his neck with sharp teeth.

A familiar heat worked its way downward. "What was that for?"

"For doubting me. I can't believe you thought I changed my mind."

"This isn't exactly a love match, sweetheart."

She grew eerily still against him. "You don't love me?"

"I do, so much it hurts." His hand tightened in her hair. "I know you don't love me, though."

"I care about you, a lot." She sat up and met his gaze openly. "I know that's not enough."

"No, it's not."

Her lips turned up into a shy smile. "I'm working on it."

"Really?" The emotion welled up again, threatening to spill out. She was working on it, huh? Maybe even trying to take him into her heart. He didn't deserve her, never would, but he couldn't refuse her either, couldn't live without her gentle understanding and seductive heat. "How hard?"

"Pretty hard." Her face lit with humor. "So hard I'm pretty sure everybody knows it now."

"You weren't that loud."

"Not me, the couch. It squeaks."

He ran a hand over her back and didn't even try to hold back the satisfied smile. "I'll get that fixed."

"Mmm. I doubt it. I think you liked it."

"I did," he admitted. "And now, I want to take you home so I can feed you and we can do this all over again."

Her smile was sweet and tender and beautiful. "I can handle that."

They helped each other dress and straightened up as much as they could. He laughed with her and played and felt relief sag through him every time her shy gaze met his, but his mind kept drifting back to what she'd said. *Merciful.* As soon as he could, he was going to figure out exactly what had happened at that meeting, even if it meant standing against his mother, one of the People's most formidable warriors.

THAT NIGHT, Indigo woke him, screaming for her mother, her body jerking in hard spasms. He shook her, trying to wake her, and panicked when she scrambled away from him, slipping out of his reach and over the edge of the bed before he could catch her. Her head clipped the edge of the nightstand as she fell in a graceless heap onto the floor. He leaped around the bed and heaved a sigh of relief when she groaned and pushed herself up.

Sweet Goddess, what had she been dreaming about?

He helped her into bed, flipped on the light, tended the shallow wound. A slow, burning dread hit him when he asked her what had made her scream and her eyes fogged in confusion.

She slept peacefully in the nights after that, but he didn't forget that one nightmare.

Over the next few days, they began to learn one another, to work around each other's habits and shortcomings and develop a deeper bond. Indigo had a hard time waking in the morning, so Bobby cooked breakfast and then came back to bed and woke her with sweet kisses and long strokes along her sleep-warmed skin. He coddled her so much, she retaliated by ramping up their sparring matches and kicked his tail on a regular basis, a pointed reminder that she was a Daughter and not one to be trifled with.

In the evenings, they took slow walks around the neighborhood after supper or cuddled on the couch with a movie, but their nights always ended with him inside her, taking her as high as he could before they both shattered and fell.

Every day, she took a little more of his heart.

Before she'd claimed him, that would've worried him. Now, he held on to the hope that she really could learn to love him, that he was taking a little bit of her heart in return.

THIRTEEN

T HE FIRST SUNDAY after Bobby moved in with Indigo, they went to her mother's house for the formal presentation. It was a modern structure made of rock and wood, and smaller than the older homes located near Tellowee's center, though still big enough to accommodate a large family. Indigo watched Bobby assess the two acre lots with a critical eye, likely noting the layout of the streets and the distance between homes, and knew exactly when he put it on his mental list of potential house sites.

Elizabeth met them at the door of her home, beautifully rounded beneath a loose, white peasant top and faded jeans, carrying her youngest daughter in the crook of her arm.

"Indigo." She leaned in to brush her lips across Indigo's cheek, though her coldly appraising gaze rested on Bobby. "Come in, darling."

They followed her inside and took off their coats, shaking off the cold November rain.

Indigo hung their coats on pegs next to the door. "Where's Glen? He'll be here for the presentation, won't he?"

"Of course, though he seems a bit baffled by the custom." Elizabeth led them into the living room and sat on a plush couch upholstered in earthy plaids. "He's upstairs changing Joey."

Indigo relaxed onto a matching chair and settled in for a

good conversation while they waited. Bobby stood behind her with his right hand on her left shoulder, a silent guard in the manner this tradition demanded.

Moments later, Glen came down the stairs carrying Joey. He stood slightly taller than his wife and was whip thin with shoulder-length hair the color of gold, pulled into a ponytail at the base of his neck. His chambray shirt was untucked over jeans and his socked feet whispered against the hardwood floor. "Sorry. Joey was a little fussy."

"It's ok, dear." Elizabeth took the hand he held out to her and kissed the back of his fingers before rubbing her cheek over them. "Let me scoot up and we can begin."

When Elizabeth was settled, Glen stood beside her and watched with avid eyes.

"Indigo, daughter of my heart and my body, I give you leave to begin."

"Maetyrm." Indigo slid forward in the chair and bowed slightly. "I have come before you with a gift to your line, a Son of a reputable family who will bring much honor to our People."

"What is this Son's name?"

"Robert Lake Upton, the second of that name."

"Who is this Son's mother?"

"Rebecca, known as the Blade, a strong and skilled warrior and a Daughter of the line of Abragni."

"Who is this Son's father?"

"Robert Lake Upton, the first of that name, who has no kin among the People."

"Why should I acknowledge this gift?"

Bobby squeezed Indigo's shoulder when she hesitated. "I have claimed him as my mate."

Elizabeth nodded. "I would hear this from the Son's lips."

Bobby stepped forward and bowed. "Maetyrm."

"Robert Lake Upton, the second of that name, a Son of the People and a child of the Blade. Have you accepted my daughter as your mate?"

"I have."

"Why should I accept this mating?"

"I love her as no other ever will."

Elizabeth's eyes glittered in her pale face. "Pretty words from a man with such a violent reputation."

Indigo hissed in a breath. Trust her mother to bring up the past, and in a manner designed to illicit the sharpest response.

"I do what I must to protect my own," Bobby said, his voice as hard as her mother's.

"And should the day come when she grows weary of your attentions?"

"She may leave with no penalty or harm, though my heart will go with her."

Elizabeth nodded. "A rumor has come to my attention, that you bear the mark of a dove on your shoulder, and have since your twenty-first birthday. Whose mark is this?"

"It is the mark of Indigo Dupree."

"Was this mark taken with her knowledge?"

"It was not."

"Have you been faithful to her since taking her mark?"

Indigo froze. She hadn't anticipated that question, hadn't even discussed it with Bobby. If he'd taken lovers after taking her *aenkanien,* she wouldn't hold it against him, but her mother would. Elizabeth would refuse the claiming, sending them into a spiral of reprisals against Rebecca and her kin, and possibly leading to a vengeance war.

Rebecca's first act would be to claim Retribution.

Indigo flinched. Her body disfigured, Bobby lost to her forever. His hand tightened on her shoulder, comforting her.

"Answer the question," Elizabeth snapped.

Indigo heard Bobby's inhaled breath. "I have."

Elizabeth gaped. Indigo's head snapped around and she said, "What?" at the same time her mother did.

"Eh," Glen said. "Can I ask a question?"

Elizabeth nodded faintly. "As the second father of my

daughter, I give you leave to ask what you will."

"How old are you?"

"I turned thirty last month," Bobby said.

Glen's eyes grew round. "You didn't have sex for nine years? Are you friggin' kidding me?"

"Ah," Bobby said. "I'm not kidding."

"Man." Glen looked down at his wife. "Don't ask me to do that."

Elizabeth patted his arm. "I would never dream of it."

Indigo caught his eye and mouthed *I owe you* before turning back to her mother.

Elizabeth cleared her throat. "Indigo, daughter of my heart and my body, I give you leave to join your life to this man's, the Son of Rebecca, known as the Blade, and Robert Lake Upton, the first of that name, and to bring him into our line with honor and love."

Indigo rose and bowed. "Thank you, Maetyrm."

"Can we eat now?" Glen said.

Elizabeth smiled. "Yes, I think we should."

SUPPER WAS A SIMPLE AFFAIR of roast pork and vegetables. Bobby listened more than he spoke, caught Indigo's gaze slipping to his at odd moments. She was wondering if he'd told the truth about not having sex after taking her *aenkanien*. It was plain on her face.

His brow furrowed. If she hadn't believed him under the duress of the presentation, when a lie could mean death, how would she ever believe him outside of it?

It's not that he hadn't wanted sex and, he was ashamed to admit, hadn't attempted it a time or two. It had never gone beyond a steamy dance and a completely passionless kiss, not for lack of trying, and he'd finally given up.

Of course, he'd had plenty of sex before he'd taken her mark, all futile attempts to erase her from his heart. He'd never

155

tell her, not if he could help it. Her knowing would only widen the influence of his past on their future, and it might hurt her at a time when she was so close to trusting him, maybe even a step or two away from loving him.

The babies rested in a double cradle to the side of the table, sleeping peacefully until the meal was nearly eaten. Beth mewed and shifted, threatening to wake her brother. Bobby placed his napkin on the table beside his plate. "May I?"

Elizabeth's gaze rested on his with the heavy weight of a protective mother. "Of course."

He stood and moved to the cradle, and gently scooped Beth into his arms, holding her carefully. It had been a long time since he'd held a newborn, not since Charlotte's next youngest had been born. He'd missed the birth of the youngest while out of town on a business trip and had regretted it ever since. There was nothing like a baby cuddled up against you, trusting and sweet. He ran a finger over Beth's cheek and smiled when she turned her head toward it.

He looked up to find them all watching him, Glen with the proud look of a new father, Elizabeth wearing a dispassionate mask. Indigo's gaze held a longing that took his breath. She wanted this, wanted to hold a child of her heart and his. He would give her as many children as she wanted, as often as she wanted them. She would be a good mother, and he would watch over her and their children with all of the strength he'd inherited from the Sisters through his mother.

"She looks like you," he told her.

Glen folded his arms across his chest. "Well, there goes your special dispensation."

Bobby grinned. "Hey, it's the truth."

"She's probably wet," Elizabeth said.

"Oh." Indigo pushed her chair back and stood. "Let me. I've been dying to get my hands on her."

Bobby handed the baby over and watched Indigo walk from the room cooing to her little sister. Elizabeth and Glen rose, clearing dishes from the table, and Bobby decided that it was now or never.

"May I speak with you alone?" he said to Elizabeth.

"Of course. Glen, dear, if you'll get started, I'll finish up."

Glen pressed a kiss to his wife's cheek. "Fair enough."

Elizabeth led Bobby to a library containing two leather sofas placed facing one another over a coffee table. Windows lined one wall, with book-laden shelves filling the others. She sat on one end of the far sofa and gestured for him to sit next to her.

Bobby sat down and turned to face her, leaving a cushion between them to preserve some formality. Elizabeth was, in her own way, as formidable as his own mother, if centuries younger. He knew little about her life other than what he'd gleaned from Indigo. That put him at a distinct disadvantage when dealing with her, considering his mother's notoriety, and his own.

He studied her while they settled, and marveled at how alike in looks she and Indigo were, close enough to pass for sisters, with hair as deep as midnight and sapphire eyes tilted up at the corners in heart-shaped faces. Elizabeth's features were sharper, harder, and her eyes pierced where Indigo's merely observed. He'd heard Elizabeth was a fighter, a no-nonsense woman who wasn't afraid to take charge or get her hands dirty, and while Indigo shared those traits, they were tempered by her softer nature. She was the dove to her sister India's hawk, and their mother was an eagle with sharp beak and claws and eyes fixed on her prey.

"What is it you wish to discuss?" Elizabeth asked.

"Indigo." Bobby hooked an ankle over his knee and held it there with both of his hands. "Has she ever had nightmares before?"

"Not in a very long time." Elizabeth's brow furrowed. "Why do you ask?"

"She had one a couple of nights ago. Woke screaming and fell off the bed trying to get away from me." He leveled a hard stare at her. "She wouldn't tell me what it was about, but I'm guessing you probably know."

"I might." Elizabeth curled her legs up onto the couch and rested a hand on her ankle. "When the girls were little, they were mischievous children. India led." She laughed. "Well, you know what India's like. Back then, though, Indigo was a willing participant. The two of them would get into all sorts of trouble together."

Bobby tried to imagine Indigo as a mischievous child and failed. Until the day she'd brought her suit before his mother, she'd always been tentative, almost shy, a student of duty and obligation.

He'd been on the receiving end of that duty often enough to understand how deeply ingrained in her it was.

"They were born in England, but I wanted to travel a little. Restless feet." The smile lifting her lips held a touch of sadness. "So I took a job for the People investigating a slave owner here in the States, a man who had ties to the Shadow Enemy, though he didn't appear to be a member himself. I brought the girls with me, of course. There was no harm, or shouldn't have been, since I was going in as an independent woman, a widow, and not a member of the household."

Bobby nodded. It wasn't an uncommon scenario.

She sighed and shifted on the couch. "We were visiting this man's plantation down near Charleston and the girls got away from me. I never really pieced together everything that happened. From what I can tell, they were spying on some of the slave boys who were bathing in the river. The overseer caught them. He had his whip with him and used it on Indigo. India slipped out of his grasp and managed to claw the man hard enough to send him running, but the damage was done."

A slow burn of horror seeped into him. *Blessed Mother.* "I hope you killed him."

"Oh, I did. Skinned him from stem to stern while his heart beat and fed him his own entrails until he choked. He got India with his back swings while she was trying to stop him.

Considering some of the scrapes that one got into, the wounds were relatively minor, but the overseer got in at least a dozen hits to Indigo. The damage was..." She sucked in a breath and let it out slowly. "Her skin healed and the scars faded, but she was never the same. No more running after India, chasing trouble. No more daredevil adventures. Her childhood was essentially over and she was only ten."

Bobby pushed down the hatred and horror. "And she had nightmares after that?"

"Every night for a while. They gradually tapered off. I can't think what would have triggered her recent nightmare. Are you certain nothing else has happened?"

"We're hunting down India and she's helping." He shrugged. "We've gone furniture shopping."

"Well, that's a nightmare on its own," she said with a laugh. "Indigo hates shopping."

"Hmm." She'd seemed to enjoy their trips together. "We went shopping a lot the first week or so after she came back. Other than that, I can't think of anything except her meeting with Mom."

Elizabeth's eyes narrowed. "Your mother imposed a heavy fine on her for your mistake."

"I don't consider it a mistake," he said evenly. "And whatever that fine was, my personal wealth is enough to make up for it."

"Like your mother would allow that," she scoffed.

"My mother has no say in how I spend my own money." He drew himself back before the argument escalated. "I told Mom to go easy on her."

"And you really think she listened? You don't know Rebecca very well."

"Well enough. She wants me to be happy. Surely she wouldn't have done anything to hurt Indigo."

"Maybe not," Elizabeth conceded, "but she might threaten it, if she needed leverage."

Bobby rocked his foot, considering that. "I told Mom flat out that I would protect Indigo if she came after her."

"You would defy the Blade for Indigo?" Elizabeth's lips, so like Indigo's, twisted into a disdainful sneer. "I have a hard time believing that."

He leaned forward and pinned her with a cold stare. "Believe it. Anyone who harms Indigo will learn exactly how vicious I can be."

She sat back, her expression nonplussed. "You're serious."

"I am. Mom knows that, too."

Elizabeth's face blossomed with a smile. "Well, well, well. I do believe that old biddy's met her match."

She slid off the couch and he rose to face her. She reached up, cupping his face with both of her elegant hands. "Robert Lake Upton, the second of that name, I accept you as my daughter's mate. Love her always. Harm her never."

"I shall protect her with my life," he murmured.

She pulled him down, pressed a kiss to his mouth and then his forehead. "Welcome to the family, Bobby."

He grinned and let her take his arm and lead him back to the kitchen where their two hearts waited.

FOURTEEN

WO DAYS PASSED before Indigo had time to take a breath. News of her and Bobby's engagement seeped out, and before she knew it, her phone rang nearly constantly with people calling to congratulate her on making such a spectacular match.

She was polite, really she was, when what she wanted to do was say, *What am I, chopped liver?*

Ok, so Bobby was the only son of a powerful Daughter, allied closely with a member of the Council of Seven, and Indigo was a wallflower, but that didn't mean she was a nobody. Her grandmother had served on the Council of Seven representing their line through the Sister Lilleni before the current councilwoman, Gwendolyn, had taken the position. Elizabeth was relatively young, but she'd earned a certain notoriety as well and might have gone much farther if she hadn't become mortal.

Which was in itself a notable feat. Not every Daughter was born with a trusting heart. If they were, it was usually beaten out of them by the sheer difficulty of their lives. To submit one's will to a man and become mortal was an honorable action, marking such women as the wisest among the People.

Indigo had accomplished things in her time, too, so why did everyone treat her as if she were Cinderella to Bobby's Prince Charming?

She wrinkled her brow at the comparison and sighed. Bobby's stature as a Son, particularly when combined with his maternal lineage, very nearly made him a prince of sorts. The way people fawned over the match still rankled, as if snagging him was her biggest accomplishment to date.

In truth, he'd done all the snagging. She'd just stopped running.

Margaret poked her head into Bobby's office, startling Indigo out of her reverie.

"Hey," Indigo said. "Bobby's out running errands."

Margaret closed the door. "I can talk to you."

"Ok." Indigo scooped up her work and dropped it onto the coffee table in front of the couch, her favorite work station. "Want to sit?"

"I'll take a chair," Margaret said, and did just that, turning one of the chairs in front of Bobby's desk around before dropping into it. "I've been trying to run Bobby down for about a week now."

Indigo plucked at the seam in her khakis. Not everyone approved of her match with Bobby. She had a feeling Margaret would fall into that category. "It's been a busy time."

"So I hear. Congratulations on the engagement."

"Thank you."

"I'm sure Mom's making your life hell."

Indigo allowed a small smile to curve her lips upward. "Only a little."

Margaret snorted. "She must be getting soft in her old age."

"I dare you to say that to her face," Indigo said with a laugh.

"What am I, stupid?" Margaret shook her head. "She can still kick my ass around the block and back."

"Mmm." That was probably true. It was one reason Rebecca had retained her power long after becoming a mortal. She was a Daughter with whom one did not tangle. "We're thinking of having a party this weekend, maybe at The Omega."

"That's the other reason I came by. Jerusha's coming into

town this weekend. She heard about the engagement all the way in London."

"Oh?"

"Yeah. We want to take you out, have a little girl time."

"By *we* you mean...?"

"Me and Moira, Jerusha, Dani and Charlotte, maybe Mom and a couple of other gals." Margaret shrugged. "You know. Girls' night out."

"Um." Indigo tried to imagine spending an entire night with the women in Bobby's family and making it through in one piece. Nope. That wasn't going to happen, but what could she say and still keep the peace? "Sure."

Margaret's smile seemed a tad too knowing, as if she'd seen right into Indigo's head and witnessed every single doubt. "It'll be fun. We can hire some strippers."

"I'll pass on the strippers, but maybe we could do pizza and pool."

"Ok. I'll arrange everything."

Indigo sighed her relief. One less thing for her to worry over. "What was the other thing you wanted to talk about?"

"Right, almost forgot." Margaret dug a folded sheet of paper out of the back pocket of her jeans. "I've been doing a little digging on my own and came up with a few ideas on solving the problem with traitors among the People. I was supposed to talk to Bobby about it last week, but..."

"He's been busy."

Indigo took the paper and unfolded it, and tried to push down the guilt that nagged at her. She'd had to let her own forays into Margaret's past go to concentrate on everything else, though a little niggle in her gut insisted the other Daughter knew more than she was letting on.

Indigo smoothed the paper across one thigh, pushing out the creases, and studied it, surprised that it contained not raw information but a chart showing relationships between people and events. She sat straight up and grasped the paper in tense fingers. "By the Goddess, Margaret. Why didn't you come forward with this sooner?"

"It's been busy."

"Yes, I know, but this is..." With one finger, Indigo traced the intricate connections outlined on the paper, studying them. "It's enough to break the whole thing wide open in a week, maybe less if we move hard and fast. How did you put this together? I mean, who could possibly know all of this?"

She clamped her jaws together and met Margaret's hard stare evenly. Hadn't she wondered if Margaret was a member of the High Guard, that mythical branch of Daughters bent solely on countering the Eternal Order? And if she was...

No. The more important question was, *What would Margaret do to protect her secret?*

"Never mind," Indigo said. "I don't need to know, and that's what I'll tell Bobby when he asks."

Margaret rose and bowed. "Use this information wisely. It cannot be traced back to me."

"I understand." Indigo stood and returned the bow. "Zenalisa and Laura are clever women."

"Yes," Margaret said with a careful nod.

"Hiro and Drew love intrigue. In fact, they're quite good at figuring out who did what and when."

"They are."

"Bobby's built up quite a business here, you know." Indigo folded the paper and placed it with her work. "I've been very impressed with the efficient way they operate."

Margaret's grin held an unholy mischief. "I think I'm going to like having you around."

Indigo returned her smile, sure for the first time that she had an ally in Bobby's family outside of Dani. "The feeling's mutual."

Margaret left, shutting the door quietly behind her, and Indigo settled down with the list to study and plan.

Bobby stood in front of the bathroom mirror, hands tangled up in a tie. Why he had to wear one to eat with his own parents escaped him. It was just a dinner, but no. Indigo had insisted he wear real slacks instead of khakis, a button-down shirt, and a tie.

She was wearing a dress, a loose flowy thing that slid around her body when she walked, clinging to the swell of her breasts and the lush curves of her ass and stopping short enough that every time he followed her, his eyes fell to the bare sensitive skin behind her knees and made him want to drop to the floor and lick there, and keep going until she was naked and writhing beneath his mouth.

And she thought her dress was demure enough for a visit with his parents.

He grunted out a laugh. Goddess help him, he was going to have a hard time keeping his dick under control with all that beautiful flesh shifting around under her dress every time she moved. Dad would understand. Mom? Probably not.

The sharp clack of heels against wood sounded in the bedroom moments before Indigo rushed into the bathroom, her heart-shaped face flushed pink.

"You're not ready." She brushed his hands aside and lifted the two ends of his tie, folding and tucking until it was presentable. "There. Your parents will be here any minute."

"It's not like they're royalty or something." He dropped his hands to her hips and drew her in, stroking her through the silky fabric of the dress. "You didn't have to go to so much trouble."

She breathed out a faint laugh. "It's the final step before we can get married."

"As far as I'm concerned, it's a done deal." He pressed a chaste kiss to her lipsticked mouth and let her fuss over the smudge that transferred to his lower lip. "And it's just my folks. We'll be doing this a lot over the next few decades."

"Yes," she agreed as she stepped back. "But there's only one first dinner."

He rolled his eyes skyward and followed her into the

apartment's main living area.

Indigo had spent the entire weekend polishing and scrubbing and fussing over every room in the apartment. If a cobweb or speck of dust had survived her laser gaze, he'd be surprised, but he had to admit the apartment looked nice. He'd finally talked her into taking the bookcases. They took up an entire wall in the living room and were filled with the books she'd collected over the years along with pictures of her family and his. Flowers decorated every surface, sprouting out of vases in shades of orange, red, and gold. The mission-style coffee and end tables he'd given her surrounded the leather couch and recliner she'd bought, and the TV rested safely behind the doors of an entertainment center, facing the couch.

She'd gone all out with the dining area. He'd scooted the table out for her and helped her drape it in layers of tablecloths. She'd dug out pewter candlesticks and made him polish them, and then filled them with pale yellow candles and placed them on either side of a low flower centerpiece.

The one thing he'd insisted on was having the meal catered. Otherwise, she would've worn herself into a frazzled wreck trying to please his mom. So he'd put his foot down. Frankly, he wanted her to have energy to spend on him after his folks were gone.

He was just crazy like that.

The doorbell rang and she jumped. He barely refrained from rolling his eyes again. It was going to be a long night. "Would you relax?"

She slid her hand into his and took a shaky breath. "I don't think I can."

"It'll be fine."

"Easy for you to say. They're your parents."

He gave her an exasperated look and opened the door for his parents, and suppressed an irritated grimace at their clothing. Mom wore a dress, for cripes' sake, and Dad had on a tie. Bobby shared a sympathetic look with his father as the two entered the apartment.

"Hello, dear." Rebecca tilted her cheek for his kiss. She slid her coat off and handed it to him. "What a lovely little place this is."

"Thank you," Indigo said. She stood solicitously at his dad's elbow, waiting patiently while he took his jacket off around his hand crutches. "We're pleased you could come."

"We appreciate the invitation," Rebecca said.

Bobby had never heard her sound so stiff and formal outside of a business meeting. The two women circled one another awkwardly, coming in for a brief brush of lips to air at the other's cheek before moving apart. The silence stretched thin between them.

He rubbed a finger across his forehead. Yup, it was gonna be a long one. "Dinner's warming in the oven. Why don't we sit down and talk before we eat?"

Indigo's expression held such relief, he had to bite back a smile. "Oh, yes. That would be lovely."

He settled Rebecca onto the couch next to his father, who dropped down with a sigh, and perched on the arm of the recliner to Indigo's left.

"Thanksgiving's just around the corner." Rebecca folded her hands in her lap. "Have you made plans yet?"

Indigo shot a glance at Bobby before answering. "We haven't really decided on anything."

"Jerusha will be in," Rebecca said. "She's staying for a while, so I thought we'd get the whole family together. What does your mother do?"

Rebecca touched a hand to the locket at her throat, and it dawned on Bobby that she was as nervous as Indigo. What a pair.

"We're usually never in one spot all at one time," Indigo admitted.

"We always have room, if she wants to join us," Robert said. "I need to talk with Glen about his family anyway."

"Dad, geez. Not the genealogy thing again." Bobby draped a hand on Indigo's shoulder and felt her muscles relax under his touch. "Don't get him started, Indi. He'll drive you nuts asking questions about your family tree, especially if there are gaps."

Indigo turned to give him a sweet smile. "I don't mind."

"There, now. A girl after my own heart." Robert leaned forward, bracing himself against the edge of the sofa. "Any chance you've got nobility in your father's line?"

"Oh, well." Indigo stuttered to a stop. "No idea."

"Robert, really. Don't put her on the spot." Rebecca patted his arm. "I hate to bring up business, but I need to borrow Indigo for a moment so we can go over the marital contract."

"I don't think so," Bobby said mildly. "In fact, I want to review it before Indigo signs anything."

"Well, really," Rebecca said.

He cut her off. "I have that right."

"Bobby, please." Indigo touched a hand to his knee. "I told you I took care of this."

"You told me you gave her what she wanted so we could be together," he said, and ignored the flicker of guilt when Indigo paled and looked away. "I want to read that contract."

Rebecca's posture stiffened. "Do you not trust me to deal fairly?"

"Not for this, no." Bobby pinned her with a hard stare. "Especially if you have something to gain."

Robert's eyebrows shot up and he coughed into his hand. "Get him the contract, dear."

"Oh, all right." Rebecca pulled her purse into her lap and extracted an envelope. "I'm sure you'll find it very favorable to both of you."

Bobby rose and took the envelope from her, pulled the contract out, and read it standing. He didn't miss the way Indigo's shoulders tensed, the white-knuckled grip of her hands in her lap, or the way her eyes fell to the floor; nor did he miss his mother's haughty gaze as she stared out the window and the way she twisted the locket between her fingers.

Most of it was legalese. He cut straight through that and hit the high spots. In lieu of physical Retribution, Indigo would create a trust for children born of her union with him, in which she would place a fine for forsaking a Son. Bobby whistled at the amount. Elizabeth had been right there. It was a hefty sum, but no larger than he'd expected. He read down, did a slow burn at the provisions for children, and noted the blank space under the section titled, "Son's Gift." When he finished, he started at the beginning and read the whole thing again, item by item, and wanted to strangle his mother at the noose she'd slipped around Indigo's neck.

In lieu of physical Retribution.

He'd heard of such things, harsh punishment doled out when a Daughter didn't treat the precious Son as his mother thought he should be treated. He cursed under his breath. No wonder Indigo clung to him so fiercely. She thought Rebecca was going to have her beaten to within an inch of her life if things didn't work out with him.

A wave of dizziness washed over him and he pinched the bridge of his nose.

"Bobby, what is it?" Indigo said.

He shook his head at the alarm in her voice.

Physical Retribution. Often meted out with a whip on bare flesh until the skin was raw. He bent over, bracing his hands against his knees, and sucked in a harsh breath as nausea roiled in his stomach. By the Lady Goddess. His mother had threatened her with a whipping.

Indigo's screams echoed through his mind and his gut clenched. He stood slowly and threw the contract down on the coffee table. "I told you."

Rebecca flinched.

Indigo looked between them, confusion replacing her alarm. "What?"

He ignored her and speared his mother with a cold gaze. "I

told you that if you tried to harm her, I would stand in front of her. Did you think I was kidding?"

"No," Rebecca said, her voice barely audible.

"But you threatened her anyway." He stabbed a finger at the contract. "Physical Retribution. Do you think I don't know what that is, what it would do to her?" He yanked a hand through his hair. "For something that wasn't even her fault? How could you, Mom?"

"I..." Rebecca cleared her throat. "I did what I had to do to make certain you were cared for."

He laughed, a harsh, bitter sound that made her flinch. "And if she left me and you went after her, what do you think I would do? Do you think I'd let you whip her because I wear her mark, a mark she had no hand in placing?"

"Bobby, please," Indigo said.

He hushed her with a sharp wave of his hand. "I would stand in front of her and take Retribution in her place. You know I would."

"No!" Indigo said. The word held a horror so deep it startled him.

Rebecca sucked in a breath and the color drained from her face. "That would kill you."

"What's going on here?" Robert said. "I thought that was standard language in the contract."

"It's not." Bobby nodded at his mother. "She put it in there to keep Indigo tied to me, to make her have my children whether she wanted them or not. This is low, Mom, even for you."

Indigo stood abruptly. "Bobby, I'd like a word with you please."

"I think we need to..."

She cut him off. "In the bedroom. Now."

She turned on her heel and marched out of the living room. Bobby shelved his argument and followed her, ignoring the whispered conversation his parents were having on the couch. He shut the door behind himself and stood facing her.

She sucked in a breath. "How could you embarrass me like that?"

What the hell. "She was gonna have you beaten."

"She was going to do no such thing." Indigo crossed her arms over her chest. "And even if she were, do you think I'd let her bully me around like that? I'm not a child. It was my decision to claim you, *mine*, and my decision to bring a suit before your mother. I wouldn't do that if I didn't want you. I'm not some weakling that I can be pushed into doing something I don't want."

"Indi, honey, I didn't mean..."

"Don't you *Indi, honey* me." She dropped her arms and faced him with such a sad expression he reached for her, and flinched when she stepped away from him. "When are you going to trust that I'm strong enough to take care of myself?"

"I do. I know you're strong enough."

"Do you?" Her gaze went flat and cold. "Do you really?"

She brushed past him and left the bedroom. He yanked at his tie, loosening it, and undid the top button of his shirt.

Well, that wasn't how he'd expected that to go. For one, he'd hoped she'd be grateful he'd challenged that damned lopsided contract. Two children in three years? Ridiculous. He wanted kids, sure, but not like that, not rushed because his mom had set a timetable to it. And he sure as hell would never let the physical Retribution clause stand, even if he thought Indigo would never love him.

Why didn't she understand his need to protect her, to keep her safe and hold her to him and say to hell with the rest of the world? He'd wanted to since the first moment he'd seen her, when she'd walked into the classroom his tenth grade year and stolen his heart with the gentle smile in her sapphire eyes.

He folded his hands behind his head and ran through his options one by one. A triumphant grin twisted his lips when he hit on a way to even out the contract and force Rebecca to leave them alone once and for all.

FIFTEEN

A FIRE DANCED MERRILY behind the tempered glass doors of the fireplace insert. Rebecca stared at it and drew her legs tighter into the curve of her body. She took a sip of the wine she'd poured earlier, a nice red grown locally. The fruity undertones were lost to her, overwhelmed by the dismay ricocheting through her mind.

She'd severely misplayed her hand where Indigo was concerned.

The fire popped and sizzled, throwing warmth into the library. It was her favorite place, this room, with its overstuffed couches and walls of books. She and Robert had spent hours here together, and the children, too, when Bobby was younger. This was where she came to relax and think.

And sometimes to brood over her mistakes.

A woman of her age and experience should have grown out of strategic errors. Her son's life wasn't a battlefield, though, where the sides and issues were clear cut, where she wasn't so close to the action that she couldn't direct it as she had countless times over the centuries.

Perhaps if she loved him less, she'd have dealt with it more rationally, but that was asking too much from a mother, to erase the love she felt for her only son, and with it her heart.

When he'd learned the exact terms of the marital contract,

he'd been so angry, and then he'd turned the tables on her nicely.

She hid the proud smile that rose behind a sip of wine. Yes, he was his mother's son.

A house and land. That's what he'd demanded as the Son's gift to his wife, not to enrich his new bride's pockets so much as to punish his mother for overstepping her bounds. She'd done what she had for the best, but of course he wouldn't see it that way. All he saw was the harm that could come to Indigo, not the harm that would come to him when she left him heartbroken and alone for the second time in his young life.

The pain of that memory still burned. Losing Bobby to the Army was one thing. Knowing what Indigo's rejection had pushed him to was another. All those years spent in a system that had channeled his rage to its own calculated purpose. He'd been wrong to think she wouldn't learn exactly what he'd done during that time, and wrong to be afraid when she'd invoked the Enforcer and pushed him into contact with the woman he'd lost.

That had been done for the best as well. It was far past time for Bobby's heart to find solace. Gentle Indigo was the perfect woman to help him find it.

Rebecca had never intended to enact the Retribution clause, regardless of what Bobby thought. It was there simply for leverage, to force Indigo to carefully consider her options should she ever wish to abandon him again.

Of course, if they had children, it wouldn't come to that. Indigo would never leave her children and Bobby would never allow them to be taken from him. If they were stuck in a loveless union until then, so be it.

Somehow, though, Rebecca didn't think it would be loveless. Bobby loved Indigo fiercely, of that there was no question, and Rebecca had noticed the shy glances Indigo had sent him, the way she'd relaxed under Bobby's hand, the soft blush that rose to her face when he gazed down at her, all the love and pride and joy shining from him. The love was there, or would be soon, and after that, surely it was only a matter of time before Indigo submitted her will to Bobby and became mortal, cementing their relationship.

The door creaked open. Rebecca allowed a small sigh to escape as Robert made his way slowly across the room on his hand crutches. Her beloved husband hadn't been happy with her either the night before.

She turned to watch his progress with a tenderness that surprised her, even now, decades after she'd fallen in love with her handsome Yankee scholar. They weren't quite into old age yet, and wouldn't be for a while, but they were getting there. She didn't regret it, not one bit. Here was the man who had given her purpose and reason, and a love deeper than she'd ever before known, even for her children, as much as she loved them. They had their share of troubles, true, but nothing they couldn't overcome together.

And his heart would always be hers.

"How was the doctor's appointment?"

He dropped onto the other end of the couch facing her and set his crutches aside. "It went well. Doc said what he always does. Take my medicine, eat well, get plenty of exercise and rest."

"And your progress?"

"Oh, that's just peachy." He settled into the back of the couch with a contented smile. "Says I'm gradually improving. If I'm lucky, I can get rid of the crutches soon, for short periods, anyway."

"That's wonderful." She put down her wine and slid over to him. He placed his arm around her shoulders, drawing her in, and kissed the top of her head when she rested it on his chest. "I wish you'd let me go with you."

"You were supposed to go to work," he chided. "I came home expecting an empty house and found you playing hooky."

"I needed a little time to think things over."

"Bobby?"

She'd never been able to fool him. Seeing through to her

174

inner self was his best trait, and his worst. "Among other things."

"He was right to be angry."

"I was doing what I thought best for him." She toyed with a button on his shirt, just above his heart. "Besides, Indigo agreed to those terms on her own. I didn't force her into it."

He coughed to hide a laugh that she still heard. "Yes, you did. At least be honest about it."

She huffed, making his laugh deepen and rumble through his chest under her ear. "It's settled now, at any rate."

"Only because Bobby forced your hand." His arm tightened around her shoulders. "You heard him. Indigo gave you what you wanted so they could get married. That has to mean something."

It did. Hadn't her own thoughts drifted along similar lines? "We'll see."

"No more interfering, Becca. I want to live out my retirement in peace without my son and wife being at loggerheads."

"It won't come to that. I promise," she said when he gave a disbelieving *hmph.* "You'll see."

She stared into the flickering flames and pushed aside the worry in her heart. Bobby would come around, Indigo would learn to love him, and life would settle down as it should.

It just had to.

INDIGO BARELY had time to breathe the next day. As if the disastrous meeting of the night before were a spur goading him into action, Bobby charged into the office snapping orders and prodded everyone into working twice as hard as they usually did, Indigo included. It didn't leave them a lot of room to talk. Maybe that's why he'd done it.

She'd certainly left him wanting on that score after that awful dinner with his parents. Confronting his mother over the contract, distrusting his lover's strength and resolve. The heat of humiliation burned her cheeks. Their little talk in the bedroom hadn't helped at all. He'd marched back into the living room, demanded a Son's gift worth nearly four times the value of the fine Rebecca had imposed on her, and completely stricken the language regarding Retribution.

And then he'd shocked them all by looking his mother straight in the eye and telling her, flat out, that they would have children when they were ready and *he* would pay any fines imposed in the contract for the lack thereof.

It had warmed her through and through, even as his lack of faith clawed at her.

On the other hand, the look on Rebecca's face might've been worth Indigo's own discomfort over Bobby's actions. She chuckled to herself and imagined the director's stricken expression, the slump of her shoulders when she'd initialed the changes Bobby insisted on, and the small flash of pride.

It was the latter that kept Indigo's spite in check and gave her hope that someday, far in the future, she and Rebecca might meet as equals, united in their concern for Bobby.

If she could just get him to see her as something other than a shy, retiring dove, as a woman who needed his heart, not his protection...

Later, after a bemused Robert led his suspiciously silent wife home, Bobby had cajoled Indigo out of her anger and into bed where he'd loved her for hours, bringing them both to release after beautiful release with his whispered words and soft touches.

She could love him. It was there in the quiet longing of her heart, perched on the verge of falling, but still fearful of the long cartwheel over the edge into love.

Near the end of the workday, she cornered him in his office, after he'd spent hours evading her, pleading work whenever she tried to get him alone.

"Don't forget our dinner tonight with Dani and her sweetheart," she said.

He groaned and threw his pen down on his desk. "Dave

Winstead," he spat, as if the words alone left a foul taste in his mouth. "Can't you go without me?"

She gave him a stern look. "If I have to go out with your sisters this weekend, then you can sit through one dinner with a former FBI agent."

He hefted a sigh and rubbed tired hands through his hair. "At least promise me this is the last one we have to do for a while."

She rose from the couch and came around the desk. He opened for her and pulled her onto his lap, and she nestled there, content for the first time that day. "I wish I could," she said softly. "Even after we're officially married, it'll take a while for people to quit dragging us out to celebrate."

"Kiss me, then, and let me forget about it for a while."

She did, drawing his head down so their mouths could meet in a gentle kiss. She loved this, the way his lips clung to hers and his tongue flicked and stroked, teasing her while his hands roamed until she squirmed under his touch with a need that ricocheted through her body, taking her heart with it.

She broke the embrace before it could get out of hand and talked him into coming home. When they arrived there an hour later, she stripped him down and led him to the shower and let him press her against the tiled wall while he rocked into her and drove them both to a sweet release.

They were toweling off when his phone beeped with a text. He flipped it open, typed out a quick return message, and dropped it back down on the counter. "Something's come up at work."

She rolled her eyes skyward. "Sure it has."

"Really." He hung his towel up and reached around her for his brush. "Laura has some paperwork she needs signed tonight so it can go out first thing tomorrow."

She refused to call the gnawing in her chest jealousy. Suspicion, maybe, but not the green-eyed monster. "And why didn't she ask you to do that before we left?"

"I don't know." He lifted one shoulder in a careless shrug. "Maybe she just got it finished."

"Right. Laura, who is normally so efficient you can't tell she has any work, has just now decided that, *whoops*, she's going to wait until the last minute to finish something time-sensitive."

Bobby's grin was knowing and a little too self-satisfied for Indigo's peace of mind. "You're jealous."

She gaped at him. "I can't believe you said that."

"It's just Laura."

"Oh, yeah. It's *just* Laura who moons over you and follows you around like a puppy begging for a good petting."

His grin slipped. "Are we talking about the same woman? Laura, the ice queen, whose middle name is formality, the same woman who wouldn't touch a man at work with a ten foot pole?"

"That would be her." Indigo turned on her heel and marched out of the bathroom. "She's got a major crush on you."

"C'mon, Indi. Don't be ridiculous."

She whirled on him and skewered him with a look that sent him stepping back, hands raised. "Trust me, Bobby. She's crushing on you."

"Ok, fine." He dropped his hands and retreated to the bed where he dropped down to watch her rummage through her clothes. "I'll talk to her, sort it out, but I still need to go in and sign those papers."

"You do that." She slammed her underwear drawer shut. "I'll be having dinner with Dani and her reputedly gorgeous hunk of a man. Who knows? Maybe I'll find another one of my own."

His eyes narrowed. "Don't push it, Indigo. It's all I can do to let you leave the apartment every day."

"Let me!" She huffed, saw that he was serious, and crossed her arms over her still-naked chest. "The day you *let* me do anything is the day I hand in my Daughter card."

His lips twitched. "Your Daughter card?"

She bit her lip to stifle a giggle, and loosed it when he collapsed against the bed, laughing so hard he rolled along the comforter. She pounced on him and rolled with him until their bodies were joined and he was inside her, exactly where she wanted him to be, always.

SIXTEEN

MUCH LATER, Indigo raced flustered and flushed into The Omega, Tellowee's one and only bar. She spotted Dani at a corner table sitting with a massive brute of a man and rushed over.

"Sorry," she said and pressed a hand to her racing heart. "I hope you've not been waiting long."

"Not at all." Dani stood to hug Indigo, a tight squeeze that let them both know everything was ok. "We haven't been here too long."

"Oh, well. I won't worry then." Indigo turned to take in Dani's companion, the famed Dave Winstead who, rumor had it, had left his job with the FBI to be with Dani. She nodded to him, determined to be polite to the man who had saved her friend's life, and her heart, no matter what Bobby thought. "I'm Indigo and you must be Dave."

He stood in a slow move that seemed to last forever as his long body rose and rose until he towered over her. "Nice to meet you."

"Wow," Indigo said, and knew her eyes were popping out of her head at his sheer bulk. "You're, ah..."

"Humongous," Dani said with a pleased sigh. "You can say it. I certainly think it enough."

Dave shot a disgusted glance at Dani as a slow flush climbed his cheeks.

"Farm boy here's a little shy," Dani said with a waggle of her thumb.

"Oh, well." Indigo took a deep breath and let it out on a shaky laugh. Her heart was still galloping from her race into the bar. "That's sweet."

Dani sat down, then Dave. Indigo pulled a chair out and sank into it gratefully.

"Where's Bobby?" Dani said.

Indigo rolled her eyes. "*Laura* called him back to work to sign some papers."

"And he went?" Dani arched a questioning eyebrow. "That's playing with fire. Doesn't he know she's got a crush on him?"

"He does now," Indigo said.

Will Corbin walked up to stand between Indigo and Dani, and rested a hand on each of their backs. "Who's playing with fire?"

Indigo turned to greet the bartender with a smile. His lean build reminded her of Bobby, though his features and coloring were different. He had the easy grace and charming manner of a cherished Son. Indigo recalled uncomfortably that his grandmother, Anya, sat on the Council of Seven and was Bobby's aunt through his mother, making the two men cousins, close in age and lineage.

Will ran the bar for his parents, who preferred to travel, and kept the clientele in line with a flirtatious smile and a wooden bat tucked snug behind the bar.

"Bobby," Dani said. "He's ditched us to go to work and flirt with his secretary."

"Office manager," Indigo corrected, "and he's hardly flirting with her."

"Want me to handle him for you?" Will flipped the fourth chair at the table around and straddled it. "Better yet, why don't you forget about Bobby and run away with me."

Indigo pretended to consider it. "It's tempting."

"I saw you first, you know, back in school." He put his

hands on the back of the chair and leaned forward, a boyish smile dimpling his cheeks. "But that rat snatched you out from under my nose before I could grow up and claim you myself."

They all laughed, though Indigo thought Will's was a tad wistful. Poor man. The life of a Son wasn't all it was cracked up to be.

He chatted with them a while longer, his casual friendliness drawing even the stoic Dave out of his shell, before he rose and flipped the chair back around. "Gotta get back to work before Moira destroys my bar."

Dani peered over her shoulder at her older adoptive sister and snorted. Indigo turned to find Moira at the bar going toe to toe with another Daughter in a heated argument over who knew what. She shook her head and turned back around. Moira's temper ran high, but she was a good person. Mostly.

Indigo caught Will's arm before he could leave. "We're planning a formal wedding ceremony for the spring. Would you be willing to stand with Bobby?"

"Of course." He braced one hand against the table and another against the back of her chair. "And since he's not here to save you..."

He pressed his lips to hers and took his time learning her, slanting his mouth over hers in a masterful display of sensuality. His hand crept up to tangle in her hair, tugging gently. Indigo sat there like a lump, unsure whether to pull away or kiss him back or bite the tongue that flicked out, testing the seam of her lips.

Dani cleared her throat loudly. "Cut it out, Will."

He drew back and tweaked Indigo's nose. "Serves him right for not being here."

She couldn't argue with that.

He moved away, earning a protest from Dani. "Hey, where's mine?"

Will flipped his towel at Dave before slinging it over his shoulder. "I like being in one piece, cousin. Catch you later."

When he'd gone, Dani fixed Indigo with a laser-bright stare.

"I noticed you didn't struggle to get away from him there."

"Oh, well. I didn't know whether to punch him or kiss him back."

"Kiss him back," Dani said in a *well, duh* voice, and yelped when Dave punched her arm lightly as a reprimand.

"He's certainly got the moves." Indigo snuck a glance toward the bar where Will was pouring drinks. She fanned her face as discreetly as she could. *Moves* might be an understatement. "And I bet he'll make some woman very happy one day."

"Just not you," Dani said.

"No, I'm quite content where I'm at."

"Ditto," Dani said with a grin.

They waited for Bobby for over an hour, chatting and sharing gossip. Dave filled them in on what he could of the Shadow Enemy's movements, including what appeared to be a growing division in the Alexiou family over the organization's direction.

Indigo checked her watch for the umpteenth time and shifted on the wooden chair. Bobby should've been there to hear that, given the work they were doing for the IECS. Where was he? Surely it didn't take that long to sign papers.

Dani pressed a hand to her abdomen and grimaced. Dave placed a massive hand on her back and rubbed in slow, soothing circles.

"What is it?" Indigo said. "Are you pregnant?"

Dani gave her a disgusted look. "Why does everybody keep asking me that? No, it's this bad feeling. Ever since..."

She shook her head and the sadness in her expression touched Indigo's heart. Dani didn't have to say anything for Indigo to know where the younger Daughter's thoughts rested, on the recent events leading to her mother's death by her own hand.

"My instincts are getting stronger," Dani continued. "Right now, they're screaming at me that something's wrong."

"Can you pinpoint it?" Indigo said, but she already knew, because her gut was pinging with it, too. Something was wrong with Bobby.

No, Indigo. You're being irrational.

Just because he's running behind after visiting work late in the evening, spending time with a woman who has a big time crush on him. What could possibly go wrong?

Dani shook her head. "Not really. Something about a hawk carrying a dove in its claws. Dammit, why do these visions have to be so metaphorical?"

Indigo watched Dani continue speaking as if from a great distance. Her friend's mouth moved in animated slashes across her face, words tumbled out, she was certain, but Indigo couldn't hear them.

A hawk and a dove.

Bobby's *aenkanien*, a symbol for the weaker sibling, and her sister, the hawk, on the opposing side in their battle over the Prophecy of Light.

Indigo stood abruptly, knocking back her chair.

Dani stopped speaking in mid-word to stare at her. "What is it?"

"Bobby." Dizziness swept over her. She leaned against the table until it passed. "He's in trouble."

Dani opened her mouth, but was cut short by the beep of Indigo's phone. She pulled it out with the mantra *Not Bobby, not Bobby, please, let him be ok* running through her head, and read a text sent by Hiro: *Bobby's been taken. BDH now.*

The breath froze in her lungs and she sat down as suddenly as she'd stood. Dani took the phone from Indigo's limp fingers, read the message, and flipped it shut. They looked at one another for long moments as a silent understanding passed between them. Someone had dared to take a protected son, their kin, a man who filled an important role in each of their lives.

Indigo's strength flooded back, braced by the slow anger bubbling up in her gut, and with it the steely will of a Daughter whose mate had been threatened. Bobby was in trouble. Goddess help the ones who'd taken him.

BOBBY DROVE between home and work with half his mind on the road and the other half on Indigo.

She was pissed at him.

It was bound to happen to any couple. He wasn't stupid enough to believe they were the exception, but man, her anger killed him almost as much as her tears did.

The image of Indigo huddled on the floor, sobbing after her nightmare, hit him full force and he shuddered. Nope. Didn't want to see that again.

Note to self: Keep Indigo happy. No exceptions.

Only, he wasn't going to bow to his mother the way Indigo did. Hell with that. Mom would weasel her nose in on everything if they let her. The only reason she didn't have more control over his life now was because he'd drawn those lines with her when he'd left home at sixteen. Goddess, he loved her to the bottom of his heart, but he didn't need her telling him how to run his marriage.

And Indigo didn't need his mother telling her how to treat him. His soon-to-be wife did that very well on her own.

His wife. Sweet Lady, he loved calling her that and it was true, or close enough now that Indigo had claimed him and both mothers had given their blessings. The ceremony was a formality, nothing more, a ritual that didn't mean dick compared to the love he held for her. He would hold on to her as long as she would let him, hold her, cherish her, give her the babies she longed for.

Earlier, she'd thrown Laura at him as if he could possibly care about another woman. Indigo *knew* she was the only one for him. Hadn't he shown her in every way he could? Yet she'd been jealous over his office manager, for cripes' sake.

He shook his head, bemused. So what if Laura had a little crush on him, which he didn't believe for a second. How could that possibly affect his heart, when it held only Indigo?

Anyway, Laura had never shown the slightest interest in him. Ok, so she'd given Indigo a hard time when she'd first joined them, but that was to be expected. BDH ran like a well-oiled machine most days. No one liked having a major player coming in to rock the boat. Surely once Laura got to know Indigo, the tension between them would ease into friendship.

He parked his truck in the parking deck, gave the aging dashboard a fond pat, and made his way to the elevators, bypassing security by using the private elevator. When he reached BDH's floor, it was quiet, the main lights dimmed during the off hours. He dropped by his own office, jotted a note on his calendar to talk to Margaret, then went to Laura's office. The lights were off in there as well, so he searched through the common areas until he found her in the break room.

She was sitting at a small round table in the corner, staring out the window at the night, with her hands folded demurely in her lap and her ankles crossed in that way elegant women had. He chuckled to himself at Indigo's ridiculous jealousy. Laura was pretty enough, true, but she was too staid and, frankly, too much like his mother for him to be attracted. Friendly, yes. She was a nice young woman, but she would never hold a candle to Indigo.

She looked up and gave him a faint smile, her lips tilted so slightly only someone who knew her well could distinguish the pleased expression from her normal business-like mask.

He dropped down in a chair across from her. "You shouldn't work so late."

"It's what you pay me for." She touched the fingers of one hand lightly to the pulse point at the bottom of her throat. "I appreciate your coming all the way back."

"Hey, business before pleasure, right?"

She blinked and looked away.

His heart sank. *Shit.* Maybe Indigo was right about the whole crush thing. He chafed his palms down his thighs and searched for a tactful way to test the idea.

"As a matter of fact, I was on my way to dinner with my sister and her new boyfriend. Indigo went ahead so I could come in and get those papers signed for you."

She turned her gaze back to his, solemn brown eyes wide in her face. "May I ask you a personal question?"

Uh oh. Here it comes. "Sure."

"Are you really going to marry her?"

"Yes." He met her gaze evenly and couldn't miss the slight furrow in her brow. "I've loved her for a long time, since I was a kid really."

"I see." She stood and stared down at him, a flurry of emotion running through her expression, changing it in tiny increments. "We should toast to a long and happy marriage. Would you share a soda with me?"

What harm could there be? Besides, he'd noticed her flinch. Indigo had been right. Laura *did* have a crush on him. Least he could do was let her know they would always be friends. "I'd like that."

She gave him that almost smile again and walked toward the refrigerator to pull out a coke. He took the time to observe her while she divided the soft drink between two glasses, to really see her, from the severe bun she kept her dark blonde hair in to the straight set of her shoulders to the curve of her ass. Which was nice, he admitted, but looking at it made him feel like a perv. She was a co-worker and she trusted him and, hell, half the time she felt like his kid sister. Nothing for Indigo to be jealous over. He'd be sure to tell her that asap.

Laura's hand appeared in front of him holding a half-full glass. When he'd taken it, she held hers out and said, "To the people we love."

"I'll drink to that." He tapped his glass against hers and took a sip, grimacing at the saccharine taste. There was a reason he stuck to coffee. "And I'd like to offer a toast, too. To family and friends."

"Of course," she said.

They tapped glasses again and sipped, and then she made a toast and they drank some more, and he thought of another one, and by the time they'd run out of things to toast, his glass was empty and he was pleasantly loose. That was what friendship was. Sharing a coke after work and celebrating life's moments.

"Well, I suppose I need to sign those papers, get back to Indigo before she gets worried." He tried to stand and his legs wobbled. "Whoa." He grabbed the edge of the table and laughed at his own clumsiness. "Guess I had a little too much coke, huh?"

Her features remained neutral, calm. The first inkling that something might not be right pinched at him.

He pushed up off the table, trying to stand again, and his head spun, taking him down with it until he collapsed bonelessly to the floor. The edges of his vision blurred and shrank, and the room slowly disappeared. Laura's face appeared in the pinpoint of light left, looking down at him so dispassionately, his mind flinched from it, doing what his numb body couldn't.

"You picked the wrong woman, Bobby," she said.

As the blackness took him, he thought, *Indigo's gonna kill me for this.*

SEVENTEEN

S TREETLIGHTS FLICKERED by outside the car as Indigo, Dani, and Dave sped toward BDH. Dave drove Dani's Jeep, his hands competent and firm on the wheel. Dani had taken the front seat and Indigo the rear, but their hands clenched together in the gap between the front seats, holding tight to comfort one another, staving off the worry until they knew more.

Dani had called Rebecca as soon as they'd hit the highway and even from several feet away, Indigo had felt the icy anger seeping through the phone when the Blade learned her only son had been kidnapped.

They arrived at the office fifteen minutes sooner than Indigo would've reached it on her own, even in the relatively light evening traffic. She used her keycard to enter the building at the front, and was grateful the security guards manning the lobby passed them through without question.

When they stepped out of the elevator, the entire floor was flooded with light. A man she didn't know, one of the people who worked for BDH, sat at the reception desk and pointed them to Zena's office. They rushed back and found her office crowded with people around the mass of technology the young woman had assembled.

Indigo had never been inside Zena's work area, and now she gawked at the row of monitors along one wall, the tables laden with keyboards and other equipment she barely recognized, all organized precisely under the strict hands of the tech expert.

Hiro stepped forward and pulled Indigo through to where Zena sat in a chair, rapidly tapping at a keyboard while images flashed across one of the monitors. The others showed stationary points around the building. Security feeds, maybe. One screen in particular caught Indigo's eye. She leaned forward, studying it, and recognized the break room. Laura sat at one of the tables, an ice pack pressed to her cheek, and was surrounded by a small cadre of BDH personnel.

Indigo focused on Zena and the rapid clack of her fingers on the keyboard. She faintly heard Dani introduce Dave to Hiro, Drew, and Margaret, but she ignored it to press a gentle hand to Zena's shoulder. "Have you found anything?" she said softly.

Zena nodded, shaking the multitude of thin, ebony braids hanging loose around her shoulders. "Got the whole thing, from the time Bobby entered the building to the time he left it. I'm looking for possible exits, maybe a direction we can follow so I can pick up feed from other security cameras in the area." Her soft Southern twang shifted to a pointed one as she raised her voice loud enough to be heard beyond Indigo. "Of course, I would *never* tap into those feeds without getting permission first 'cause that would be *illegal.*"

Hiro snorted. "Cut the crap, Zena."

She ignored him and lowered her voice. "Hold on. I'm gonna skip straight to the good stuff. Here, look at this."

Zena pointed to one of the monitors where an image of Bobby and Laura, seated at a table in the break room, popped onto the screen and then moved forward.

"Sound?" Indigo said.

"Nope, not in there. Sorry."

They were talking, a short conversation. Laura stood and walked to the fridge, pulled out a soft drink, and divided it between two glasses. She appeared to hesitate for a moment, and then turned and brought the drinks back, giving one to Bobby. Over the next few minutes of footage, they talked and drank as if they were toasting something. Then Bobby put down his glass, tried to stand, and slid to the floor, landing with an inaudible thump. Laura crossed to him, checked his pulse, then pulled out her phone.

A slow burn ate its way outward from Indigo's heart. She'd told Bobby to be careful with Laura. She'd *told* him. Sweet Goddess, when would he learn to listen to her?

"Ok, that was one thing, but here's where it gets interesting."

Zena typed commands and the feed skipped ahead. Another person entered the room and Indigo's heart froze in her chest. *India.* Her sister stalked over to Laura, barely sparing a glance for Bobby lying passed out on the floor. The two women talked, seemed to argue even. India pulled out the knife she kept strapped to her thigh and raised it to strike a cowering Laura. At the last minute, she pulled her blow and landed a pop to the mortal's cheek hard enough to send her sprawling. India dug a sheet of paper out of her pocket and pinned it to the table with the point of her knife before hauling Bobby up into a fireman's carry. On her way out the door, she turned and grinned smugly into the security camera.

Indigo sagged backward and bumped into Hiro. He draped an arm around her shoulders and rubbed his hand up and down her arm.

"I'm sorry," he said, so low Indigo could barely hear him.

"For what?"

"I should've known she was up to something."

She huffed out a surprised breath. "How could you possibly have known that?"

"Long story," he said, and moved away.

Indigo stared at the image of India with Bobby over her shoulder, fixing her gaze there as Margaret took the spot Hiro had vacated.

"Mom's gonna have a shit fit over this."

That was putting it mildly. "Don't worry. She'll find a way to blame me for it."

Margaret shifted her balance, crossed her arms over her chest. "Doubt that."

Right. India had kidnapped Bobby. Not a big leap to go from there to blaming Indigo. "What was on the paper?"

"And I quote, 'The Son of the Blade for the Oracle,' end quote. Woman's got balls."

"True." Metaphorically, anyway, though Indigo tended to agree with Betty White's thinking on that score.

"Hiro and Drew have already organized crews to do a search and retrieval." Margaret tapped a finger against one bicep. "That information you have might come in handy now."

Indigo whipped her head around to stare at the other Daughter. "It would expose you."

Margaret lifted one shoulder, dropped it. "Pass it off as your own. If nobody believes you, so what? It's not like they're gonna argue, not when Bobby's out there in the hands of...someone who'll probably harm him."

Indigo let the slip pass, filling in the gap in her mind. *The Eternal Order.* So her sister really was searching for a way to stop the Prophecy from happening. Why hadn't she taken that threat more seriously, especially knowing India's single-minded focus?

Indigo pressed a cool hand to her eyes, trying to find her own focus. If she could just think around the panic and worry.

"The more information they have, the easier he'll be to find," Margaret said.

Indigo rubbed a finger across her forehead, realized she'd picked up the habit from Bobby. A swell of sorrow rose within her, pushing its way upward until it hit her like a wave and threatened to drown her under its heavy weight.

"And the quicker he's found the less likely Mom is to get involved." Margaret leaned in and said in a low voice, "Do you really want her charging in here?"

"You're trying to blackmail me," Indigo said around the

knot in her throat. How could she stand Rebecca peering over her shoulder while they hustled to find Bobby? "It's working."

Margaret winked. "Knew it would."

"She won't stay away, not for long, no matter what we're doing."

"No, but you won't need long. We know what India wants. All we have to do is wait for her to give us a location."

A quiet fear cut through the sorrow. India could do a lot of damage between now and then depending on how pissed off she was and whether or not she felt the need to prove something. There was a lot here for her to prove. Her superiority over their mother, who had submitted to a man and become mortal. Her diligence in chasing after a goal that would keep her from ever having to submit herself. Her worth as a Daughter and her cunning as a warrior, and the eternal struggle between one sibling and another over who got to play with the best toys.

Bobby was a valuable toy. India would want to play, and that was what worried Indigo the most.

INDIA FLEXED the knots securing Bobby to a sturdy, wooden chair, testing their strength. She'd searched him before bringing him to one of the empty houses the Order used and dropped the contents of his pockets into a trash bin outside BDH where they would be easily found. He needed to be weaponless in the off chance of an escape, though one wasn't likely. Too many eyes surrounded this house. The recent housing bubble had left them plenty of places like this, foreclosed homes held by banks that didn't watch them too carefully. This one was less than half an hour from BDH Security, nestled among several other houses also taken over by the Order, and was fully furnished to boot. Some of the Order's members even slept here.

India firmed her lips against a soft smile. She'd found a more comfortable bed not too long back. It had come with its own accessory, a sexy man with a nubile body and an endless imagination, plus as many monster movies as she could stomach, which was a lot.

Happy times.

Someone had cleared a space in the living room where they'd situated Bobby, away from the doors and windows, in part to keep him from being seen from the outside, and in part to give the Order room to maneuver in and out of the house without him knowing who, exactly, they were.

Olivia the Good stepped into the room carrying a glass and a pitcher, each full of water. Her bright copper hair was pulled into a braid that fell down her back over the leather vest she wore, a precaution every member of the Order had taken in case this whole thing blew up in their faces and ended in a ruckus. Like all of them, Olivia was a trained fighter, though she was one of the younger members, having just reached her fifth decade. Her value lay chiefly in her strategic placement within the inner circle of the Council of Seven, where she acted as an aide to one of the Seven.

"When will he wake up?"

India pushed herself into a stand and checked the clock on the mantle. "Probably not long."

"Do you think he's ok?" Olivia set the water down beside Bobby's chair before grasping his hair and gently easing his head back. She checked his pulse, pulled up one of his eyelids. "What did that girl give him?"

"No idea," India said with a shrug. "Don't care, either. He's here, right where we need him to be. That's what's important."

"Not if he dies from an overdose."

India snorted. "He's a Son."

"Yes, exactly." Olivia let Bobby's head drop and stepped back. "He might be more resilient than other mortals, but if something happens to him, it will bring the fury of the Blade down upon us all."

"Rebecca Upton," India said evenly through gritted teeth, "will do anything we ask to get her son back. She's the only one who can give us the Oracle. That's why we took him."

"Ok, ok." Olivia shook her head. "I know the plan as well as you."

"Then why are you questioning it?"

"Because it doesn't feel right to take a Son."

India stifled a curse at Olivia's naïveté. The preference Sons were accorded was one of the reasons the Eternal Order existed in the first place. No Daughter liked to be supplanted in her mother's heart by a mere mortal male.

Bobby grunted softly. His muscles tensed. India motioned for Olivia to move back, out of his line of sight.

She reached forward and slapped his cheek lightly, hard enough to help him wake up, not hard enough to leave a bruise. India had no qualms about using Bobby as a hostage, but she didn't want to rile his mother any more than was necessary by sending back a damaged Son.

He jerked away from her hand and shook his head, then winced. "Holy shit. What was in that coke?"

"No idea," India said.

He managed to open one eye enough to give her a *go to hell* look. "Couldn't you have given her something that didn't leave a headache the size of Wisconsin?"

"We'll get you something for that." India jerked her chin at Olivia, who scampered out of the room to look for aspirin. "Want some water?"

He laughed weakly. "You put something in that, too?"

"Of course not," she snapped, then inhaled sharply through her nose. Hiro kept warning her about her temper. It shamed her to admit she was working on handling it better because of him.

Changing to please a man. If anyone else knew, she'd be laughed out of the Order.

"Why did you take me?" He grimaced, shifted in the chair testing the limits of the rope. "Is it because of Indigo?"

"What does she have to do with anything?"

Bobby spared her a glance. "We're engaged."

Something ugly pushed its way up from deep inside her, shooting through her muscles until her lungs ached and her heart raced and her muscles trembled with it. "No," she said on a low growl.

"Yup. Elizabeth approved and everything." His steady hazel gaze held an odd mix of pity and triumph. "Figured you'd heard by now."

Fury. That's what was running through her. A twisted, bitter fury that her sister had chosen to mingle her life with this Son and risk submitting. Her sister, who had shared a womb with her and been her other half until that stupid man had unfurled his whip over a prank, a nothing, and Indigo had left her, retreating into a shell and abandoning India to a world that would never love her half as well as her twin had.

India swung out and backhanded Bobby in a powerful blow that jerked his head around and sent the chair teetering. "You're *lying.*"

"Nope." His gaze settled on her as he spat onto the carpet, sending bloody spittle through the air. "We're getting married in the spring."

She hit him again, so numb the sting of the blow was lost to her. The satisfaction of seeing his head pop around was not. "I'll kill you before I let her marry you."

He laughed, a hard sound that stoked her anger higher. "Too late. I already wear her *aenkanien.*"

India gasped. He was lying, in spite of everything. Men. You could never trust them. She yanked out her spare knife and walked around the back of the chair. A quick downward slash and the knit fabric of his shirt tore down the middle. She ripped it away and felt the air squeeze from her lungs at the sight of the tattoo imprinted into the skin covering his left shoulder blade. A dove. The rings symbolizing eternal devotion. Sweet Goddess, it was true. Indigo had taken him not just as a lover, but as her mate.

"Is she..." India cleared her throat, opened her lungs, searching for air. "Did she submit?"

"No." The softly spoken word fell between them like a wall dropping. "She claimed me anyway."

Her palm itched against the knife's leather-bound hilt.

She could cut it off.

The idea sprang into her mind fully formed. If she cut off the *aenkanien*, Indigo would be free of him.

India's fingers tightened on the knife.

They could be sisters again, the way they once had. Working together, sharing everything.

Her last night with Hiro shuddered through her.

Well, maybe not everything, but he was just a man, nothing compared to the love one felt for a sister.

"I don't know what you're doing back there, but think hard on it." Bobby twisted around to peer at her over his shoulder. "Forget for a minute that my mom is gonna come after you. Indigo's the one you need to worry about."

"My sister will never harm me." Guilt twisted in her gut. No, Indigo wasn't the sister who lashed out and hurt her family. "And she won't miss you, once you're gone and this stupid prophecy is stopped."

"She wants my children." He turned around and slumped against the chair's low, rigid back. "Do you really want to get in her way on that?"

Indigo pressed the tip of the knife to the dove's forward wing, hard enough to draw blood. "She'll find another lover."

"Not like me."

Indigo twisted the knife, working it upward under the skin. Bobby yanked away from her with a hiss, far enough that the blade slipped out, leaving a thin line of blood. If Olivia had secured his torso to the chair, he wouldn't have been able to pull away. *Stupid girl.* Always secure a Son thoroughly, otherwise they could break free. That was the problem with having compassion for a mere mortal male. They never stayed where you put them.

India reached out to haul him back and was seized from behind by strong arms.

"Leave him," Olivia hissed, and squeezed until India dropped her hand. "No harm must come to the Son and you know it. What were you thinking?"

India drew in a shaky breath. Rational thought trickled in through the miasma of hatred and anger, and she closed her eyes at her own stupidity. She'd almost blown the whole thing because she hadn't controlled her emotions.

Hiro would be so ashamed of her.

Of course, he would be really pissed when he saw the security footage of her carrying Bobby off.

Not that she cared.

The sick roil in her gut said otherwise. She shuddered out a breath and clamped down on her emotions. Now was not the time to go all gooey over a man.

Olivia gradually let India go. "Give me the knife or you'll have to leave."

"Watch it, kid," India said as she handed her knife over. She didn't need it to have fun with Bobby. "You're not nearly as tough as you think you are."

"Try me," Olivia said. She slapped a bottle of aspirin into India's hand and stalked out.

"The fuck did you think you were doing?" Bobby said. "Maiming me isn't gonna keep Indigo from loving me."

"So now she loves you, huh." India set the bottle down and stalked around the chair to face him. "We'll see how much she loves you when I send you back to her in pieces."

She raised her fist and, with a familiar, malicious glee, rained the wrath of a scorned sister down upon him.

EIGHTEEN

THROUGH THE GLASS WALL between the hall and the break room, Laura appeared fragile, human. Her shoulders slumped, fine wisps of her hair spilled around her face, loosened from Laura's habitual bun, and a bruise bloomed across her jaw.

Fragile or not, this girl had betrayed Bobby. Temper lashed at Indigo in tandem with the cold chill creeping up her spine. India held Bobby in her tender mercies and they needed to find him. They needed information, and though Laura refused to talk, she was the best source they had.

Indigo pushed back the emotion, the urgency and fear, and reached for control. Laura would talk. Indigo would see to it.

She pushed the door open and stalked into the room, nodding politely to the one man Drew had left behind as a guard. Laura's eyes met hers then skittered away. Satisfaction shot through Indigo. The younger woman was right to be frightened.

She stopped three feet away, pulled out a chair, sat down to look at the woman who had betrayed Bobby in the worst possible way. She kept her gaze steady and direct, and waited.

After a few moments, Laura crossed her arms over her chest. "I have nothing to say to you."

"That's fine," Indigo said. "The police will be here soon. They'll be very interested to see the security footage of this room."

Laura blanched. "You can't prove I did anything, footage or not."

"Oh, but we can. No doubt your fingerprints are on the glass Bobby drank from and the residue of whatever you gave him is still inside." Indigo shrugged and tried not to enjoy herself too much. "Whether you'll be charged with kidnapping or being an accessory doesn't matter. I'll see to it you spend a long time behind bars atoning for what you did tonight."

"I'll never go to jail. My lawyer will get me off with probation, maybe community service."

"Really? Hmm." Indigo leaned forward and speared Laura with a deadly stare. "Do you think I'll let you off that easily?"

Laura laughed, a breathy sound that barely made it past her lips. "You can't touch me without bringing the police down on your head."

"Can't I?"

Indigo met the guard's eyes. He left with a nod and assumed a position on the other side of the break room's doors, out in the hallway with his back to them. Indigo slipped her jacket off, folded it, and laid it on the next table over.

"The thing about betraying a friend is that a lot of people are willing to look the other way to see justice done." Indigo slipped the rings from her fingers, unfastened the charm bracelet and matching necklace Elizabeth had given her for her birthday last year, and set them aside. "Zena, for instance. She was rather upset when she watched Bobby's kidnapping through the security feed. Apparently, she stays late most nights, monitoring the premises, tinkering with her gadgets. Did you know?"

Laura shook her head faintly, her brown eyes large and round in her ashen face. "What are you doing?"

"Getting comfortable. I had a long chat with Zena tonight." Indigo slipped off her flats and nudged them out of the way. An ancient Italian gentleman had hand-crafted them for her on her last visit there and they would be impossible to replace. "Now,

Drew insists she's tight-lipped, won't spill a thing to him about her past, but I had no problem getting her to tell me how a job with BDH saved her and her family, lifting them out of poverty and a harsh life in one of Atlanta's worst neighborhoods. When she came to work here, she bought her mother a house in a nice subdivision out in the suburbs and now she's putting her little brother through school. Such a sweet girl."

Laura choked on a breath. Zena was many things. Intelligent and sharp, in more ways than one, but sweet was stretching it a bit. Indigo slipped the top button free from her blouse.

"What are you doing?" Laura said again in a voice shaky with the first threads of fear.

"Taking my shirt off. It's pure silk, quite delicate, and I really want to be able to wear it again after tonight." Another button and another. "Zena was so upset about Bobby, she agreed to cut the security feed to this room during our chat."

Laura stood suddenly and Indigo shoved her back into the chair one-handed.

"Try to leave again and I'll make it twice as hard on you," she warned.

Laura clutched the chair's arms. "What are you going to do to me?"

"Whatever I see fit." The last button slid free. Indigo pulled the shirt off and draped it over the back of a chair, then undid the fastening of her slacks. "The thing is, you drugged my husband."

"You're not married yet," Laura said in a thin, choked voice. "Bobby said so."

"We haven't had a formal ceremony, true," Indigo acknowledged. She slid her slacks off, folded them, and placed them on top of her jacket, and stood in front of Laura in the matching lace bra and panty set she'd worn to tease Bobby with later, before this woman had drugged him and allowed India to carry him away. A thin shaft of rage penetrated the icy calm. "But in the eyes of our People, the deed's been done, and was long

201

before you came into Bobby's life."

"I don't know what you're talking about."

"You wouldn't because you're an outsider, a mortal human, and no matter what you think, you were never good enough for him. He would never have chosen you because he'd already given his heart to me." Indigo leaned forward and grasped the other woman's jaw in a firm grip. "How old do you think I am?"

"Urm." Laura's breath rasped out of her. "Twenty-five?"

Indigo laughed coldly. "One hundred and sixty two. Do you know how much you can learn about pain in a century and a half, even when you're not trying to?"

"You're crazy."

"I assure you that I'm quite sane. Pissed, yes." Indigo squeezed Laura's jaw until she cried out before letting go. "You harmed my husband. Another Daughter would've killed you by now. Me, I want to see you suffer a bit before you die."

A tear leaked from the corner of Laura's eye as she leaned as far away from Indigo as she could. "You'll never get away with killing me."

Indigo lashed out with her fist, popping Laura hard enough to break her nose. The other woman screamed and bent over, hands clasped to her face, blood dripping between her fingers onto the carpeted floor. Indigo walked behind her, dug her fingers into the remnants of Laura's bun, and yanked.

"When I was a little girl, my mother skinned a man while he was still living, merely for daring to strike her children." Indigo ran a fingernail down the long, slender column of Laura's neck, and let the shudder of fear that ran through the other woman stoke her own resolve. "How long do you think you would last, once I start peeling your flesh away?"

"Please." Laura's tears turned to quiet sobs. "Let me go. I promise I'll leave. You'll never see me again."

"I'm afraid that's not possible." Indigo released Laura's hair and brought her hand down in a hard chop that bruised Laura's back, drawing a high-pitched mewl from her. "No matter what I do to you, Bobby's mother and sisters will insist on coming after you. They'll go easy on you if Bobby's returned to us undamaged, but if he's harmed in some way, well. There's no telling what they'll do to you, little girl."

Indigo stalked around the chair to face the sobbing woman and casually backhanded her hard enough to snap her head around. "The women of his family have led interesting lives." A punch to the upper arm, followed by a loud cry of pain. "They call his mother Rebecca the Blade for her skill with the sword, earned in battle centuries ago when she was still little more than a child." A swift rib shot snuck in under Laura's raised hands, dealt hard enough to crack the bone and elicit another screaming sob. "I wonder if she's sharpening her blade now?"

"No," a steely voice said.

Indigo whirled. Rebecca stood at the entrance to the break room wearing a threadbare plaid shirt and worn jeans, calmly examining Laura slumped over in the chair, moaning, and Indigo in her lingerie with Laura's blood spattered along her hands. Bobby's sisters, all save Jerusha, and several other Daughters were ranged out along the glass wall in the hallway, backs to the break room in an unbreakable chain. No one was trying to get in, though several BDH personnel snuck peeks over and through the wall of Daughters.

Rebecca walked forward, grasped Laura's jaw, and raised the young woman's face to assess the damage.

"Please help me." Laura's voice wheezed out of her throat and her eyes were wild. "Please."

"No, child." Rebecca dropped Laura's jaw and leaned in until their faces were inches apart. "Do you know who I am?"

Laura shook her head slightly.

"I'm Bobby's mother. Whatever Indigo has done to you is a mere trifle compared to what awaits you at the end of my hand." Rebecca stood. "Where did India take my son?"

"I don't know. I swear." Laura sniffed once, winced and placed a delicate hand to her broken nose. "She said she would

203

exchange him for something important and he would never be hurt. That's all I know."

"Pray India told you the truth and no harm comes to my son." Rebecca stepped back and gave Laura a final dispassionate look before turning to Indigo. "The police are on their way up. Hiro's delaying them as long as he can, but they'll be here soon. We need to get you cleaned up."

"Yes, Maetyrm." Indigo bowed solemnly. "There's a shower in the gym one floor up. It should be empty."

Rebecca gathered Indigo's clothes into her arms. "We'll take the stairs."

Indigo turned her back on Laura and followed Rebecca out of the room, ignoring the furtive stares from the mortal men and women clustered around the break room's door. Rebecca didn't speak on their way upstairs, through the gym, and into the women's locker room, leaving Indigo alone with the security feed playing in her head. Bobby falling to the floor, given into India's care by a woman he trusted. Her sweet Bobby, who held her in the night and loved her as no man had ever done. Temper leaked abruptly out of her, leaving a cold, tight fear. If something happened to him...

Her lungs froze in her chest. No, nothing would happen. She would find him and bring him home and he would be ok. They would both be ok.

The footage looped around and restarted, and her fingers curled into fists.

Laura, on the other hand, hadn't suffered nearly enough.

In the shower room, Indigo stripped off her bra and panties and placed them in Rebecca's outstretched hand.

"I'll check these for blood while you clean up." Rebecca set the underwear aside before tugging out the clip holding her own hair back. "Turn around and I'll pull your hair up so you can keep it dry."

"Thank you." Indigo turned, bending down enough so that Rebecca could bundle her hair up out of the way. "I'm fine here if you want to go back downstairs."

"I'll stay, if it's all the same to you. We can chat while you shower."

Indigo's heart slipped a notch. "Yes, Maetyrm." She stepped into the shower, left the curtain open so they could talk, and turned the water on, waiting for it to warm before she stepped under the steady spray and squirted soap from the container mounted in the stall into her hand. "How's Robert?"

"Oh, he's fine." Rebecca picked up Indigo's bra and ran it through her fingers, examining the fabric for blood spatter. "Miffed because I made him stay home. He's in no shape to traipse all over this building. He only agreed to stay after I pointed out that someone might call our home with a ransom demand."

Indigo bit the corner of her mouth as she scrubbed her skin. That someone would probably be her sister, which had to cut at Rebecca. How right Bobby's mother had been to bring India into the marital negotiations. Of course, if Indigo had known India's plan to kidnap Bobby, she would've nipped it in the bud before he could be taken.

"This is very nice lingerie." Rebecca shifted the bra in her hand and focused on the other cup. "Where did you get it?"

"A little boutique in Buckhead." Indigo squirted more soap into her hand and began to work on the beds of her nails, where tiny spatters of blood had already dried and caked. "Very exclusive. A lot of their inventory is handmade."

"It's too bad you didn't buy this in dark blue to match your eyes. The lavender is lovely, but the blue would've made your eyes pop."

Indigo wasn't sure what to say, so she held her tongue. How often did a woman have a conversation about underwear with her soon-to-be mother-in-law, especially if that underwear had been bought to entice said mother-in-law's son? Rebecca probably didn't need to know that, though.

"I bet Bobby went wild over this," Rebecca said.

Indigo snorted out an embarrassed laugh.

"Watch your hair, dear. It wouldn't do to get it wet." Rebecca raised a knowing eyebrow. "Do you think I don't know what the two of you do when you're alone? Child, I learned about the birds and the bees well before your mother was born."

Indigo turned her face carefully into the water, using it as an excuse to hide her flaming cheeks. Of all the things for them to talk about, this was the one Rebecca had to pick. Anything else would've been a more comfortable topic, even her rogue twin.

When Indigo was as clean as she reasonably could be, she turned the water off and accepted the towel Rebecca handed her.

"Besides, I want grandchildren."

Indigo blinked, suppressing the urge to roll her eyes. "I had no idea."

"Sarcasm is unbefitting a woman of your status," Rebecca said, though her voice held no bite. She handed the lingerie to Indigo. "I think these are safe to put back on."

"Thanks."

Indigo folded her wet towel and set it on the counter before shimmying into her underwear and pulling her clothes on over top. She pulled the clip out of her hair and handed it to Rebecca, who twisted her own blonde locks up into her customary chignon.

"Ok, let me look at you." Rebecca ran her hands over Indigo's hair, smoothing wayward strands, and straightened her shirt until it hung properly. "Yes, I think you'll do. No one will be the wiser unless one of Bobby's crew reports us to the police."

"I doubt that." Indigo slipped her jewelry back into place and stood patiently while Rebecca adjusted the necklace. "They're a loyal bunch."

"Not as loyal as some. I had no idea you could be so vicious."

Indigo ignored the odd note of pride in the older Daughter's voice with a casual shrug. "She hurt Bobby. I couldn't let her get away with that."

"Tell me something, Indigo." Rebecca paused, seeming to weigh her words before continuing. "Were you beating her out of duty or because you have feelings for my son?"

"Both. I would never have claimed him if I didn't care for him."

"You seemed so unfeeling. I have a hard time believing you were doing it because your heart was involved."

Indigo's temper spiked and she bit it back. "I was plenty pissed. Still am, but I went in there to gather information. Mortal humans are frail. If I'd let the anger take over, I would've killed her before learning anything."

"I see." A smile bloomed across Rebecca's even features. "Cold-hearted logic. Your sister could take a few lessons from you on that score."

"We're different people," Indigo said, and knew she'd failed to hold back the exasperation when Rebecca's smile widened. "People always assume that I'm weak because I'm quieter and sometimes more gentle, but I'm still a Daughter. The blood of the Sisters runs as swiftly through my veins as it does through hers."

"Yes, it does." Rebecca threaded her arm through Indigo's. "When Bobby told me you'd claimed him, I had my doubts, but now I can see how unfounded they were. I couldn't be more pleased at being wrong about you."

"Oh, well." Indigo cleared her throat. "I'm not sure how to take that."

"As a compliment. Now, come along, dear. We have work to do."

Indigo allowed Rebecca to lead her back through the gym, stopping long enough to throw her towel into the laundry before they went back downstairs to see if India had called.

IT TOOK HOURS to organize. In that time, no one called with a place to meet and exchange Bobby for the Oracle.

Rebecca had no intention of giving her up, not even for the life of her own son, but it wouldn't come to that. Bobby's people, his friends Hiro and Drew and all the others who worked with them, were scanning video feeds, tracking down leads from a sheet of paper Indigo had given them, and gearing up for surveillance and a rescue attempt when they had a location. Rebecca held back from the fray, observing the way they worked together as a near-seamless unit, tightly focused on their mission.

It brought back memories, some fond and others not, of her own days in the field, first as a squire, then as a soldier, and finally as a leader.

Indigo worked well with the others, slipping in wherever she was needed, and caring for everyone else when she wasn't. She and Hiro seemed particularly close, bending their heads together to confer more than once, seemingly reaching for an odd sort of comfort from one another. Once, Hiro drew her in for a hug and Indigo's shoulders trembled under his steady embrace. They seemed to be caught somewhere between friendship and something deeper, though what that might be puzzled Rebecca. There could be no doubt who held Indigo's heart after the little scene with Laura, none at all. This friendship, or whatever it was that had developed between Indigo and Hiro, was no threat to Bobby, and so didn't worry Rebecca.

What did worry her were the quiet looks passing from Margaret to Indigo and back again, except for the moment when Indigo had presented that paper with the miraculously appropriate leads they needed to track down India and her little gang in the Order. Then, Indigo had studiously kept her attention on the group, not once sliding her gaze to Margaret's.

That paper illuminated intricate connections only a handful of people could make. Indigo was not among those, but Margaret, with her particular duties to the People, was. If others found out where Indigo had obtained that information, both their lives were forfeit.

Rebecca studied the pair as they worked apart toward the

same end.

She hoped they knew what they were doing.

HOURS PASSED, dragging Indigo with them through the long night while they waited for word from anyone on Bobby. She stayed at BDH, helping where she could. The next day dawned and still no news. Her nerves stretched thin and taut as the hands on the clock in Bobby's office inched around its face, marking off the time until the sun fell again behind the mountains.

She missed him so much.

It had been easy to stay strong when the police arrested Laura and during the mini-interrogation Indigo and everyone else had endured.

No, she hadn't spoken to Laura since Bobby's kidnapping, though she'd heard the other woman had tried to escape a couple of times and gotten beat up pretty badly in the process. Such a shame, she'd said, and her expression had been so sincere, the police woman questioning her had let it drop.

Strength had come easily when Nicodemus Hutley, the Special Agent in Charge of the local FBI field office, had come in with his slow drawl and quick mind, asking nosey questions about the kidnapping that had taken him perilously close to learning about the People. Dave had taken care of it, but Indigo suspected Hutley would be back. Next time, he might not be put off so easily.

She made a note to remind Bobby to instruct Zena on better procedures. The next time someone was kidnapped, Goddess forbid, keep the police out of it. They only ever got in the way.

Her energy had gradually flagged, worn down one tiny incident at a time, from Rebecca's watchful gaze, darting between Indigo and Margaret as if she knew what the two of them were doing, to helping with efforts to track down India and Bobby, to Hiro's mournful apology.

Damn him, he'd finally let it slip that he and India had been, as he put it, *watching a lot of Godzilla*, which Indigo took as code for *having wild and dirty monkey sex*. She'd wanted to ask what had possessed him to take up with a rogue Daughter, but it had been plain on his face. Hiro was falling in love with India, Goddess help him. India wasn't known for her kindness toward men, though Indigo hadn't the heart to share that with Bobby's friend. In the past, her sister had never stayed with a man longer than one night. That she'd chosen to hang around Hiro long enough to *watch a lot of Godzilla* might be a good sign.

Indigo wanted to be happy for them. Maybe if things were different she could be, but until Bobby came back to them, it was hard for her to dredge up anything outside of exasperation for Hiro and a cold fury at her twin.

Now, twenty-four hours after Bobby's kidnapping, Indigo's energy had fled and her mind was gritty and numb. Everyone else had taken the time to rest, even Rebecca, who had gone out with Charlotte to tend Robert and her younger daughter's family.

Indigo had tried, by settling in on the couch in Bobby's office for a short nap. As soon as her eyes closed, she saw Bobby, trying to stand and then falling to the floor, and India lifting him easily and carrying him out, away from Indigo and the people who loved him. Over and over again, it played through her head until she'd finally gotten up and plowed back into the rescue efforts.

An hour later, Dani caught Indigo in the break room making the umpteenth pot of coffee and yanked her mug away.

"Forget it," Dani said flatly. "We're taking you home."

Indigo pressed tired fingers to her eyes. "I'm needed here."

"No, Indi," Dani said, and tears welled up so suddenly at the nickname that one escaped and slid down Indigo's cheek. "You're no good to Bobby like this."

It was the only thing anyone could've said to get her to leave. Indigo gathered her things, checked in with Hiro to let him know where she was going, and let Dani and Dave take her home.

Indigo sat in the back, watching the lights flash past along the highway and listening to their softly voiced their conversation, a soothing murmur of comfort.

Dave parked Dani's Jeep and they walked up with her, making sure she was safely in the apartment. Dani hugged her hard before they left. The quiet support nearly broke the thin thread of Indigo's control.

She locked up and wandered, trying to pin down why the apartment felt so wrong before her tired brain put it together. Bobby wasn't there. It was too big without him, the rooms hollow and lonely. The yearning to have him close washed up so suddenly, she swayed and nearly toppled under its weight.

They would find him and bring him back. She repeated those words over and over again to herself, using them to block the images from the security feed that perpetually looped through her mind as she undressed, slipped on one of Bobby's t-shirts, and crawled into bed. She pulled his pillow close, holding it with a desperation born of fear and sinking hope. His scent washed over her, the spicy cologne he used mingling with the sharp fragrance of his shampoo, and under it all, Bobby's unique masculinity. She breathed it in, taking it into herself, and clung to it as tears leaked out and her heart throbbed in her chest and turned over in surrender.

She loved him.

A sob mingled with a half-laugh. What perfect timing, to figure it out now.

Another sob escaped and on its heels came the emptiness. Goddess, she missed him, missed him so much it hurt. She turned her face into the pillow and let go, let the hurt and the anger and the worried fear out in great, heaving sobs into Bobby's pillow, and when she was spent, finally fell into a restless sleep.

Intermittent beeps woke her. She peered at the clock, tried to bring the digital numbers on its face into focus and failed. Bleary eyed, she flopped onto her back and checked the light seeping in through the closed blinds. Sunrise, she guessed, and searched for the beeps.

She finally found the source in her cell phone. Someone had sent her half a dozen texts while she slept. She opened one and read the message. *Come now.* The next one said the same thing and the next. Neurons fired in her brain hard enough to bring her fully awake while she hurriedly scrolled through all of them. *Come now.* She checked the phone number, didn't recognize it, and sent back a message.

Where?

The answer was an address that Indigo immediately forwarded to Hiro, Drew, and Margaret. She bounced out of the bed and threw on clothes, and called a taxi to drive her to BDH.

It was time to get Bobby back from India.

NINETEEN

BDH WAS A MADHOUSE of activity by the time Indigo arrived. Drew barked out orders from his office toward the back of the floor. Indigo weaved through the people rushing back and forth, saw Hiro conferring with a team already half geared up, and finally found Rebecca and her daughters holed up in Bobby's office.

She pushed the door open in time to hear Margaret say, "Forget it, Mom. You're not going."

"She's right," Indigo said.

Heads snapped around, Moira's, Charlotte's, even Rebecca's, who regarded Indigo with a flat stare meant to intimidate her into submission.

It wouldn't work this time.

Margaret gave her an amused look, but the person Indigo wanted to see was Bobby's next youngest sister, seated on the far side of the couch past Moira, slumped down with her eyes closed, and Charlotte, who smiled prettily at Indigo in greeting, and Rebecca, whose gaze never wavered.

Indigo and Jerusha were only two years apart in age and had attended school together at the IECS during the turbulent war years of the 1860s. They'd been fast friends until Bobby's failed play for Indigo had placed a harsh strain on her relationship with his family. It was the one regret Indigo had about leaving

Tellowee and avoiding the women in his family. She'd missed her friendship with his sister. Now that the embarrassing *incident* of fourteen years past had been resolved, it would be nice if she and Jerusha could renew their friendship.

"Jerusha, it's so good to see you." Indigo picked her way over legs and knees and furniture until she could hug her favorite of Bobby's natural siblings. "When did you get in?"

"Couple of hours ago." Jerusha pulled back from the hug and touched her forehead to Indigo's. "Mom called as soon as she heard about Bobby. I packed a bag and started hopping flights to get here."

"I'm so glad. We could really use your help." Indigo moved away and settled into the empty chair in front of Bobby's desk beside Margaret, who had taken the other one. "Has Margaret filled you in?"

"Yeah. Hiro's got this idea about spreading us out between teams, with Mom here at command to oversee us and Charlotte back home with Dad to head off any calls there."

"Sounds like a good idea," Indigo said. "What's the problem?"

Margaret snorted. "Mom wants to go with us."

"Absolutely not," Indigo said. "You're mortal. You stay."

Rebecca narrowed an icy gaze at her. "I've been taking care of my own hide for nearly a millennium."

"That's not the issue here." Indigo leaned forward and met Rebecca's gaze with a steely one of her own. "You're a more valuable asset than Bobby. If for some reason you were to be captured, we would have no choice but to hand over the Oracle."

"That won't happen," Rebecca said.

"You're right, it won't," Indigo snapped, "because you're staying here to coordinate the teams and guard Zena."

"Wow, this is better than a tennis match," Charlotte said. "Maybe we should televise it. You know. Do the pay-per-view thing and make some money."

"I'd pay to see it again," Moira said. "Maybe after the sun's

214

fully up. Don't know why you Yanks can't sleep to a decent hour."

Indigo ignored them. "It's settled then. Charlotte, check in with Hiro, make sure he doesn't need anything else, and then you can head to the Upton home. We'll call as soon as we have word."

"I'll make a good, solid breakfast and have it waiting for y'all," Charlotte said, and slid out of Bobby's office in search of Hiro.

"Is there a place I can get cleaned up?" Jerusha stood and pulled her lean body into a full, bone-cracking stretch. "Don't have time for a shower, but I'd love to brush my teeth."

"Oh, here." Indigo rose to rummage in Bobby's desk. "He keeps spare toothbrushes and toiletry items in here. I always wondered why before."

"Now you know," Jerusha said with a wink. "Which way?"

Rebecca rose as well. "I'll show you. It will give us time to catch up a little."

Moira went with them, mumbling about coffee and rubbing her eyes like a child pulled from her bed too soon.

When they were gone, Margaret swiveled her chair around to face Indigo. "Didn't know you had it in you to stand up to her."

Indigo huffed out a laugh, caught somewhere between insult and pride. "I'm learning to draw a few lines."

"Atta girl."

They hunkered down over a copy of the intel coming in from the team Drew had placed around the residence where Bobby was being held and strategized as time ticked quietly by.

THEY TIMED THEIR STRIKE for just after nine a.m., when nearly everyone in the neighborhood around where Bobby was being held would have gone to school or work. Hiro divided their groups into units containing two immortal Daughters and two mortal BDH personnel each, with extra teams standing by in case they were needed. The Daughters who weren't trained in BDH tactics were to take rear positions and allow the others to lead.

They parked a block away from the residence where Bobby was being held and walked in through back yards, up and over or around fences when needed, moving quietly in the morning's stillness. Hiro led one team with Indigo, Jerusha, and a young BDH man Indigo knew only as Sanchez. Margaret, Moira, Drew, and another BDH man comprised the other team.

They held their weapons at the ready, each according to preference, and eased around the sides of the house, Hiro's group to the front, Margaret's to the rear, avoiding windows and shrubbery as they moved into position. Hiro took the door, gently tested the handle, and mouthed *unlocked*. Sanchez peered carefully around the sill of the front window, frowned, and shrugged.

He couldn't see in.

Hiro nodded and mouthed a countdown, and then pushed the door open, allowing it to swing wide before they rushed in one by one, Hiro first, then Sanchez, with Jerusha and Indigo close behind. From the back of the house, sounds filtered forward of Margaret and Drew's team entering.

The first thing Indigo saw when she came in was Bobby slumped over in a chair with his back to them, his shirt torn completely off and a bandage wrapped around his ribs. India stood over him with her hands on his head. She looked up, her eyes round with surprise, and then she was gone in an agile sprint that carried her out of the room and into the hallway, away from the back of the house.

"Got her," Hiro said as he broke into a run.

Indigo caught Jerusha's gaze. "Go after him. I've got Bobby."

Jerusha nodded and shot out the front door.

Indigo raced to Bobby and dropped her sword behind his chair. The damage done to his beautiful body had her heart

216

stuttering in her chest and a slow, crawling dread creeping up her spine. Ropes dug into his forearms, holding him to the chair. Probably the only thing keeping him upright. His eyes were swollen and bruised a dark purple, his nose bloodied, his lips split and cracked. More bruises blossomed along his jaw, down his neck, and over his arms and torso, running under the bandages before peeking out below them.

She inhaled sharply through her nose as a slow and steady heat rose in her, burning through her until her vision blurred red and her blood boiled.

Someone had beaten him, torn at him while he was helpless to defend himself.

Her fists clenched as the anger became so big, so hard, that it threatened to burst from her. She swallowed it back, and with it the bile that had gathered in her mouth on seeing her beloved husband's beautiful body treated like a punching bag.

No, Laura hadn't suffered nearly enough, but she would.

Indigo palmed her knife, used it to carefully slice away the ropes, and caught him when he slid from the chair. Hands pushed in, helping her settle him on the floor. She gently prodded his injuries, stripped his pants and boots off to check his legs and feet, and was relieved to find the bruises confined to his upper body and the breaks to his ribs.

She closed her eyes, steeling herself for what else needed to be done, and pulled down his briefs to check his penis and testicles, the first place a Daughter usually struck on an enemy male. And sank down with a small prayer of thanks to the Lady Goddess that he was hale and whole there.

Whoever had beaten him hadn't wanted to maim him permanently.

Not whoever. *India.* No one else would've dared to treat such a valuable hostage so poorly.

Damn her twin's temper and complete lack of respect, for Indigo, for the strength of Bobby's family, for Bobby himself.

Hiro came back in puffing and dropped to his knees beside

Bobby, his gaze steady in spite of his heaving breaths. Jerusha followed and stood behind him, and Indigo's heart sank at the hard set of the other Daughter's expression.

India had gotten away. For once, Indigo wished her sister wasn't such slippery prey.

Margaret came in from the back. "Checked the whole house. Nobody else is here."

Drew settled down beside Indigo. "Let us get him. He needs a hospital."

"I can help," she said.

"No, we've got him," Hiro said. "Won't be the first time."

"Probably not the last either," Drew added with a grin.

"Good times," Hiro agreed.

Indigo moved out of the way to let them care for her lover, and tried not to ponder what trouble the three men had gotten into before Bobby had walked back into her life.

BOBBY CAME TO with a groan amid the beeps and wheezes of machinery. His body was one big ache from his waist up and his eyes felt like they were frozen shut. He lifted a hand and felt a gentle touch on his arm, holding him back.

Indigo.

He turned his head toward the soft sounds of her breathing and said her name. A rusty, unintelligible grunt came out instead.

"Shh. I'm here. Everything's ok now." Her hand stroked his hair back, a cool brush along his skin. "Water?"

He opened his mouth, tried not to flinch when the cuts on his lips cracked apart, and felt the touch of a straw there. He sipped, let the water dribble down the back of his throat, and fell back against the pillow with a sigh. Questions sped through his mind, pushing their way through the fogginess of whatever drugs were in his IV. He cleared his throat and managed to grate out, "Long?"

"It's been three days since you were taken." Clothing

rustled, a chair scraped back. "We came in and got you as soon as we could."

He nodded once.

"They were trying to exchange you for the Oracle. Did you know? Rebecca refused, of course, but there was no question about that. We were coming for you." Her hand fluttered across his thigh, landed there, a warm, solid comfort. "I hope you know we would never have left you."

Strain thinned her voice. He patted awkwardly around the bed, searching for her until she twined her fingers with his. It had never occurred to him that she wouldn't come for him, not once. Why would she even bring it up? Even if she never loved him, she would always come for him. He wanted to tell her he knew that, tell her he loved her enough for both of them. The words faltered in his throat, caught by the pain or the meds seeping through his blood or a parched and injured mouth. He heaved in a frustrated breath and gasped it back out when pain shot through his torso where his ribs had cracked under the hail of India's rage.

"Stop trying to talk," Indigo said. Her fingers tightened on his. "Get some rest. We can talk later."

He wanted to talk *now*, needed to tell her, and struggled with it until someone came in and adjusted the medicine in his drip, sending him into a numb void where Indigo couldn't follow.

BOBBY DRIFTED through the night, waking more times than he could keep track of. *Indigo.* He had to find her, tell her something, *do* something. Every time he remembered what it was, *where* he was and what had happened, someone hit the pain meds on his drip and he fell back into the darkness.

At long last, light drifted across his eyes, piercing his subconscious. He followed it up into full wakefulness and inhaled, searching for air and hissing out a sharp breath when pain throbbed through his torso.

219

"Bobby, darling, can you open your eyes for me?"

"Mom?" He rubbed a sore hand across his eyes and pulled back when his fingers found a sticky gel slathered thickly over his eyelids. "The hell?"

"Dr. Phillips used a salve to keep the wounds around your eyes from sticking to the bandages." Cool fingers trapped his hand and pulled it gently away from his face. "Stop fiddling with it."

He tried to lift his eyelids, earned a thin shaft of light and a stab of pain for his troubles, and shut them again. "Get it off."

"Don't be a baby," Rebecca said.

"It's uncomfortable." He winced at the whine in his voice. "Where's Indigo?"

"Talking to the nurses. Here, hold still."

Something soft rubbed across his eyes, taking some of the sticky goo with it.

"Why were my eyes bandaged?" he said.

"Because you kept trying to open them. Dr. Phillips said they'd never heal like that. There now. Try again."

He slitted his eyelids open, let his pupils adjust. Rebecca moved away, out of his line of sight, and the room dimmed into blessed darkness.

"Thanks." He blinked, trying to focus. "Time is it?"

"Eight thirty four a.m., nearly a full day since Indigo and your friends rescued you." Something moved near him, a lightness against the darker shadows, and finally resolved into the blurry figure of his mother. "You've been under nearly that whole time, although that wouldn't have been necessary if you hadn't fought against your IV every time you woke."

He ignored the gentle chide. "Was trying to find Indigo."

"She's barely left your side. Poor thing." Rebecca sighed. "She's trying to assume responsibility for your kidnapping."

His heart sank. Indigo and her damn sense of duty. "Wasn't her fault."

"We all know that, darling." Her fingers grasped his gently, comforting him. "She feels guilty anyway."

He closed his eyes, tired of fighting to keep them open. "Did they get India?"

"She slipped away, though I suspect she hasn't gone far."

The door squeaked open and soft footsteps sounded on the tile floor. A hand stroked his forehead, then a light kiss pressed there.

"Indi?" he said and reached for her with his good hand.

"You're awake." Her voice held that soft lilt she used when she was happy. Her fingers found his and squeezed. "I was starting to worry."

"Don't." He tried to open his eyes again, needed to make sure she was really there and not another dream. "Missed you."

"Stop trying to open your eyes." Her lips touched his briefly before she let his hand go and moved away. "You're healing quickly, but they need a few more hours, ok?"

"Sure." He turned, trying to find her in the room by the sounds she made moving through it. "We were just talking about how my kidnapping was not your fault."

"Try being a little more subtle, Bobby," Rebecca said with a wry twist in her voice. "Else you'll bludgeon us all with your bluntness."

Better bluntness than Indigo on the run again, trying to outpace the guilt. "The truth is harsh sometimes."

"Yes, but it's not a hammer." A shoe hit the tiled floor. Cloth shifted as someone stood. "Now that you're awake, I'm going to go home and catch a nap. I'll be back in a couple of hours with your father so Indigo can take a break." Rebecca pressed a kiss to his cheek, then whispered, "Try to talk her into going home for a while when we return. She won't leave you and it's wearing her down."

Air brushed across his skin as she moved away. The door squeaked open, shut softly, and then Indigo was there next to him.

He felt for the edge of the bed and gingerly scooted over as far as he could to make room for her, holding a hand to his ribs to keep from jostling them. "Sit with me."

"Oh, no, I couldn't. Your ribs..."

"I'll heal better if you're close."

Her laugh held as much relief as it did humor. "Nice try, but no. You've had enough damage done to you to last us all a while."

"I've been through a lot worse than that, honey." He reached for her, found an arm, and tugged. "This is just scrapes and bruises."

"And busted ribs and burst blood vessels in your eyes and internal bleeding and bruising. You're lucky you didn't puncture a lung." She sat on the edge of the bed so that their hips touched, and placed his arm on her lap. "She punched your beautiful mouth."

He grinned. "Out of all the cuts and bruises, that's what bothered you?"

She huffed out a sigh. "No."

"So it didn't bother you at all to see me beaten up and wounded."

"Of course it did, you oaf." She squeezed his hand. "She did a number on your face, though. When I saw you, I thought she'd broken your jaw."

"Nope. Just the ribs." He ran his tongue over his teeth, testing them. "Loosened a couple of teeth, maybe."

"I could just kill her for this. What was she thinking to hurt you?"

"Ah, well." He cleared his throat, winced when even that tweaked his ribs. "I might've goaded her just a little."

"You *what?*" Her voice was sharp enough to make him wince again. "Why would you do that?"

"She tried to cut my *aenkanien* off and I got pissed."

"She..." A long sigh. "By the Goddess, I should take her down for that alone."

"Don't even think it. I know you. If something happens to

her, it'll kill you."

"Not this time. It was one thing to kidnap you, and something all together different for her to tie you to a chair and beat you unconscious. Stop trying to open your eyes."

"I want to see you." He lifted his eyelids cautiously, found it easier to keep them open than before, and focused carefully on Indigo, sitting on the bed beside him. He drank her in, running his gaze over her hair hanging in a loose cascade down her back and the paleness of her face. "Is that my t-shirt?"

"Oh, ah. Yes." She fluttered a hand at it. "I hope you don't mind."

"Not at all." He tried to pull his hand free and gave up when she easily overpowered him. Damn drugs. "Are you wearing a bra?"

"Really, Bobby. This is no time for a question like that."

"It's always the perfect time to know if you have a bra on or not." He shifted and cursed under his breath at the stabbing pain radiating from his ribs. "Does this thing have a switch on it so I can sit up?"

"Hold on." She slid off the bed and searched, and a moment later the top half tilted upward, taking him with it. "Better?"

It stopped before he was sitting all the way up, but since it was easier to breathe, he didn't complain. "When can I go home?"

"Forget it," she said, and though her expression was stern, a quiet laugh tinged her words. "You're staying here until Dr. Phillips says it's ok, even if I have to sit on you to keep you here."

Interest stirred in his loins. "That sounds promising."

"Do you think of anything other than sex?"

"Yes, all the time, but right now, sex seems like a good topic."

"Sex is a horrible topic right now." She sat at the far end of the bed next to his legs. "What with those busted ribs and all."

Bobby winced. She just had to remind him. "How many did

she get?"

"Three and that's plenty. Now, close your eyes and get some rest."

"Bossy." But he closed his eyes, content now that he'd found her. "It'd be better if you were up here."

"Maybe tomorrow," she murmured as he drifted into sleep, comforted by her nearness.

TWENTY

THE HOSPITAL was silent by the time India arrived. Visiting hours were over. The night shift nurses had clocked in and were quietly making their rounds. It was easier to sneak in and do what needed to be done in the still of the night.

If she hadn't been betrayed, the Oracle would already be in the hands of the Eternal Order, but no. That bitch Olivia had gotten cold feet and texted Bobby's location to Indigo. The safe house had been overrun by BDH personnel and Bobby's sisters before they could make the switch, Bobby for the Oracle. India wouldn't have made it out if Hiro were a Son. As it was, she'd barely managed to elude him.

He'd probably make her pay for that later, if he'd even speak to her again.

She bit back a sigh and checked the corridor before sliding into it.

That feeling in her gut wasn't disappointment. Couldn't be. She'd never needed a man before, never intended to in the future. It just wasn't in her make up.

Goddess, she missed him.

She closed her eyes and leaned her head against the wall as a massive ache lodged itself in her chest. What a fool she was. All this time, she thought she'd been so clever using Hiro for sex and an in with Bobby's company, but in the end, she was the one who'd been played. He'd snuck into her heart, taken over, and now, she felt so lost, so alone. It wasn't love, not yet, but she was getting there, and with a man who would probably never forgive her for kidnapping and beating his best friend.

He wasn't the only one pissed at her. Indigo would be after her for trying to peel the *aenkanien* from Bobby's skin, and Bobby's sisters, well. They would simply follow their mother's lead.

India beat her head against the wall, cursing her own stupidity. She'd known better than to take her anger out on Bobby and had done it anyway, in a fit of jealous rage over his place in her sister's heart.

Hiro was right. Her temper would get her in trouble one day. Looked like that time had come.

Once she'd left the safe house, she'd doubled back, watched Bobby being carted away, seen Indigo's heartbreak and felt its echo inside her own heart.

And then she'd found the traitor Olivia and taken great pleasure in beating a confession out of the sniveling Daughter.

Voices sounded at the other end of the hall, forcing India to move. She ducked into the stairwell and went up another flight. The Oracle was here, somewhere. The mission could still be salvaged. If India got caught killing her, it would be no loss, and at least the People would be rid of a possible key to the Prophecy of Light.

INDIGO WAITED with Rebecca in the hallway while Dr. Phillips examined Bobby. She and Bobby's mother hadn't spoken much since his return, not about his kidnapping or about the shape he'd been in when they'd found him. People had been streaming in and out since he'd been admitted, paying their respects, angling for gossip. She hadn't been alone with Rebecca long enough for them to really talk.

Indigo was glad to put it off. With everything else going on, the last thing she wanted was a conflict with Rebecca. Bobby needed them both right now, cooperating, not sniping at each other.

She smoothed a hand over her shirt, straightening it more out of habit than concern. Nurses came and went, their tread softened by rubber-soled shoes. Visitors filed out of rooms to head home for the night. The steady rhythm of the hospital ground its way through her frayed nerves. How long did a checkup take?

When she was on the verge of barging in to see what was wrong, Dr. Phillips came out of Bobby's room wearing a rueful grin. "He's asking to go home."

"You told him no, didn't you?" Indigo said. "Surely he's not well enough yet."

"Truth is, he could've gone home last night if I'd thought he'd rest," Ethan said. "I only kept him this long because I know what he's like."

Rebecca inclined her head in a graceful nod. "What excuse did you give him this time?"

"The two of you, and those are my last excuses. Tomorrow morning, he goes home and you'll have to find a way to make him rest once he gets there." A friendly smile stretched across his handsome face, crinkling the corners of his eyes. "Try to keep your children out of trouble, Director. This is the second one I've treated here in as many months."

"I shall do my best, Dr. Phillips," Rebecca said with a rueful smile of her own.

"Not much chance of that, is there?" Indigo asked softly when Dr. Phillips left.

"I'm afraid not." Rebecca pierced Indigo with a penetrating look. "When was the last time you took a break?"

"Not long ago. Um." Indigo flipped her wrist over and checked her watch, and was stunned to see how late it really was. "Around lunch, I think?"

"And it's after supper now." Rebecca placed her hands on

Indigo's shoulders and squeezed. "Go take a walk, a nice long one. I'll hold down the fort here for a little while, try to keep Bobby from going stir crazy.'

A nice solitary stroll through the quiet hospital corridors, alone with her thoughts. What a lovely idea. No one to entertain while they visited Bobby, none of the noise of people trooping in and out nonstop. Being with Bobby was easy by comparison, even with his restlessness. They'd spent the day talking during the few moments they'd been alone and he'd been awake, simply chatting about whatever came up. But having all those people there, pressing in, their words friendly but their expressions questioning. It had been difficult to bear, on top of everything else.

Guilt cut in and Indigo bit her lip as fear quickly followed it. The last time they'd been apart...

She pushed the thought back and the flutter of panic with it. Begging trouble wouldn't do any good. Being prepared by carrying a weapon wherever she went, that was smart, but lingering on what might have been was pure foolishness. "It's my place to take care of him now," she reminded Rebecca.

"Go," Rebecca said firmly. "Robert's expecting me home soon, and when I'm gone, you won't have another chance for a break until tomorrow morning."

Indigo hesitated, torn between protecting Bobby and the need for space.

Rebecca leaned in close to her ear and said in a barely audible whisper, "The Oracle's on the next floor up."

The Oracle. Here? What was she doing...? Indigo searched her memory. Right. The Oracle had awakened during a visit by Maya Bellegarde and her fiancé, James Terhune, less than two months before. She'd been moved out of her special room near the IECS Archives to receive better care, though Indigo hadn't heard that the Oracle was still in Tellowee.

"Will you stay with him?" Indigo said.

"For a while," Rebecca promised. "He'll be fine if I have to leave."

Indigo wasn't so certain. There was always the worry that Bobby would get up and walk out of the hospital on his own, though surely he would wait for her.

"I'll be quick," she said, and waited until Rebecca went into Bobby's room before heading for the elevator.

BOBBY WAITED PATIENTLY while Ethan Phillips flicked a light across his eyes, checking to see if they reacted properly. Ethan was a couple of years older than him. They'd gone to school together at Tellowee before Ethan graduated and went on to study medicine. In the way of Sons in all of the People's settlements, they'd banded together with the other Sons both in school and out, to train, to make mischief, and to have friends who understood what it was like to be the protected child.

It was hell growing up among a bunch of kick ass girls who tolerated zero sass, but it could also be a lot of fun. Panty raids at the dorms brought all-out wars on the campus' quads in the middle of the night, to the exasperation of the dorm parents, but what could they do? When you trained kids from birth to fight and spy, it was pretty hard to stop them from sneaking out and wreaking havoc on their fellow students, all in the name of fun.

The Sons had always gotten their asses handed to them because they were always outnumbered, but they'd had a hell of a time doing it.

Bobby grinned. "You remember that time Darren Stovall got stuck in the AC vent trying to raid his girlfriend's dorm?"

Ethan clicked his pen light off and put it away. "Haven't thought about that in ages. What ever happened to him?"

"Heard he got married, moved to the California branch to be with his wife a couple years ago."

"Who in their right mind would take him?" Ethan said with a grin. "I guess you and Indigo'll tie the knot soon."

"Officially, yeah. Unofficially, it's a done deed."

"Congratulations, man. She's a good woman." Ethan leaned against the side of the bed and crossed his arms over his chest. "If you play your cards right, I'll let you go home with her tomorrow morning."

Another night stuck in this hospital bed, with Indigo sleeping in the chair? Not if he could help it. "Any chance I can leave now?"

"Nice try, but no dice. Your mom would kill me."

"Come on, be a pal." Bobby dropped his voice to a whisper. Indigo was out in the hall with Rebecca. If he was quiet, maybe their supersensitive Daughter ears wouldn't catch him begging. "I'm a newlywed, for cripes' sake. Do you know how long I waited for her?"

"Sorry, man." Ethan snagged Bobby's chart and scratched notes onto the top page. "Indigo's already threatened to put the hurt on me if I release you any sooner than I have to."

Bobby dropped his head back against the pillow. He'd wanted Indigo to find her courage, really he had. He just hadn't wanted her to use it against him. "Don't be a wuss."

Ethan narrowed his eyes. "If you weren't lying in that bed, I'd show you what a wuss I'm not."

"Bring it, man. I could use a diversion."

"Concentrate on getting better so you can go home to your wife." Ethan tucked the chart away and moved to the door. "See you tomorrow, bright and early. Get some rest."

"Yeah, thanks."

When Ethan was safely out in the hall, Bobby sat up carefully in the bed. His ribs still ached and made breathing a little hard, but the rest of him was healing rapidly. This time tomorrow night, he'd be back in Indigo's arms, showing her how much he loved her, as often as his body would let him.

Damn India's hide.

He shook the thought off and placed his feet flat on the cold tile floor. It wouldn't hurt to walk a little, move around to ease the stiffness. Since his wife and mother were out in the hallway being distracted by the good doctor, now was as good a time as any to try his legs out.

He gripped the edge of the mattress and was leaning forward to ease off of it when his mother came in. She took one look at him and frowned as she shut the door behind herself.

Busted. *Dammit.* He'd hoped to at least make it to the bathroom on his own.

"What do you think you're doing, young man?" Rebecca said.

"Getting up. What does it look like?"

"Getting into trouble." She sat down in the chair at his bedside. "You're lucky Indigo took a walk to stretch her legs or she'd have you back in that bed quickly enough to make your head spin."

He rolled his eyes skyward. Oh, if only she would. He snuck a glance over his shoulder to find his mother pinning him with a glare. "Gimme a break, Mom. I've been stuck in this bed for more than a day now."

She inhaled a sharp breath. "You're lucky that's all you'll spend there. When we find India..."

"Don't start." With a sigh, he shifted back onto the bed so he could talk to her face to face. "She's Indigo's sister and as far as I'm concerned, that makes her off limits."

"Off... Are you out of your mind? Look at what she did to you. If I don't go after her, it sets a horrible precedent."

He gave a half laugh. "Yeah, right. Leave off, Mom. I'm not gonna have an all-out war with Indigo's family over a couple of cracked ribs."

Rebecca's mouth thinned into a harsh line. "Elizabeth agrees with me on this. She's done everything but banish India."

"Well, she can just unbanish her." He cut her off with a wave of his hand. "When we find India, she'll take responsibility for her actions, but I don't want it to go beyond that. No revenge killings. No harsh fines. I mean it, Mom."

She considered him for a moment before tucking her feet

under herself. "Indigo's already influencing your judgment."

"No. We haven't even talked about this." He clutched his thighs, willing his patience to win out over the exasperation. "Are you ever going to accept her in my life?"

"Oh, Bobby. I didn't mean it like that." She reached forward and grasped his hand, squeezing it gently. "It's a good thing, her influence. You're happier now. A blind man could see how much better your life is with her here. I'm very glad the two of you have finally found each other."

He covered her hand with his, felt it warm against his skin. "I love her so much."

"I know." She turned her hand over and threaded her fingers through his. "I know you do. She loves you, too, you know."

He shook his head and let his hand slide away, afraid to hold on to any hope where Indigo's feelings were concerned. "No, but it's ok. Someday she will."

"What a pair the two of you are. You're afraid to look into her heart and she's worried she's not good enough for you. Honestly, what am I going to do with you?" She sat back with a smile that made him nervous. That was her devious smile, the one she wore when she was up to something, and it sent a chill of unease down his spine. "Do you know where she is right now?"

"Walking the halls, trying to find some peace, if she's got any sense in her," he retorted.

"The Oracle."

He sat straight up and grimaced at the tug in his ribs. "You're kidding."

"It shouldn't be a difficult walk for you." She stood and gathered her purse and coat together. "Your father's expecting me at home. I'll have a nice lunch waiting for the two of you when Dr. Phillips releases you tomorrow."

He held his cheek up for a kiss and said goodbye while a quiet buzz grew in his head and his heart beat double-time in his chest.

Indigo had gone to see the Oracle.

Daughters went to see the Oracle all the time, to read to her, to bring her gifts, but there were two times when the sleeping woman was always visited: When a Daughter submitted her will to a man and became mortal, and when she married. Usually, those two occasions happened at the same time.

His heart sank. Of course. Indigo was only visiting to tell the Oracle she'd married. Dammit, she still could've waited for him, even if she didn't love him. It was traditional for the couple to present themselves together. He ignored the stab of hurt to his heart and focused on the irritation instead. What was she thinking, doing an end run around him and making such an important visit without him?

He scooted off the bed and eased onto his feet. Indigo might not love him, but she needed to understand that they were in this together. His wife needed an object lesson on that score. There was no better time than the present to give her one.

TWENTY-ONE

IT WAS A QUICK TRIP to the next floor. Indigo used the time to clear her mind. Traditionally, couples approached the Oracle with news of a happy event, but from time to time, Daughters went there alone for counsel.

The Oracle never spoke, save when she'd awakened the previous month. It was the solitude, the time for reflection in the presence of a woman who was thought to be one of their oldest Daughters that drew people to her. It was for this that she'd allowed Rebecca to persuade her to leave Bobby. Indigo was in dire need of time to sort her mind out.

She hadn't had the nerve to tell Bobby of her love. He would accept it, not as his due but as the natural course of their relationship, and he would be happy. She just wasn't ready yet to share it with him. As deep as her feelings ran, they were still new, fragile. She wanted to hold on to them a little longer, treasure the love for the rarity it was.

She could tell him tonight, she thought, and immediately reconsidered. No, not while he was still in hospital. It had been hard enough to resist him when it was his heart alone involved. Now that hers was, too, she had a feeling he would try to charm her right out of her clothes and into the hospital bed with him, where they would do many things other than rest.

She smoothed her ponytail back and firmed her lips against

a smile. If she told him she loved him, he would want to... How had Hiro put it? Oh, yes. *Watch a lot of Godzilla.*

A laugh left her before she could stop it. She put a hand to her mouth and looked around before remembering that she was alone. No one had seen her being silly.

The elevator dinged and Indigo stepped out into the silence. The ICU was on this floor, though she doubted a long-term care patient like the Oracle would be there. Maybe in a private room?

She followed the signs to the nurse's desk and found it empty. Odd. Weren't there always supposed to be nurses on duty, especially here?

She tapped her fingers against the laminated countertop, racking her brain for another solution. The Oracle never went anywhere without at least two Handmaidens guarding her. *Find the Handmaidens, find the Oracle*, she thought, and set out to do just that.

The soft clack of her shoes against the floor echoed eerily in the empty hallways. Indigo bypassed the ICU, searching for a private room instead, but after circling the floor and encountering not one living soul, her sense of wrong blossomed into unease. She slipped her shoes off and hid them behind the desk, then pulled her Keltec from its holster at her ankle. It wasn't much and she probably wouldn't need it, but better out and unnecessary than holstered and needed.

She checked the ICU first and found only one patient, an elderly gentleman who was very much alive, judging by the beeps and whirs of all the machinery he was hooked up to. She checked the other rooms one by one, easing each door open and peeking in before clearing it. The first two rooms were empty, so she moved to the next one down the hall.

She pushed the door to the third room open and scanned it. Unlike the other two rooms, this one's bathroom door was closed. She checked the handle, turned it easily, and opened it on three nurses sitting in the tiny space, bound and gagged. Two were out cold, and had been put that way with a hard right hook, if the bruises on their jaws were any indication. The third, a young brunette, eyed Indigo warily above her gag.

"Indigo Dupree," she whispered. "I'll cut you loose if you promise not to try anything."

The other woman nodded. Indigo placed the Keltec on the floor outside the bathroom's entrance, pulled out her pocket knife, and gently sawed through the gauze wrapped around the nurse's head and across her mouth.

"Thanks," the nurse whispered when Indigo was finished pulling it away. She wiggled around and offered her bound hands to Indigo, and rubbed her wrists when they were loose. "Are you the cavalry?"

"Hardly." Indigo set her pocket knife to the bindings around the nurse's ankles, then carefully began cutting through the gauze securing the other two nurses. "My fiancé's downstairs, waiting out some busted ribs. I decided to take a break and come up here to visit someone special. Who did this to you?"

"You did, I thought," the nurse said. "And then it hit me that if you'd done this, you wouldn't come back for us, not to set us free."

Indigo rubbed the back of her wrist against her forehead. India. *Sweet Goddess.* There was only one thing her sister would want on this floor. "Can you walk?"

"Sure. What do you need?"

"Call down to the next floor and tell Rebecca Upton that India Furia is after the Oracle."

"I know Director Upton." The nurse shrugged at Indigo's curious look. "You work here long enough, you get to know the regulars."

Indigo bit the inside of her cheek to stifle a laugh. Regulars, indeed. "Will you be ok?"

"Yeah, I know what to do. Thanks."

"Anytime."

Indigo retrieved her gun and padded out of the room into the hallway, peering up and down it before she entered, then resumed her search for the Oracle.

After checking several empty rooms, she pushed open the last door at the end of the hallway and found India standing over the Oracle, a sharp, long-bladed knife in her hand. Indigo propped the door open and cursed under her breath. The Handmaidens were nowhere in sight. What had her sister done with them?

"She's beautiful," India said without looking up. "I didn't think she would be."

"Step away, India. Please." Indigo raised her gun with one hand and aimed the barrel at her sister's chest. "I don't want to hurt you."

"Don't you?" India flipped the knife in her hand, tapped the blade against her thigh. "I tried to kill Bobby."

"You did a piss poor job." Indigo inhaled sharply, barely reining in her growing anger. "You should never have taken him."

"It was the perfect plan. Bobby for the Oracle. The Son for the woman whose death might ensure that no more Sons would be born. What could go wrong?" The last words were said so softly they were barely audible. India reached out a hand and gently smoothed it across the Oracle's forehead. "I told her about Hiro."

Indigo's grip on the gun faltered. "You've submitted?"

India's laugh held equal parts humor and bitterness. "No."

"Then what?"

"I realized I could love him someday, if things were different. If I had less of a duty and more of a heart."

"You have plenty of heart, India," Indigo said gently. "It's just not always in the right place."

"Is it not, kaetyrm?" India turned to face Indigo, her face twisted with anger. "Did I not love you enough?"

"Of course. I know you love me."

"Is that why you turned on me, when that man hit you?" India reared back and hit the headboard of the Oracle's bed with enough force to crack it, jarring the comatose woman. "Is that why you left me?"

Indigo shook her head, confused. "What are you talking about?"

"He whipped you and I couldn't stop him. Over and over again he hit you. I tried to get him to quit, to make him stop, and I failed." India threw her head back and screamed her rage into the empty air. When she stopped, her chest heaved with more emotion than Indigo ever remembered seeing her sister demonstrate. "You *left* me that day, Indigo, left me alone with Mámá, and she hated me for not stopping him."

"No, India. No," Indigo said as shock hit her. "That's not what happened. It was nothing, a few hits from a whip. I healed."

India shook her head. The tears streaking down her face glinted in the light spilling from the hallway. "You don't remember what it was like before, how close we were. Like two halves of one person. After, you were never the same and I was lost. I *needed* you."

"I was always there, India." Indigo dropped the hand holding the gun, numb. All that rage, building for a century and a half inside her sister's heart, and she could've stopped it, if she'd only known. "Tell me what to do to make it right."

"Leave him." India stepped forward, her hand raised in a silent plea. "Come away with me, tonight, and we can leave all of this behind us. It'll be just like it was when we were kids, you and me, together like sisters should be."

"I can't," Indigo whispered. "He's my heart, India. You don't know what you're asking."

"Your heart. A man is more important to you than your own sister?" India sneered as her hand dropped. "I should've killed him when I had the chance."

"Don't push me on this," Indigo warned. "I'll defend him to the death if I have to."

"You and your duty." India stepped back, moving slowly until she stood at the Oracle's side again. "I have my duty as well, kaetyrm."

She raised the knife high above her head. Indigo brought the Keltec up and squeezed hard against the trigger, firing into the wall above India's head.

"Step back, India." Indigo lowered the gun, pointing it at her twin's torso. "Next time, I won't aim for the wall."

India frowned with visible disbelief, though she held the knife steady. "You would really kill me over this?"

Indigo met her sister's gaze calmly. "If you force me to."

"Sister." Emotion flickered across India's face, softening it. "I won't blame you for it."

She raised the knife and bore down on it, and Indigo fired just as strong arms came around her, knocking her aim off. India cried out and clutched at her arm, her eyes wide in a face that had gone pale.

Indigo noticed her sister's wound and reaction only peripherally as she struggled to regain control of the Keltec and wrest herself away from whoever was holding her. She jabbed an elbow back, connected solidly, and froze when a low male hiss sounded in her ear.

"Bobby?" she asked and pivoted her head toward him.

"Easy with the elbow there, Indi." He shifted to hold her arms in a firm grip. "Give me the gun, sweetheart, and I'll let you go."

Indigo shrugged to loosen his hold. "She's trying to kill the Oracle."

"I can see that. Now give me the gun."

"No. She's crossed the line this time, Bobby." Indigo squirmed in his embrace, searching for a weakness in his hold outside of his ribs. "If I don't kill her, she'll keep trying and eventually, she'll really hurt someone."

"You're not killing her. Indigo, listen to me." He squeezed his arms until she stopped struggling and lost her breath. "If you kill her, you'll never be the same. I can't let you do that. Please, Indi. I know how much you love her."

Indigo hauled in a breath as emotion welled up, love for her sister and for the man beside her; regret over the past and the many wounds that could never be healed; and sorrow for the hand she'd had in turning her sister into the angry, bitter woman she'd become.

A tear slipped from the corner of her eye and then another, and she sniffed them back before they overwhelmed her. Her arms went limp and she let Bobby take the Keltec from her hand. He was right. She couldn't kill India, even knowing what her sister would do if left unchecked. In spite of all their differences, the love between them was too great. Bobby had known that, reminding her over and over, and had understood their bond much better than anyone else, even their mother.

Indigo turned her back on India and clung to Bobby, intending to tell him how very much she loved him. A sudden dizziness filled her head and her vision dimmed. She gasped as a huge, invisible weight pressed upon her, threatening to crush her and then lifted just as quickly, leaving her shaken. From a distance, she heard India call her name. Bobby caught her close to him and cupped her face with one hand. His lips moved, though she couldn't make out his words, and then her eyes rolled back in her head, sparks flashed through her brain, and her body jerked so hard she slipped from Bobby's grip and dropped with a hard thud to the cold, tile floor.

BOBBY DROPPED into a crouch beside Indigo and patted her face gently, trying to rouse her. India scrambled across the room and skidded to a stop, kneeling on her sister's other side.

"Is she ok?" she said in a tight voice. "What happened?"

"I don't know." Bobby checked Indigo's pulse and sagged with relief at the steady beat. Color had bled from her skin, turning it a shade paler than the floor, and she was as cold as ice under his fingers. "One minute I was trying to convince her not to kill you and the next she passed out."

India dropped onto her bottom and covered her eyes with her hands. "She's submitted."

Bobby did a double take. "No, can't be. She doesn't love me, not yet."

"Oh, please. You think I don't recognize the signs?" India dropped her hands and shot a withering glare at him. "Besides, she as good as told me she loved you not five minutes ago. It was just a matter of time before you broke her will."

"You have a really warped vision of love."

Bobby shook his head and turned his attention back to Indigo. She should've woken already, if she really had submitted to him. Hope blossomed in his chest. Did she really love him? He took a shaky breath, brushed her hair back, and tried it out in his mind.

Indigo loves me.

That sounded stupid, like a kid reciting a Sunday School verse, but he didn't care. Indigo loved him and she'd submitted, and she would never leave him again. He leaned down and pressed a tender kiss to her lips, pulling back when India hooted out a laugh.

"She's not Sleeping Beauty, you oaf."

"Shut up," he said, though he couldn't keep his lips from twitching into a smile. "You're bleeding."

"Yeah, flesh wound," India said with a shrug. "I would say thanks for saving me, but she was shooting a Keltec. Can't hit the side of a barn with that thing if you're not up close and personal."

"She didn't want to kill you."

India snorted. "Could've fooled me."

Bobby gave her a flat look. "She had a duty to protect the Oracle."

India returned his stare with one of her own. "I have a duty to protect the People, too."

"How is killing an innocent woman protecting the People?"

"Figure it out, Bobby. You're not dumb." She rolled her shoulders and winced before raising her arm to look at the bleeding gash bisecting it. "Doesn't matter anymore. Now that I've bungled this mission, the guard on the Oracle will double and we'll never get another chance at her."

"I don't want to know," he said in a hard voice. "But if you ever make Indigo choose between doing the right thing and saving your hide again, I'll come after you myself."

"It's not the first time it's happened. Can't promise it won't be the last."

"Try."

India grinned. "You know, I kinda like you."

"Yeah, I can tell. Next time, leave my ribs alone."

"Next time, don't pissed me off." She slapped his shoulder, then pushed herself into a stand. "She's coming 'round. Let's get her downstairs so the two of you can make goo-goo eyes at each other in private."

Bobby stared up at her, nonplussed. "You go down there, you'll get arrested."

"Hunh. Doubt it. I'm too slippery for that." She hefted him up. "I haven't forgiven you for taking her heart."

"Get over it."

She looked away, tapped her fingers against her thigh. "She was mine first."

"For cripes' sake, she's not a damn toy."

"I know," she said softly, and grabbed his arm when he made to bend. "I'll get her. You'll puncture a lung or something if you try to lift her."

India leaned down and pulled Indigo up. When she was halfway to standing, Bobby grabbed an arm and draped it over his shoulder while India took the other one.

"Bobby?" Indigo said in a slurred voice. "What happened?"

"You passed out," he said. "Can you walk?"

"Think so." She peered at him owlishly before turning her gaze on her twin. "Did you kill her?"

"No, now stop talking and start walking," India said. "I need to leave soon."

"Probably too late," Indigo said, and she sagged to one side. "Sorry. Still a little dizzy. One of the nurses called Rebecca."

India cursed under her breath and leaned forward to look at Bobby. "I'll help you as far as the elevator and then I gotta go."

They hobbled out into the hallway at a slow pace and made it only a few feet before Rebecca stepped into their path, her bare feet silent on the floor.

Bobby took one look at his mother's set expression and sighed. "Get out now, India," he murmured.

She carefully pulled Indigo's arm over her head and stepped back away from them. A booted footstep rang against the floor behind them. Bobby glanced over his shoulder. His gut clenched when he saw Margaret blocking the hallway to their rear.

"Get her out of here." India met his gaze calmly. "If I don't make it, tell her I love her. Tell her..."

"You can tell her yourself," he said. "They won't kill you."

She barked out a harsh laugh. "For what I've done, I deserve to die."

He shook his head, but it was too late. She'd already pivoted around on quick feet and made a running charge at his sister. Indigo tried to pull away from him and he gripped her harder.

"Forget it, Indi," he said and began hauling her down the hallway toward his mother, ignoring the twinge in his ribs. "You're not helping her this time."

"She's my sister."

Her voice held a kind of hopelessness that ate at him. Damn India for doing that to her.

When they reached his mom, he said, "Make sure Margaret doesn't kill her."

"Oh, we don't want her dead," Rebecca assured him. "She's too valuable for that."

A shiver of dread ran down his spine. "You're not talking about her being Indigo's sister, are you?"

"No, dear." She patted his arm. "But I'll keep that in mind."

"You do that."

Indigo shifted in his embrace, her eyes fixed on India and Margaret's fight. Bobby followed her gaze. Moira had joined Margaret, and though India was holding her own, she wouldn't be able to keep it up forever, especially if Rebecca entered the fray.

Indigo didn't need to see her sister being beaten into submission.

"Come on, love." He pressed gently against her waist until she turned with him. They leaned on each other as they walked down the hallway. The sounds of the fight receded behind them, the thuds of blows and grunts fading until the elevator doors closed them off completely.

BY THREE P.M. the next day, Indigo had had more than enough of other people. The night before, they'd waited an eternity before Rebecca came in with news. Margaret and Moira had subdued India and turned her over to the local police on charges of kidnapping and attempted murder. After Rebecca left, Indigo had allowed Bobby to coax her into the narrow hospital bed where he'd held her until the sun crested the horizon. She'd done her best not to disgrace herself by crying all over him.

When Dr. Phillips released Bobby, they'd gone straight to his parents' house and eaten lunch with his family, his mother and father, his sisters, Charlotte's family, and even Dani's new beau, Dave, who Bobby had scowled at until Rebecca sent them out to the basketball court behind the house to settle their differences.

Indigo had worried the entire time about Bobby's ribs, but apparently the two men hadn't played basketball or fought either one. They'd come back in looking less hostile, if not exactly friendly. It was a start, a foundation to what she hoped would become a lifelong friendship.

She and he had finally managed to sneak away half an hour before. Indigo opened the door to their apartment and heaved a sigh. It was good to be home.

Bobby came in behind her and closed the door before wrapping his arms around her. "Alone at last."

Indigo turned in his embrace and rested her head against the broad plane of his chest. It had been so long since they'd been here together. A lifetime seemed to've passed since then. "What shall we do?"

"I have ideas, lots and lots of ideas." He nuzzled her hair, bent to nip at her ear. "Days worth, maybe. Let's lock the door and work our way through them one at a time."

"Mmm." She tilted her head to one side, giving him better access as he moved from her ear to her throat. Pleasure rippled through her at each touch of his mouth until a throbbing ache settled between her thighs. She untucked his shirt and ran her hands gently along the firm skin at his waist, mindful of the tender bruises lingering there, and reveled in the way his breath hitched with every stroke of her fingers. "It's the middle of the day."

"So? We're adults. Who's gonna stop us?"

"How are your ribs?"

"Still a little twingey."

She dropped her head to his chest. "Maybe we shouldn't do anything."

"Oh, we're gonna do something all right." He wrapped her ponytail around his hand, tugged her head back until their eyes met, and said in a soft, low voice, "I need you, Indi."

"Bobby," she whispered, and stood on tiptoe to press her lips to his. "Make love to me."

She led him into their bedroom where they undressed each other and fell into the bed, skin brushing against warm skin, their mouths locked in a desperate, needy kiss. When Bobby slid into her, she gasped and arched against him, and they moved together, letting passion build slowly until it overwhelmed them in a soundless wave that swept them into sweet release.

Afterward, Bobby rolled onto his side and pulled her to

him. She rested her head on his bicep and slid a leg over his to keep him close, half afraid he'd slip away from her again.

"I love you," she said. "So much."

He leaned back and caught her gaze with his. "Yeah?"

"I do." She snuggled into him and let his heat warm her, as it always had. "I'm mortal now."

His arms tightened around her. "That's what India said. Didn't believe her, though."

"You talked to her?"

"While you were out." He ran his chin over the top of her head, pressed a kiss there. "She was worried about you and none too happy we'd mated."

"I know. Will you ever forgive her, do you think?" She sighed, regret filling her. Playing the *what might've been* game would do no good, but the possibilities roiled through her mind anyway. The what-ifs stretched from her childhood right up through India taking her rage out on Bobby and the Oracle. "I won't blame you if you can't."

"I'm not important here, sweetheart. She's your sister. If you can forgive her, I'll support that."

"This is why I love you," she said and laughed when he reared back, disbelief written across his face.

"You love me because of your sister? That's kinda kinky."

She curled her fingers into his chest, careful not to scratch. "Stop it. I meant, I love you because you understand, because you love me enough to want me to work it out with her."

"Is that all?"

She smiled at the humor in his voice. "No. You're the best man I've ever known."

"Hunh. I've done a lot of things you don't know about."

His words from the first time they'd made love drifted through her mind, all the things he'd done in the Army, and with it came the guilt. She'd pushed him into doing that through her own inability to deal with his young heart, through her own fear of his love. "I know enough to tell you it doesn't matter. We've both done things we regret."

"I don't want you to regret anything." He bent to take her lips with his in a tender touch that brought an ache to her heart. "Not a thing."

He slid his hand down her back and cupped her bottom, pulling her up until her hips pressed against his erection.

Her breath caught in her chest and the heat of desire throbbed through her. "Already?"

"I'm pretty sure always," he said with a laugh.

"What about when...?" She bit her tongue to hold the question back. "No, never mind."

He propped up on his elbow above her, his other hand a gentle caress on her hip. "What?"

"When you were in the Army." She shook her head slightly. "I don't think I want to know."

"You mean, how did I get through nine years without having sex," he said flatly. "I tried not to."

She flinched away. "I told you I didn't want to know."

"You need to hear this." His hand tightened on her hip. "I tried to have sex with other women after I took your mark, tried to love somebody else, and it never took, not once. You've had my heart since the first time I saw you."

"Oh, Bobby." Tears pricked at her eyes and she sniffed them back. Of all the things she'd ever done in her life, this is the one she'd do over if she could. "I'm so sorry for the way I treated you then, for running out on you and breaking your heart."

"Don't be. You were right the first time. I was too young." He rolled onto his back, taking her with him. "But now you're here and it's enough."

She straddled him and rested her hands on his lean stomach. "Tell me you love me."

"I do, baby. I love you." He squeezed her hips as his eyes went soft. "With all my heart until the day I die."

"Marry me." She lifted her hips and brought them down, sheathing him fully within her, stretching herself with his hard

247

length. "My needing time is soon. I want to be married before we have children."

His wide mouth tilted into a wicked smile, lighting his hazel eyes from within. "Elizabeth already blessed us. We're married, sweetheart, have been for a while."

"Why didn't you tell me?" she said, and let happiness pull a laugh from her. Of course he'd already secured her mother's permission, not the grudging acceptance of a mother for her Daughter's mate that Elizabeth had given in the formal presentation, but a true blessing. In the eyes of the People, that final permission was more binding than anything mortal law required them to do. He would want them to be bound as tightly as they could be. Now that she'd found her heart and him in it, she wanted that, too, just as deeply.

"I've been telling everybody who'd listen." He took her hands and kissed the tips of her fingers. "Thought you'd figured it out already."

"No, but now that I have, it's too late for you. I'll never let you slip away again."

He pulled her forward and thrust up into her with slow, lazy strokes. "Just try and get rid of me."

"Not a chance," she said, and took her time giving him all the love in her heart.

EPILOGUE

INDIA WOKE SLOWLY, climbing her way carefully through the dense fog in her head. With every breath, her lungs burned and her ribs pinched. Aches blossomed across her face, down her torso, along her arms and legs, and memory hit.

Indigo shooting her to protect the Oracle.

Bobby throwing off Indigo's aim and Indigo losing her immortality to him.

Shuffling down the hallway with them. Rebecca stepping into their path.

Trying to get past Margaret, and then Moira, and the hits that kept coming, even after she'd fallen to the floor and curled into a ball to protect her internal organs and head.

And then nothing.

She tried to open her eyes and winced when light pierced through her. She lifted a hand to shield herself from it and heard the *shink* of metal on metal as her hand came up short, stopped by a cold grip on her wrist.

She lost her breath as dread crept through her. They'd chained her, probably had her in a cage somewhere. Her heart tripped, stalling in her chest, and raced hard and fast when it found its beat again. A cold sweat broke out on her skin and her lungs heaved, trying to catch air.

Locked up in a tiny cell surrounded by concrete and the

hopeless stench of the enslaved. Her worst fear, come to life.

She struggled against whatever was holding her, trying to break free, and screamed when a hand came down on her arm.

"Hush now. You're safe."

She turned her head toward the gentle male voice. "Hiro?"

Her own voice sounded oddly broken as it rasped out of her throat. What had they done to her?

"Don't speak." A hand brushed hair off of her forehead. "If I unlock the handcuffs, will you promise not to try an escape?"

She nodded carefully, sighed when the metal bands slid away from her. "Where?" she whispered.

A long silence followed, so long she thought he'd left. "Somewhere safe. It's better if you don't know the details."

She nodded again, not sure why she was agreeing, and curled onto her side. The ground gave next to her. No, not the ground, a bed. Hiro had sat down close enough for his heat to radiate onto her. A shiver ran through her and then another one until her body shook from head to toe with it. She bit her lip, trying to quell the tears, and felt them streak hotly down her face anyway. Something soft fell against her, covering her, and then he was behind her, holding her gently.

"You're safe now. I've got you."

After an eternity, the tears quieted and her body warmed. Questions ran through her mind too fast for her to hold on to them, except for one. How had he gotten her away from Rebecca and her daughters? She struggled to form a question and finally managed a single, "How?"

"You want to know what happened. I get that, but it's too complicated to talk about now." Something brushed against her hair, his face maybe, and then his mouth found her neck, pressing a kiss there. "I'll tell you all about it later, when you're awake enough to understand. For now, try to focus on getting better. Dr. Phillips said you'll be fine, but you took a beating."

She winced. That part, she remembered. It was everything else that was fuzzy.

"Look, I'm still kinda pissed at you, so pissed I almost let them lock you up, but you don't have to worry about that anymore. You're safe. Your record's been wiped clean. As far as the law's concerned, you never existed." His sigh blew across the back of her neck. "I can't believe I'm telling you this now. You're not gonna remember."

"Will." She coughed to clear her throat, groaned as pain stabbed through her so hard her vision dimmed. She waited it out, clinging to his silent strength, using it to claw her way back to reality. "Thanks," she managed at last, and let his chuckle bring an answering humor from her.

"Stubborn. Thank God for that. I thought I'd lost you."

She shook her head, careful not to jostle it too much. There was so much she wanted to tell him, so many things bottled up in her heart. How she'd thought of him when she'd fallen under Margaret's sledgehammer-like blows, and how she'd wanted to live then, wanted so badly to live long enough to tell him how much he meant to her. She might never be able to love him, not the way a woman was supposed to love a man. Her heart was too damaged for that, but what was left of it, she wanted him to have.

Even if it could never be love.

"Shh, baby. Go to sleep now. I'll be here when you wake up, promise."

Dizziness washed over her. She let it take her down until she fell into a deep, healing sleep, secure in the embrace of the only man she'd ever trusted.

Acknowledgments:
Many thanks to Richard E. Hopkins, Jr., and my son
for their continued help and inspiration.

About the Author:
Lucy Varna lives in the Blue Ridge Mountains of
northeast Georgia, surrounded by her large, extended
family. She may be contacted online through her
website:

www.lucyvarna.com
www.daughtersofthepeople.com

www.ingramcontent.com/pod-product-compliance
Lightning Source LLC
Chambersburg PA
CBHW051425170626
46809CB00006B/2320